The Winter Berry House

CAROLINE FLYNN

ONE PLACE. MANY STORIES

This novel is entirely a work of fiction. The names, characters and incidents portrayed in it are the work of the author's imagination. Any resemblance to actual persons, living or dead, events or localities is entirely coincidental.

HQ
An imprint of HarperCollins*Publishers* Ltd
1 London Bridge Street
London SE1 9GF

1

This edition published in Great Britain by
HQ, an imprint of HarperCollins*Publishers* Ltd 2020

ISBN: 9780008409043

MIX
Paper from
responsible sources
FSC® C007454

This book is produced from independently certified FSC™ paper
to ensure responsible forest management.

For more information visit: www.harpercollins.co.uk/green

Printed and bound in Great Britain by
CPI Group (UK) Ltd, Melksham, SN12 6TR

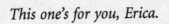

This one's for you, Erica.

Chapter 1

Kait

'Two coffees and a slice of lemon meringue pie to share, please, Kait.'

'So, the usual,' Kait replied with a grin. She didn't even bother to write the order down on her notepad, leaving it tucked away in the left side-pocket of her apron. 'Two forks?' she asked, though she knew the answer before the question left her mouth.

'You betcha.' Arnold's enthusiasm belied his advanced age. His genuine smile did, too.

'Coming right up.'

Arnold and Jemima Jackson came into the diner – The Port, as it was officially called – every day at two o'clock on the dot without fail, and they ordered the same two coffees and one slice of pie with two forks. Not even the homemade Christmas cake with brown sugar sauce that had been added to today's dessert menu could sway them from their usual lemon meringue slice. They always stayed until three-thirty, leaving a two-dollar tip on the table under one of the coffee mugs before they left for their daily stroll down the boardwalk to watch the boats come into the harbor, their matching walking canes tapping in perfect synchronicity the whole way.

And every day that Kait Davenport worked, she watched the elderly couple in whimsical awe as they held each other's hands, their fingers gnarled and wrinkled with the decades gone by, lost in their own simple, soft-spoken conversation like no one else was in the room. They were both well into their eighties, and she pondered what a love like that must be like.

'They're at it again,' Kait whispered to Janna as she rounded the counter and worked on getting the Jacksons' order together. 'Making me feel all warm and fuzzy inside.'

Janna, donning an identical lavender uniform and deep purple apron, gave Kait a brief sideways glance, too caught up in her bid to arrange six cups of coffee on a tray and not spill a drop to offer up her full attention. Her mouth curved up at the corners, though, and she shook her head. 'You're such a sucker for that kind of thing.'

'I can't help it if I love the idea of love.' Kait took the coffee pot from Janna when she offered it. 'And you're lucky you're family or you wouldn't be getting away with calling me a sucker.'

That earned her a full-blown eye roll. 'It's because I'm your sister that I know exactly why you *shouldn't* be such a sucker for love,' she replied. Plunking a pile of creamer pods in the middle of her well-balanced circle of coffee mugs, Janna heaved the tray up onto the palm of her outstretched hand. 'We Davenport women will never learn.'

Kait watched her older sister head back to the table of six she was serving. There was only a three-year difference between them, but Janna may as well have been decades older the way she assumed her motherly role where Kait was concerned instead of acting like the thirty-two-year-old woman she was. Kait didn't blame her, though. She couldn't. Becoming a single mom of twins and raising those two babies on the meager income of a small-town diner gig was reason enough for Janna to adopt her overprotective parenting ways. Kait's romantic track record only added fuel to the fire.

Living in Port Landon her entire life had its perks. There was always a friendly face to be found no matter where she was, she didn't have to use her bank card to 'check in' at the local bank because every teller there could pull her up in their system by name alone, and she never had to explain their complicated family dynamic, as the community knew very well that she lived with her sister and neither one of them was married.

Having everyone know their business was a drawback, too, though. Kait had grown up amongst the people who surrounded her, and those same people knew all the things that twenty-nine-year-old Kait would just as soon forget. All the things that her eighteen-year-old self had done, believed, and lost were at the top of that lengthy list. As close-knit as Port Landon was, the town as a collective whole sometimes wasn't too keen on leaving things buried in the past, intent on the constant reminiscing and recollecting that an aging population was known for. They didn't forget.

Neither did Janna, by the sounds of it. Kait didn't either, but she was at least hopeful, even if bleakly so, that real love did exist. If it could for Arnold and Jemima Jackson, lasting the span of some sixty odd years, then surely she had half a chance at it, too.

'Earth to Kait.'

Hand suspended above the lemon meringue pie, Kait's attention snapped back to the here and now. A pair of familiar hazel eyes stared at her, eyebrows arched high on his forehead. She sliced the pie and placed it onto the dessert plate beside it. 'Creature of habit, aren't you?' She said it in jest, one corner of her mouth lifting, but Kait had to hold back the defeated sigh she felt pleading to be released from her throat.

Zach Canton stared at her from over the counter, leaning forward on his elbows. 'Got to see my girl,' he quipped. 'Wouldn't want you to think I forgot about you.'

It would be funny if Kait didn't find it so sad. Or frustratingly repetitive.

'I'm not your girl, Zach,' she playfully admonished him, setting the knife down before she shook a finger at him. 'I'm your friend. Just friends, remember?'

Zach didn't wilt at the reminder, and his smirk didn't falter. It never did when they had this conversation, which was almost daily. 'I know,' he advised with a wink, holding up his hands in mock surrender. 'I don't mean anything by it, you know that. Old habits die hard, I guess.'

The only thing Kait did know was that it had been years since they'd tried to date. Despite their incompatibility as romantic partners – even after being friends throughout high school before they attempted to take things further – Zach had yet to fully realize that there wouldn't be a second chance for them as lovers. Kait believed in love, but she also believed that true love couldn't be forced. She couldn't fake it, not even for the sake of a man she had been friends with for half her lifetime.

Besides, she had already experienced love once, the kind that came effortlessly and passionately without conscious decision, and look where that had got her. More than ten years after that fiasco, she was still here in Port Landon, still wishing for a romance that would survive the test of time, and still knowing in her gut that kind of love didn't come along twice in one lifetime.

Maybe Janna's pessimism was starting to rub off on her.

'Sorry,' she sighed, fully aware she was being a bit more stand-offish about Zach's advances than usual. It had been years since they broke up, and years since he first started visiting her at the diner during her shifts. Today was no different than any other day in their tiny town, so Kait really had no reason to be as on edge than she was. 'I'm just tired,' she explained. 'Janna had the evening shift last night, so I was with the kids till she got home after ten. Who knew twin boys were so exhausting?' She offered a grin up as she said it, and luckily her friend took the bait.

'No need to apologize,' he replied. 'You never need to explain yourself to me, you know that.'

4

Now she felt even worse for reprimanding him about his flirting. It was harmless, he was harmless, and he'd been doing it for years. Yet, Zach was right. He never made her explain herself to him, never asked for anything other than her company. Though she knew he would jump at the chance to rekindle their bygone romance, Zach had been a good friend to her over the years. One of her only friends save for Allison, who owned the local coffee-house, and more recently, Paige, the owner of Port Landon's very own bakery. Zach had stuck by her since high school, despite everything he'd been through during that tumultuous time. Despite everything Kait had been through. Together, the two of them had that much in common; their senior high school years weren't ones they liked to reminisce about.

'Let me get this pie and coffee to the Jacksons, then I'll be back.' She scooped the plate, forks, and coffee tray up and carried them over to Arnold and Jemima's booth near the window facing out onto the sidewalk.

'That boy doesn't miss a beat, does he?' Arnold blurted as she set the plate down in the middle of the table. The coffee mugs swayed dangerously on the tray, but thankfully Kait managed to maneuver them onto the table before her surprise caused her to spill them. Jemima, never one to comment about other people, swatted her husband's arm.

'Arnie!' she hissed over the faint melody of Christmas carols that floated through the diner.

Unfazed, Arnold nodded his gratitude for the coffee and pie, but he pinned Kait with a knowing stare. 'Don't be shushing me, now,' he replied. 'Young Kait knows exactly what I'm referring to. That Canton boy's only got eyes for you.'

Kait might have known that, even without Arnold's comment, but a warm blush still crept into her cheeks at having it pointed out. 'We're friends, Arnold,' she choked out. It had been a long time since someone outwardly suggested something more between them. To her face, anyway. 'Just friends.'

5

'Ah.' He nodded, a knowing glint in his eye. 'And that's because you still only got eyes for somebody else, huh?'

'Arnold Frederick Jackson!' Jemima hissed. Reaching out to pat Kait's arm, the elderly woman gazed up at her with pleading and apologetic eyes. 'Sorry, Kait, dear, it seems he's forgotten his manners today.'

Kait's throat thickened with embarrassment, but she forced a smile onto her face, placing her own hand over Jemima's. 'No need to worry,' she assured her, giving them both the most nonchalant expression she could muster. Leaning in, she shook a playful finger at Arnold. 'We're just friends,' she whispered with a grin. 'Now, enjoy your pie.'

The entire way back behind the counter, one word reverberated through her mind on a constant loop. *Still.* He hadn't suggested she merely had eyes for somebody else, Arnold had said she *still* had eyes for someone else. Still. And there was only one man she'd ever fallen head over heels in love with, and everyone knew it. Even Arnold Jackson.

Damn you, Branch, she screamed in her mind. *You're still making a fool of me after all these years.* Not only a fool, but also an unwilling believer in things she didn't want to believe in at all. There was a man sitting before her right now, ready and able to love her with every fiber of his being, yet Kait couldn't and wouldn't allow it. Because she didn't love him the same way. Because she believed there were a lot of things in life that were ordinary, and love wasn't supposed to be one of them. Love, she believed, was meant to be consuming and wild and passionate, and she believed it for one reason and one reason only.

Because she had experienced it with Branch Sterling. Even as teenagers, they had known their love was different, somehow. There wasn't a thing mediocre about it.

And he'd still betrayed her and broken her heart.

Damn you, Branch, she thought again.

'Something wrong?' Zach's voice cut through her searing thoughts. 'You look like you've seen a ghost.'

Interesting choice of words, considering it felt like the ghost of her first love was never far from her. Most of the time, folks around Port Landon were too polite to mention his name to her face, but Kait still heard the sporadic tidbits of information about him that drifted through the town. After his grandmother, a long-time and well-loved resident of the small town, passed away last year, there had been a landslide of mentions regarding him, speculation about the fact that he never returned for more than a few days at a time, and when he was there no one seemed to know about it until he was already gone. Branch knew how to stay under the radar, which was saying something seeing as there was no greater force to be reckoned with than the nosy neighbors and other members of a small, close-knit community.

'I'm fine,' was all Kait could manage. 'You want a coffee or something? I can get you a menu.' Coming there daily, there was no way Zach required one, and he could probably recite the list of dishes offered by heart, but Kait needed to say something to get beyond the meddling memories that were catapulting around in her brain.

Zach, however, furrowed his eyebrows. 'Is this about Branch?'

'Is everyone thinking of Branch freaking Sterling today?' Kait snarled, throwing down the bar towel she had just picked up.

'Sorry.' Her friend's hands shot up in surrender, fingertips pointed toward the ceiling. 'I just thought ... that haunted look on your face ...' He cleared his throat, softening the edge in his voice. 'I figured it must be because of him.'

Immediately, Kait despised the fact that he was right, that it was that obvious, and that she was that predictable. It took a lot to get on the bad side of Kait Davenport, who was known for being a happy-go-lucky, spirited woman. But only one person had ever managed to hurt her so irrevocably that the simple mention of his name could incite feelings of turmoil and rage.

And that person was the man she had loved passionately and wildly at the tender age of eighteen … Branch Sterling.

'Arnold brought him up,' she replied quietly, pouring Zach a coffee he hadn't asked for, purely so her hands were busy doing something, anything. 'Well, kind of.'

Zach simply nodded as she slid the coffee mug toward him. 'Everyone seems to be talking about him lately.' He reached for the sugar dispenser. 'The guy didn't even stick around after Addie's funeral, yet he has the audacity to think he'll be welcomed here now, after all these years?'

Mouth gaping, Kait struggled to take in an adequate breath of air. 'Wait, what?'

Zach went still, hand suspended just above his mug. 'Branch,' he said, suddenly looking unsure of himself. 'You said that's who Arnold and Jemima were talking about, right?'

Kait waved a hand dismissively. This was no time to discuss the not-so-misguided conversations of a couple in their eighties. 'Zach, forget them. What are *you* talking about?'

He stared at her for a beat too long, but there was no way to get out of the uncomfortable exchange without divulging what he knew. 'Kait, Branch is back,' he explained calmly. 'And if the rumors are true, he might be around for a while.'

8

Chapter 2

Branch

Hometowns were supposed to be where it all began, where folks got their start in life, survived their adolescence and grew into the people they were meant to become.

For Branch Sterling, Port Landon was the beginning of the end. Nothing in this town had been his for his entire life, yet the memories he had of it were the ones that had shaped him into the man he was. The good and the bad.

He pulled the rented Ford Escape into the familiar paved double driveway he used to spend summers practicing his basketball skills on. Okay, more like his lack of skills, but he loved the game, nonetheless. His grandparents had even surprised him with not one, but two, portable basketball nets so he and his friends could turn that big ol' driveway into a full-fledged court.

God, he missed them. The two people who took him in when he had no one else, and who believed in him and his abilities regardless of his aptitude or belief in himself.

Letting out a heavy sigh, Branch forced himself to kill the engine and get out. He couldn't sit in the driveway and hide forever. Besides, this was Port Landon. The SUV had been in Grandma Addie's driveway for only a few minutes, but the ever-watching eyes of the neighbors would have seen it by now. If people didn't already know he was back in town, which he highly doubted, they would soon enough. Nothing and no one went unnoticed in a small town. Or unspeculated. Or un-gossiped. Those weren't real words, but they were very real things within the town limits of this place.

Branch didn't bother locking the Escape. He hadn't been here since Grandma Addie's funeral the year before, and even then he'd only stayed a handful of days, but he doubted things had changed so much that folks had to lock up their vehicles and homes in broad daylight.

One glance at the old Ford Bronco in the driveway and he was glad he had chosen to rent a car instead of taking a gamble on his grandparents' vehicles. The Bronco was Grandpa Duke's, and though he had passed away three years before Branch's grandmother, the old vehicle hadn't moved since the day he went into the hospital and didn't come home. Grandma Addie never touched it, and she certainly wouldn't sell it. She couldn't. It wasn't hers to sell, she said. And his grandfather had been adamant to anyone who'd listen about who's Bronco it was. It was to be Branch's should anything ever happen to him.

Along with everything else, it turned out.

His grandparents' only child was Branch's mother, Lucinda, and when she died alongside Branch's father in a car accident when Branch was only eleven, they lost not only their immediate family, but the rightful heir to all the assets they'd accumulated throughout their lives. Which left Branch, the kid who inherited it after they had inherited him all those years ago.

And now, as he stared up at the looming Victorian home he had grown up in from the tender age of eleven onward, the house that had held so much warmth and comfort and unconditional love, Branch knew he would give it all up in a heartbeat if it meant he could have one more day with the man and woman who made him into the man he'd come to be.

On paper, Grandma Addie's estate had been dealt with a year ago. Branch could have requested time away from work and taken the time to sort through their house and belongings then. There was no reason why it couldn't have been dealt with by now.

No reason except that it wasn't just a bunch of tangible belongings to him. Just like Port Landon wasn't just a town. His grandparents' home had been his home, and everything in it was a painful reminder of what, and who, he was never going to get back. He didn't care about the monetary value of any of it. That just wasn't who he was, or how he was raised. He'd never required a lot of money to survive, and his job in a fly-in, fly-out remote location in Northern Alberta as a mechanical engineer gave him what he needed. Besides, his grandparents made sure he wasn't somebody who saw money as a measure of success.

Branch didn't want money, he wanted his family. He wanted the life he'd dreamed of right here in this house when he was a teenager, back when he thought the universe cared at all about his hopes and dreams. At the time, he didn't think he was asking for much: a good job, a family he could support and be supported by, and a love that made the movies of Hollywood pale in comparison. At eighteen years old, he thought he was on course to have exactly that.

Then, it was all ripped from his grasp.

So, when he passed the Port Landon town limit sign, he didn't look back.

Until now.

More than ten years ago, Branch had left the only home he'd ever really known, and now he was back. He was back, and that home was his. It was the only thing he had left.

Unlocking the front door and stepping over the threshold, he didn't know how he was going to do it. Sort through the six decades' worth of stuff inside his grandparents' home. Deal with the prying eyes of everyone who passed by and offered him a fleeting glance. Most of all, he had no idea how he was going to face all the emotions and memories he had tried so hard to outrun. He had run full circle, ending up exactly where it all began.

And ended.

Somehow, Branch knew the house would be the same as the Bronco in the driveway – untouched and exactly the way he remembered it save for signs of wear and elapsed time. Grandma Addie had always been an advocate for change, and welcomed it when it came, but she had never seen the need to change something unnecessarily. Therefore, though the lights all worked and the furnishings were well maintained, most things inside the sprawling Victorian home were either antique or blatantly outdated.

As soon as he kicked off his work boots and began to dawdle slowly from one room to the next, he didn't see it so much as felt it – the familiarity, the solace … the feeling of home. The same rush of relief spread through him that he'd felt the moment he drove into town, passing the town limit sign at a crawl. Branch might not have wanted Port Landon to be his home, but he couldn't seem to tell his heart otherwise.

What was he going to do with this place? A thick coating of dust covered everything and there were spiderwebs strung about the corners of each room. Even the spiderwebs had dust on them. Grandma Addie would have had a conniption fit.

Thinking of her, with her easy manner and constant puttering around this big old place, caused a violent clenching in Branch's chest. It was impossible to be here and not think of her. He had made sure to call her and check on her regularly, but Branch knew his absence had been hard on his grandmother. It had been his choice, and she never once reprimanded him for it, but he knew that Grandma Addie would have done anything to have him home more permanently. He visited as much as his work schedule allowed, sporadic visits that mostly consisted of late-night arrivals, remaining hidden inside the sanctuary of 14 Crescent Street, and disappearing again like a thief in the night the day before he was due back at work. Usually, his visits were unplanned and spontaneous; anytime he thought he heard even a hint of longing in Grandma Addie's voice – a hint of longing that matched his own. But there was one visit a year that was always guaranteed.

Christmas.

This house had held so many massive holiday dinners that Branch had lost count. His grandparents went all-out, with Grandma Addie spearheading the huge orchestrated event. It was never simply a meal around the dining room table for a few friends and family members. Oh no, that wasn't enough for his grandmother. Instead, there had always been an open invitation on Christmas Eve, and anyone who was around, available, with their own families or without, were welcomed to fill up the home and enjoy more homemade food, fun, and togetherness than they'd witnessed in the other three-hundred and sixty-four days of the year combined. As an adult, he had missed the Christmas Eve extravaganza every year, using work as an excuse for his late arrival long after the guests had retreated home. But as a child, he had helped his grandparents with the decorating. It took weeks to transform every room into a festive backdrop, but they'd done it. Every year, without fail.

Until last year, when his grandmother was stricken with chest pain. She'd called her next-door neighbor, who then called the ambulance once he arrived and called Branch from the hospital. Eighteen hours later, Grandma Addie passed away in her hospital room, with that neighbor by her bedside.

Four hours after that, Branch made it to the hospital, but he was too late to say goodbye. He wasn't sure he would ever forgive himself for that.

Standing here now, knowing she was gone and she wasn't coming back, Branch didn't know how he was going to stand being in this house, in this town, without her. Losing Grandpa Duke had been hard enough three years ago, but at least Branch and his grandmother had each other to help themselves through it. In theory, anyway. Branch had stayed as long as he could then, as well, ultimately hightailing it back to the airport in Detroit to escape his grief and occupy himself with his career. Branch realized now that he'd left Grandma Addie to pick up the pieces of her heartbreak then just as she was leaving him to do now.

It was merely another item to add to the list of reasons he felt so guilty.

He could have stayed in Port Landon, helped both of his grandparents more as they aged, been there for them as they'd been there for him for so many years. Instead, he'd thrown himself into a job that couldn't have been further away from home. It was the easy way out, the coward's way out. Purely because the town that had welcomed him with open arms in the wake of his parents' tragedy had chosen to turn its back on him. Because he'd made mistakes he would never be forgiven for.

Even as Branch thought it, he knew it wasn't the entire truth. At eighteen, he hadn't cared at all what everyone in Port Landon thought of him. He didn't much care now, either, honestly. Sure, his grandparents' opinion mattered, and he strived to make them proud – God, he hoped he had – but there was only one other person in this town whose opinion of him had mattered back then.

And she had given him no room to misread what that opinion was when she told him she hated him and didn't ever want to see him again.

Kait.

It had been more than ten years. They had just been kids back then. But they had known love. Known it, felt it, become fevered by the all-consuming nature of it. And they had lost it amongst

14

the destruction of his mistakes and the rumors his actions had flooded the town with.

Shaking his head, Branch moved back out to the front door where he had entered. He couldn't think about that catastrophe, especially not on the heels of the guilt he carried about his grandmother. His failure to be the man that Kait Davenport deserved on top of the disappointment he undoubtedly caused his grandparents was too much to bear separately. Rehashing both of those shortcomings together … the weight of his guilt would drown him, for sure.

He shoved his work boots back on and headed back out to the driveway to collect his luggage from the Escape. Branch just needed to make it through December. By then, he would have his grandparents' house sorted and cleaned, and he would have made a decision as to what to do with it before he left Port Landon. For good. He would have no reason to ever set foot in the small town again after that.

Thirty-one days. Surely he could manage to get through one month without causing anyone here any more trouble.

As quickly as the thought entered his mind, it was thwarted by a simple reality. He was pretty sure his presence alone would be enough to cause a boatload of trouble in this neighborhood. Not even a decade could change that.

Chapter 3

Kait

Kait was exhausted, and it wasn't just from the six shifts she had worked in a row – which were definitely contributing to her burning eyes that yearned to close for a solid ten hours or so and the sluggish heaviness of her limbs that she figured had to be obvious in the way she dragged herself along from table to table instead of effortlessly bouncing from one to the next the way she normally did. No, it was also because she'd had to defend herself from the constant mention of Branch's name since yesterday. Arnold's faux pas had only been the beginning.

To Port Landon's credit, no one was cruel enough to talk about her ex-boyfriend's arrival to her face. On second thoughts, maybe it had nothing to do with social graces and everything to do with the whole lot of them being plain and simple cowards.

Because everyone was talking about Branch Sterling. At least, they were until Kait showed up. Every patron of the diner seemed to get suspiciously quiet each time she approached their table or booth, staring up into her pale jade eyes with a wide, *you-caught-me* expression.

She heard the whispers, the incessant buzz of gossip and chatter.

It was like she had screamed at Branch only yesterday while standing in that hospital hallway, the way folks were chattering on about it. You would have thought the eleven years that had passed since were a figment of her imagination, or that their small town had come to a group decision that Kait couldn't handle what had happened all those years ago.

Well, maybe no one else had got over their scandalous breakup, but she sure had. More than a decade had passed, and it'd passed by without the likes of Branch Sterling in it. He might have shattered her heart into a million pieces, and a friend might have been badly injured in the process, but Kait wasn't the same woman she was at eighteen. Her eyes were wide open now, and she didn't need Branch to be happy. She didn't need him then, despite what she'd naively thought, and she sure didn't need him now.

Branch Sterling was her past. Just because the folks around here didn't want to focus on the future didn't mean she had to follow suit.

Kait was thankful Janna wasn't working alongside her today. They rarely worked together, as their boss was good about scheduling them on opposite shifts as much as possible in order to keep childcare costs down, but sometimes it just wasn't possible to avoid an overlap in their work schedules. Yesterday had been the first time in months she and her sister had been paired up to take on the lunch rush. After eight constant hours of Janna's perfectionism and overbearing demeanor, Kait felt a little guilty at how relieved she was to know it would undoubtedly be a while before the schedule called for them to work together again. Lunchtime hadn't been as busy as expected, though, and the two women had managed to get the Christmas tree and two big boxes of decorations out of the storage room. Janna, always the one to plan and organize everything to death, had sorted the decorations into countless piles, deciding in a meticulous fashion which decorations would go where. Kait knew better than to question her reasoning. That's why she focused on getting the ratty-looking artificial pine tree up, sticking its bent wire branches into the rickety wooden base. She half expected the poor thing to collapse the moment she started stringing garland and lights on it.

It didn't, however, and the vintage tree was still standing tall today while she carefully hung a mismatched collection of ornaments on the branches. With only a few tables to serve and the lunch crowd now come and gone, Kait welcomed the change of pace. Janna would have had a fit if she'd seen her choosing ornaments and hanging them without a concrete color scheme or well-thought-out plan, but Kait didn't operate like her sister did. Okay, so she would have chosen a color scheme and planned her ornamental execution a little more thoroughly if there had been a choice of ornaments that allowed for such luxuries, and if she didn't have to stop what she was doing each time the bell above the door rang out. Besides, it was Christmas decorating, not choosing a seven-course meal for the Queen.

Kait had always been the more impractical of the two. Always the one to use her heart more than her head. As she plucked a faded plastic nutcracker from the cardboard box and looped it onto one of the branches, she could barely contain an indignant snort.

Follow your heart, they said. She'd had that phrase engrained in her by every adult she knew since she was a little girl. And look where that had got her. Still working in the same diner she'd managed to get a part-time job at back in high school, still joined at the hip with her older sister, still fending off the same unwanted affections from a friend she'd never deserved, and still wishing things had been different. She liked her job, and loved her sister and Port Landon more than words could say; she would never contest that. But Kait wished she had made different choices, with her head and not her heart. Wished that she was maybe just a bit more like Janna and that she had never met—

'Branch.'

18

She had been scanning the room sporadically, making sure the two tables she was still serving – a booth near the front door and a table beside the window across the room – didn't need her assistance. As she raised her gaze, the door swung open, the bell above it ringing sharply to announce the new patron's arrival.

Kait was convinced she knew it was him before she consciously recognized him. Like something inside her felt his presence before her mind fully registered it. But if it wasn't her mind that recognized him first, that only left …

Damn you, heart.

If Branch had expected to see her, he was a really good actor. Kait, however, knew him well enough to know he never could master the art of a poker face. He had never been a good liar. At least, she hadn't thought so until she discovered the massive lies he'd managed to keep from her. She didn't know what to think anymore.

Unfortunately, the only thing she could think about clearly at the moment was that Branch Sterling looked even more handsome than she remembered. He seemed taller, somehow, although it could have just been the way the sun's rays were bursting through the windows, highlighting his lanky outline and making the contours of his jaw more pronounced. His jacket was thick to block out the frigid winter cold, his boots bulky and tucked under a pair of faded Levi's. Dark curls of unruly hair peeked out from under a Lakers cap, and the beak of it cast a shadow across his dark eyes, deepening the hue from a chestnut brown to an undeniable espresso.

And those eyes were trained on her, unblinking. Round and haunted, as though he was seeing a ghost.

Kait didn't think she looked anything like her teenage self, but she also didn't doubt it would be a shock to see her, here, in the same uniform that hadn't changed since the beginning of time. Her straw-colored hair was longer than she had worn it back then, but not much else had changed. She still pulled it back into a tight ponytail while at work, still refrained from wearing much in the way of makeup, and still knew the value of sturdy, although bland, footwear. She might be older, but there was enough resemblance remaining that she didn't blame Branch for staring the way he was.

She suddenly realized she was standing there, hand suspended in mid-air, about to place an ornament on a Christmas tree she had forgotten existed. It was about the same time she noticed that a few people in the diner were staring, too.

'You going to close that door sometime soon? You're letting the cold in.'

Branch turned at the sound of the question, from the older man seated at the booth closest to the entrance. He let the heavy door swing shut behind him. 'Sorry about that,' he muttered with a curt nod. It was the only moment of reprieve Kait got from the intensity of his gaze.

'I ... didn't know you worked here still.' There was an apology in his tone she hadn't asked for. Approaching her slowly, as though fearful he might spook her, Branch pulled his hat from his head, letting his wild waves spring free as he raked a hand through his hair. Yeah, he was definitely wearing it longer these days. 'If I had known ...'

He wouldn't have come there at all? He would have shown up before now, hoping to catch even a quick glimpse of her? Kait wasn't sure she wanted him to finish that sentence.

'I heard you were in town.' She was proud of herself for the lack of emotion her voice conveyed. It wasn't a greeting, but it wasn't a blatant dismissal, either. Just a neutral comment. Which was the complete opposite of the battle going on inside her. Kait wanted to step away from him but was also yearning to throw her arms around him and hug him tight. She wanted to scream at him and call him every name she could think of, while longing to whisper her gratitude for coming back to her after all this time. For being there, in front of her, allowing her to drink him in and remember all the promises and dreams that had once been the foundation of who they were.

She swallowed past the lump in her throat. 'Want coffee?' She didn't wait for him to answer, suddenly desperate to do something, anything that didn't include standing there staring at the man who, in her eyes, was the definition of conflict and heartbreak.

'We will,' the man sitting closest to the front door hollered, confirming what she already expected – people were hanging on every word between her and Branch, eavesdropping, and they weren't afraid to admit it. Kait offered him a polite smile from across the room, then left Branch standing by the front counter to refill their coffee mugs and check if they needed anything more.

Branch was perched on one of the stools when she returned to her station behind it, leaning on his elbows, jacket unzipped. His hat sat on the counter beside him. 'Coffee sounds good.'

Pouring him one, she slid it toward him, along with a sugar dispenser.

'Milk instead of cream, right?' The second the words left her lips, she regretted them, hating their familiarity. They had thought they were so cool back then, drinking copious amounts of coffee, pretending to be adults. Kait had loved knowing the way her boyfriend preferred his coffee, like it was one of the little things that proved how close they were, how much she adored him.

Now, the knowledge was etched into her mind. She wished she could forget his coffee preference. Wished she could forget a lot of things.

'Right,' Branch confirmed, the corner of his mouth twitching upward. 'How've you been, Kaitie?'

It was on the tip of her tongue to lash out at him. *No one's called me Kaitie in a long time, Branch. I'm Kait now, all grown up and not nearly as naive as you remember.* She couldn't bring herself to do it, too caught up in how the sound of that nickname made her heart beat faster. All she wanted to do was forget the way he made her feel and everything that went along with those feelings. It was really hard to do when he was her past personified, traipsing into the present and carrying with him the same soft eyes and alluring manner she had fallen for so long ago.

'I've been good.' It was the most she could commit to. The full truth would open a wound she wasn't prepared to contend with. 'You?' Civility. She could give him that much without breaking the pact she'd made with her teenage self to never forgive him for what he did.

Staring down at the cup in his hands, Branch shrugged. 'I'm all right,' he replied. 'Sorting through Grandma Addie's place. Or pretending to, so far.'

He might have meant it as an attempted joke, but there was no mistaking the deep grief in his eyes at the mention of his beloved grandmother. Kait's resolve to be merely civil went out the window.

'I'm sorry about your grandma.' She meant it, knowing full well how much the woman had meant to him. Grandma Addie had been just as much his mother as his grandmother, and she had never shied away from loving him like her own. 'Must be almost a year now since she passed.'

'A year tomorrow,' Branch corrected, raising his gaze to meet hers. 'And more than ten years since I've laid eyes on you. You look good.'

There it was. The fact that a decade spanned between them had been pushed out into the open, no longer the elephant in the room. Kait's cheeks flamed crimson, knowing she would never have mentioned it on her own. 'Don't,' she whispered, her throat suddenly thick.

He held her stare, a battle of wills. 'Don't what?' He lowered his voice to match hers. No one else in the diner seemed to be paying them any mind, but the question was meant for her ears only.

'Don't come in here and make me want to forgive you.'

'Kaitie, if you haven't by now, nothing I can say is going to change that.' His jaw clenched slightly. 'Doesn't make it any less good to see you, though.'

Damn you, she screamed silently. *For still being you*. Something was breaking inside her again, caused by the same man who had broken her once before. She could feel it. The difference this time was that Kait was pretty sure it was the armor she'd constructed around herself that was being fractured by him this time, not her heart. It was such a contradiction, the way he was able to calm her down and ease her mind with his simple kindness and affection, yet be capable of shattering her heart so irrevocably.

Well, that was just fine. Let Branch Sterling walk in here and throw his polite words and kind mannerisms around. Being civil to each other might put cracks in her defensive armor, but Kait was sure he could never do more damage than that. Not now. It had been more than ten years, and there was no reason they couldn't handle this like adults. He might still be easy on the eyes and hold the same allure, but that was just pure and simple physical attraction combined with a healthy dose of nostalgia.

He was a man, and only a man. Not the love of her life, not the man who'd broken her heart, and not the man she had truly thought she would never see again. Just Branch, nothing more.

She would believe it if she repeated it enough times.

'It's good to see you, too.' See, that was a very acceptable grown-up retort.

In the midst of taking a drink from his mug, Branch's eyes seemed to change as he stared at her over the rim of it. When he set it down, an unmistakable grin played on his lips and he let out a soft chuckle, fidgeting with the handle of the mug.

'Something funny?' The sight of his genuine smile was causing her stomach to flutter.

'It pained you to admit that.' Branch's smile stayed put, but he downed the last mouthful of coffee and tossed a five-dollar bill on the counter.

Okay, she obviously didn't have much of a poker face, either. 'Maybe I didn't actually mean it,' Kait replied defiantly, her chin jutting out in hopes of keeping up the pretense.

Leaning in, Branch's dark eyes were alight with amusement. 'You did, and so did I.'

Why couldn't she pull her gaze away from him? Why did she feel like she had just been caught red-handed stealing from the proverbial cookie jar? And why in the world were the corners of her mouth tugging upward to match his?

Because he knew her, inside and out. She knew he knew her. She could pretend all she wanted if it made her feel better, but facts were facts. Branch knew her better than anyone else.

'Is it okay if I come here and see you again?' Another whisper from his lips, another question meant only for her.

Transfixed, Kait couldn't help herself. She nodded. 'How long are you here in town, Branch?'

'Till the end of the month,' he said. 'I'll see you soon.'

She watched him reach for his hat and walk out of the diner, zipping his jacket up as he went. The bell above the door rang loud and shrill as he disappeared out into the snowy streets, but Kait didn't feel the icy chill that wafted into the room from the opened door.

Branch was back, for the entire month of December. All she had to do was survive it. Two days down, twenty-nine to go.

Chapter 4

Branch

Branch didn't believe in fate. How could he? He was a man who lost his parents as a kid, lost the woman he loved as a teenager, and lost the grandparents who had been his only remaining family in his late twenties.

If fate was real, it was cruel. For him, it was easier to disbelieve.

But when he strolled into that diner to get a cup of coffee to go, hat pulled down low and jacket collar tugged up to conceal his identity as much as he could, he would have believed in leprechauns that rode unicorns, or that pirates buried treasure in the harbor that ran parallel to Port Landon's downtown. He would have believed in anything, because there was no way he could come face to face with those pretty emerald eyes and not believe in something bigger than himself.

Kait Davenport was even more breathtaking than he remembered, something he didn't think was possible. Seeing her standing there in that pale purple uniform, her hair pulled into a tight ponytail with flyaway strands at her temples, it was like he had taken a step back in time. She could have easily passed for her eighteen-year-old self, he was sure of it. The only thing different was what he saw in her eyes. A hardness mixed with weary resignation. Like she couldn't trust anyone around her, and she was tired of having to keep her guard up. Or tired of people proving her distrust right all the time.

He had been the first one to cause that haunted expression. Now, unexpectedly, Branch felt something he hadn't experienced in a long time. Desire. Not just in the seductive sense, though there was a need pulsing inside him to be closer to Kait, as close as he could be. One glimpse was enough to make him want her in every way imaginable, to make him remind her of what they once had. Who they'd once been.

But the desire that overwhelmed him most was the need to soften that hardness in her eyes. He might have been the cause of it once, but Branch wanted to be the one to melt it away.

When he left Port Landon more than ten years ago, there had been no chance of that happening. Kait hated him, right along with a large percentage of the rest of the town. But as surprised as he was to lay eyes on her in that diner, nothing could have prepared him for what flashed in her gaze when he asked if he could see her again.

A chance.

It was only for a second, and barely visible, but Branch saw the flash of desire that broke through her hard façade. It was the desire to let go of the pain and heartache and unhappiness that had remained in Port Landon with her when Branch hadn't. He wasn't naive enough to believe it meant she still loved him after all the years and all the turmoil that had passed by, but it was a chance. A miniscule sliver, maybe, but a chance, nonetheless. He would take it.

Seeing Kait seemed to light a fire in him, somehow. Not just one that burned in his chest and reminded him of who she had once been to him – and who he'd been to her – but also a fire that encouraged him to do something. Make a plan. Get things sorted. Grandma Addie wouldn't want him sitting alone in this big old house ruminating over days gone by and holding on to all the tangible things that didn't matter in the greater scheme of things. She had been a woman who had loved love. She knew the value of loving someone and being loved, and she made no bones about telling him, even as a kid, that the stuff we accumulated over the course of our lives meant nothing in comparison to the relationships we made. That was where we truly prospered, she said, not in the collection of money and things, but in the accumulation of memories and experiences with those we loved and cherished.

It turned out he had been listening to all those late-night lectures she'd given, after all.

First things first. After his impromptu trip to the diner to seek out coffee, Branch hit up the grocery store and restocked the fridge. He was going to be around for the next month, so he needed to start acting like it. Food, cleaning products, and a copy of this week's *Port Landon Ledger*. He needed some updated information on this town, even if the town wasn't as willing to glean updated information on him. Planning to read through the paper that night, he tossed it near Grandpa Duke's armchair. The man had been gone four years, but it would always be his chair to Branch.

His burst of renewed energy came to a crashing halt when he bravely swung the attic ladder down from the ceiling and slid the latches into place to secure it. One look at the piles of boxes and totes amongst the mysterious piles covered in dusty sheets and Branch wished he'd never popped his head into the attic in the first place. Cobwebs hung in long, thick linear patterns, and dust floated through the air in a speckled pattern where the sun's rays struggled to shine through the grime-coated window at the other end of the room.

'It's just stuff, right, Grandma?' he muttered, scanning the mess. 'A whole lot of stuff.' He could almost hear her throaty chuckle and see the deep crow's feet at the corners of her eyes as they squinted, glinting with amusement at his reaction to the mountains of boxes.

Not for the first time, he wished she was there. He wished anyone was there. Knowing he had help to sort through this would certainly ease the burden a bit. And the loneliness.

Maybe it was better to start off smaller, take on the task of sorting through his grandfather's magazine racks downstairs instead. He could tackle this hoard of antiques and mementos another day.

Then, he saw it.

'No way.' Being careful where he stepped in case of weakened floorboards or unseen hazards, Branch crawled up into the attic and made his way across the dimly lit room. The obstacle course of piles and sheet-covered furniture left him panting in the stale air by the time he reached it, but as he ran his palm over the metal backboard of the basketball net, a different sense of nostalgia hit him like a lethal ocean wave.

Port Landon was home, he reminded himself, his fingers tangling in the frayed net. *Even if it isn't now, it was. Once.* He had a life here, then. Family. Friends. All of which he had essentially hidden from each time he swooped into town under the shadowed veil of night-time and left just as quickly as he showed up. But there had been more to his childhood and teenage years than the fateful debacle that turned his name into a curse word amongst the community.

Branch wiped a hefty coat of dust from the basketball net and awkwardly managed to get it down the attic stairs without breaking it or his neck. Suddenly, he knew exactly where to start when it came to getting things sorted.

Branch had to keep reminding himself that more than a decade had passed. Somehow, Port Landon looked exactly the same as he remembered. The postcard-like beauty surrounded him everywhere he turned. The tiny town was cloaked under a thick blanket of snow, with Christmas lights and decorations accenting every wrought iron streetlamp or porch railing. The sight was picturesque and festive, reminding him that he was just as much a part of it as the town was a part of him.

It might have felt different to him, but it looked like the same small town he grew up in and reeled him in the way only a hometown could do.

Perhaps that meant it was him who had changed instead, viewing it with warier, pessimistic eyes.

As he pulled up in front of it, Branch took in the brick bungalow with slight trepidation. He had spent many evenings and weekends in this yard. He'd probably logged just as many hours and weeks and years at the Forresters' house as he had at his grandparents' if he added them up. The house matched his memory of it. The Christmas lights were even strung across the eaves and down the columns on either side of the front step the same way they had been decorated when he was a kid.

It's me that's different, he reminded himself. And it was him that had chosen not to contact his friends after he left. He hoped Jason's parents still owned the house, and that they would be forgiving enough to at least tell him where Jason lived now. Whether Jason was in town or not, Branch had left his grandparents' house five minutes ago vowing to make contact with one of his old friends. If it had to be via phone, he would call, but Branch was determined to try to track him down.

The driveway was newly plowed, and a blue Dodge Ram sat in the driveway. Branch was half expecting to see Jason's mom's old silver Corolla sitting beside it, but, of course, that car was probably in a scrapyard somewhere by now.

Snow covered the lawn, and the windowsills had inches of ice packed into the corners. A shovel was propped up beside the front door, at the ready. Holding his breath, Branch grabbed the brass door knocker and slapped it down a few times, the sound loud and obnoxious in the chilly silence of the residential street.

The door opened quickly enough that Branch wondered if the man who opened it had been standing on the other side, waiting for him.

The wide eyes that greeted him confirmed that wasn't the case.

'Sterling, is that you?'

Jason Forrester was no longer the lanky teenager waiting to grow into his gangly limbs and deep voice. The man could have been a linebacker with those broad shoulders and his thick, muscular build. His close-cropped black hair and dark eyes revealed his identity, though. From the nose up, Branch would have recognized his childhood friend anywhere.

'I could ask you the same thing, Jay.'

'Well, I'll be.' The hug he wrapped Branch in was strong and sincere. Whatever reservations Branch had about coming here, they were laid to rest in an instant. 'Come on in. It's too cold to be standing out there.'

The interior of the house came as a shock to him. As Branch shuffled out of his coat and boots at the entryway, he took in the neutral colors on the walls and the leather couch and loveseat in the living room. From his vantage point, he could see through to the kitchen, now lined with modern white cupboards and a small pub-style table and chairs. It was a stark contrast to the melamine and aluminum he remembered. So, some things did change in Port Landon, then.

'You still living here with your mom and dad?' The question was out of his mouth before Branch fully thought it through. If Jason was offended, he didn't show it as he pulled two colas from the fridge and offered him one.

'I can tell it isn't just me you haven't spoken to since we were teenagers,' he laughed. 'I bought the place from my parents when they moved into North Springs.'

'Wow, never thought your parents would leave Port Landon.'

Jason gestured toward the leather couch. 'Mom has glaucoma

and can't drive anymore, so they bought an apartment there. Closer to more amenities.' He lowered himself onto the loveseat. 'I never thought you'd show back up here. Especially on my doorstep.'

'I should've paid you a visit long before now,' Branch admitted, sheepish. 'I'm sorry, Jay.'

Jason regarded his soda can absently. 'Word got around you were in town a few times over the years,' he explained. 'And I knew you were here for Grandma Addie's funeral, but by then I didn't know if you wanted to see any of us or not.'

She was Grandma Addie to everyone, and Branch's grand-mother would have gladly taken in every one of his friends as honorary grandchildren if she had the chance. Which only made Branch's chest tighten more. 'That's why you weren't at the funeral. Because you didn't think I would want you there?' His friend didn't have to answer. The truth shadowed his gaze.

'We didn't want to make it harder for you.'

He'd spent those few days in a grief-stricken haze, but Branch remembered vividly wishing he had friends left to stand beside him as he said his final goodbyes to the woman who'd raised him like a son. It made so much sense now that he was sitting here, face to face with the man who had been his friend for more years than he realized. A man who'd been his friend even when Branch thought he didn't have any friends left.

'I'm sorry I made you think you shouldn't come to the funeral,' Branch choked out. Clearing his voice, he set the soda down, fearful he would drop it. 'She would've wanted you there,' he added. '*I* wanted you there. I'm sorry, Jay.'

Jason nodded. He knew that. He had always been the level-headed and forgiving one in their group. 'I got to see her over the years. She was aware that she was family in my eyes, too. I've got no regrets, man.'

Of course he didn't. Jason Forrester had lived by the motto that life was too short to regret the past and dwell on what

31

couldn't be changed. Branch had always wished he was a little more like his friend. Probably now more than ever.

'You can't say the same.' It wasn't a question, but Jason wasn't reprimanding him or judging him, either.

'Nah, I suppose I can't,' Branch replied. 'Looking back on it all now, I know I could have handled it all differently. But when everyone started to turn against me—'

'No one turned against you,' Jason cut in. He leaned forward, elbows on his knees. 'At least, not everyone. I'll bet that's how it felt, but everyone didn't turn against you after the accident. Kait did. But to you, Kait *was* everyone back then.'

'Things were never going to be the same for me here after that,' Branch explained. 'It didn't matter what was true and what wasn't. I was always going to be the kid that hit one of Port Landon's own with my truck.'

Jason sighed, letting his head sag slightly. 'Man, you were eighteen and you weren't paying attention. And frankly, the guy's still walking around town acting like he's king of the world, so I really think you need to give yourself a break. It was what, ten years ago?'

'Eleven.' It had been an accident, pure and simple. A fleeting moment of preoccupation, too concerned about getting an intoxicated schoolmate home, too caught up in his own thoughts to fully take in his surroundings. Nothing would have ever led Branch to purposely use his vehicle as a weapon, though. Nothing. 'I was stone cold sober, man. I have no idea what he was doing behind my pickup, but I did not hit him on purpose, and I was not drunk.'

'I believed you then, and I believe you now.' Jason took a long drink from his soda and set it down on the coffee table. 'If it's forgiveness you're looking for from me, there's nothing for me to forgive you for. Maybe you should try forgiving yourself for a change.'

Branch didn't know if that was possible, but knowing he had

a friend now, after all these years, went a long way in helping him feel better about being back in town. 'So, we're good, you and I?'

A slow grin spread across his friend's face. 'We've been good all this time. All you had to do was show up so I could tell you.' Jason picked his soda can up and held it out toward Branch, humor alight in his eyes. 'Next time things go south around here, do me a favor and don't run north. Deal?'

Branch couldn't help the chuckle that escaped his lips. 'Deal. So, you know I work up north, then. In Canada.'

'Grandma Addie went on and on about it. She didn't like that you were gone for such long periods of time or that the area was remote as all get out, but she was sure to let everybody know that you were some hotshot engineer in northern Canada.'

That sounded about right. Leave it to his grandmother to make a remote area in the most northern part of Alberta sound glamorous. It was anything but, and far enough north that the best way to access it was by airplane, but he was paid well for his time. The two-weeks-on, two-weeks-off schedule wasn't for the faint of heart, but the seclusion had been exactly what he'd been looking for when he left.

'It's a good gig,' he replied, nodding. 'And they've been good about giving me some time off to deal with Grandma Addie's place.'

'So, you're here for a while?'

'Until the end of the month.'

'You'll be around for Christmas. It'll almost be like old times,' Jason laughed.

Almost. Branch caught that part. Because this time there was no Grandma Addie to pull off the festivities and be the glue that held them together. This time, it was just Branch, with a ticking time clock that reminded him he would be leaving again in a matter of weeks. This time, he didn't know if he would be coming back to Port Landon.

He sunk back into the couch cushions, getting comfortable. 'Never took you for a holiday kind of guy.'

His friend shrugged. 'I'm more of a Halloween kind of man, myself, but there isn't a person in their right mind who's going to turn down the homemade food that comes once folks start getting that Christmas spirit.'

A laugh erupted from Branch, and he shook his head. He missed this. Having someone to talk to. About nothing. About everything. In a way, it was as though no time had passed at all since they had last seen each other. An easy silence ensued, and he could feel the tension subsiding in his shoulders.

'I saw her, you know.' Branch didn't realize he was smiling until Jason's eyebrows arched. 'At the diner.'

'I don't see a black eye, so neither of the Davenport women punched you first and asked questions later.' Jason pressed his lips together.

'Janna works there, too, now?' Kait's older sister hadn't liked him before the accident. Afterward, her dislike turned into full-fledged disgust. 'I didn't see her, just Kait.'

'Imagine that, you only seeing Kait in a room full of people,' Jason joked. 'Some things never change.'

'It wasn't like that,' he argued, leaning forward to match his friend's stance. 'Things were different, obviously. But they were the same between us, too, if that makes sense.' He raised his head and met Jason's eyes squarely. 'I don't think it's over, Jay.'

Jason's eyes bulged and he let out a long breath. 'Eleven years, Branch. Remember that. What in the world makes you think it's not over?'

He couldn't put his finger on it, but it was something in the way Kait had tried so hard – too hard – to be defiant and distant. She was trying and failing, just like he was trying and failing to keep from loving her all over again. 'Call it a gut feeling.'

Jason was obviously attempting to make him see how outlandish his train of thought was. 'You haven't seen her since you were a teenager, and you're telling me, after one glimpse, you think she'll take you back?'

'I think there's too much between us not to at least try.'

'You always were a hard-headed one,' Jason snickered. 'Especially when it came to her.'

'Like you said, she didn't punch me or send her older sister after me, so I've got a thread of hope to hold on to.' Branch downed the last of his soda, unable to hide his smirk.

'That isn't a thread of hope, man, that's just proof of what I said earlier.'

Branch's eyebrows furrowed. 'What do you mean?'

Jason stood, taking the empty can from him. 'Even Kait's forgiven you for hitting Zach with your truck. It's time for you to forgive yourself and move forward.'

Chapter 5

Kait

'I don't believe a thing that comes out of his mouth, Kait.'

'I know.' She huffed out a sigh. 'You've said so five times since you sat down.'

Kait finished adding up the bill in front of her and pushed the calculator back under the counter. Using it as an excuse for a moment's reprieve, she placed it into a vinyl check holder along with a couple of after-dinner mints and headed to the table by the window to drop it off, leaving Zach sitting at the counter to cool down.

She knew he wasn't thrilled to know Branch was back in town. She couldn't blame him considering their sordid past. She wasn't even sure why she had mentioned speaking with him yesterday. Branch Sterling had never been Zach's favorite topic of conversation, unless he was belittling him or reminding Kait of what he'd done to her. And what he'd done to him.

Like she could ever forget. Vivid recollections of the months that followed the accident were never far from her mind. She might not have been the one behind the steering wheel, but Kait harbored acidic guilt just the same. She hadn't even been at the party that night, and she certainly hadn't witnessed the event that left Zach with a fractured leg and countless bruises. It didn't matter. She would never forget Zach's emotional retelling of what should have been an innocent celebration of their upcoming graduation, his words so clear that her memory played tricks on her sometimes, as though she was plagued by her own memories and not the recounting of someone else's.

The heated exchange between Branch and Zach. The way Branch had slammed the passenger door of his truck, so frustrated and final before he climbed into the driver's seat. Before he revved the engine and threw the truck in reverse …

She could see it all so clearly even though she had never seen it at all. Each time she thought of it, her mind struggled to pair Branch's face with the man who got into that driver's seat. It just wasn't the Branch Sterling she'd known, or the Branch Sterling she'd loved.

And still, it had happened. Which was why Kait had remained by Zach's side and helped him in every way she could, from physiotherapy to mundane errands, to the point of fatigue and burnout. She couldn't do enough for him after seeing what her love for Branch had ultimately put him through.

Still, after vowing to be there for Zach and see him through his recovery, there was one thing she would never be able to do for him despite her best efforts. With all their time together and close proximity while he healed, Zach's feelings for Kait only flourished. And while she wanted to feel as strongly for him as he did for her, that overpowering sense of love and companionship never bloomed. A year passed by before they attempted to formally date, and it took two more for her to admit it to herself, but Kait would never be capable of loving Zach the way he deserved to be loved.

'I'll bet he knew you were here at the diner all along,' he suggested before Kait could even make it back around the counter. 'Next, he'll be saying the stars aligned and the heavens opened, revealing his path to you.'

She offered him a levelled stare. 'You're being dramatic.'

'The guy hit me with a truck after warning me to stay away from you. Doesn't get any more dramatic than that.'

Fighting back the urge to cringe, Kait focused on reorganizing the menus instead of having to meet his gaze. 'I know, Zach.' *It's the gazillionth time you've mentioned that to me, too.* 'I just think it's time to stop being so angry, you know? Years have passed. He seems … different.' She didn't know how to explain it. There was something in Branch's eyes that not only proved he wasn't feigning his utter surprise at the sight of her, but also hinted of a maturity far beyond the mere decade that spanned between their teenage years and now.

Branch Sterling wasn't even thirty yet, but he had lost everything and everyone who had meant something to him at one point in his young life or another. Some losses were the result of his teenage antics, but most were tragic, painful, crushing blows that the average person wouldn't survive unscathed individually, let alone combined. And yet, he was here, back in town, and facing every demon he had.

She wondered if she was one of them.

Zach scoffed. 'Come on, you know better. He isn't different. You just want him to be.' She turned and glared at him, causing Zach to reach out a hand and grip her fingers in his. 'I don't mean that as a bad thing,' he added in a softer tone. 'It's your nature. You see the good in everyone. You're a nurturer, and you always want to help. But, Kait, some people can't be helped.'

It was a strange feeling to have someone conjure up defeat and molten determination in her at the same time. Defeat, because she would never get through to Zach and his pent-up rage where Branch was concerned, but also determination, because she wanted desperately for Branch to prove him wrong.

'It's been eleven years.' She sounded wilted and weak, and the words came out on a sigh.

'It has,' he replied, 'And we've moved on from all things

revolving around Branch Sterling. By the end of the month, we can go back to our lives and pretend like he was never here at all.'

Slowly, Kait withdrew her hand from his. She couldn't bring herself to look up at him, and she certainly didn't agree with him.

Something strong and undeniable pulsed within her, something she had once thought dormant. And that something told her, now that Branch was back in town, things were never going to be the same again.

Kait was disappointed that Janna and their coworker, Eve, had finished decorating the Christmas tree during the morning shift. Even the sparkly red and green garlands had been meticulously strung across the front of the counter and around the trim of the main door. She didn't dare touch the box of remaining Christmas decorations that had been shoved under the counter by her feet with a handwritten sign in Janna's recognizable scrawl that read *Don't touch!* Her sister's need for control knew no bounds.

It left Kait with little left to occupy herself once Natasha, the other waitress who rounded out their four-person waitstaff team extraordinaire, had left for the evening. The clock hadn't even struck seven o'clock yet. There was still more than an hour to go before she could lock the doors, finish cleaning the front of the restaurant, and head home to the three-bedroom house she rented with Janna and her twins.

Kait didn't do idle well. Sitting down, relaxing, giving herself a moment to breathe … that only resulted in letting her thoughts take over and leaving her with more frustration than resolution. It was better that she remained occupied, doing even the most repetitive, mundane tasks in order to keep her body moving and her mind busy. At the diner, that meant unnecessary cleaning and reorganizing. At home, well, there was never any chance of quiet time with a pair of two-year-old twin boys around.

On second thought, maybe she should take the opportunity of a five-minute break for what it was. A gift.

Her one and only table, a couple with a young boy, gave her a thumbs-up from across the room after she held up the coffee pot in askance, so Kait went ahead and poured herself a full cup. Coffee in the evening – a recipe for a poor night's sleep if she ever heard one.

Sliding into the booth closest to the counter, she had a clear view of the door and a cozy spot near the heat register beside her feet. Her comfortable moment to herself was thwarted a few seconds later when the front door swung open and her clear view suddenly became less than ideal.

There was nowhere to run and nowhere to hide while she made a futile attempt at composing herself. Her wide gaze landed on Branch at the same moment his locked on her.

'Back again,' she teased, holding out a sliver of hope that she sounded more nonchalant than she suddenly felt. She moved her foot beneath the table to see if the heat had kicked on in order to explain the immediate uptick in warmth around her. It hadn't. 'Don't know if there's an available table for you.'

Branch didn't bother to look around at the slew of vacant tables. He stayed focused on Kait as a slow, mischievous grin spread across his face. 'Good thing I don't mind sharing.'

He slid in across from her, hands still shoved in his jacket pockets to stave off the icy cold that lingered on him.

She thought of telling him she wasn't interested in sharing anything with him, not even a table in an empty diner, but Kait didn't trust herself to sound convincing. Instead, she began to shuffle out of the booth. 'Let me get you a coffee.'

Branch reached his hand out so fast she didn't realize he'd moved until his fingertips were pressed gently into her wrist. 'I've got it.'

He slid out of the booth instead, shuffling out of his jacket before he stretched his body across the top of the counter and dipped his hand under it to pull a white china mug from the rack. Coffee pot in one hand, mug in the other, he came back to the table with a wry smile. 'Everything's still in the exact same spot.'

'Some things never change.'

'Obviously.'

It was one word, a simple answer. But Kait didn't know if it was meant to pack the weight it did as it hit her in the chest, or if her reaction was merely her own over-analyzing brain thinking he was referring to something he wasn't.

Smirking, Branch stole fleeting glances at her as he poured his coffee then went about putting the pot back. Kait wondered if he could hear her racing thoughts, somehow.

She stood up again. 'There's only creamer on the table—'

'Kait,' Branch laughed, holding up a hand, 'It's fine. Will you please sit down and relax? I'm starting to think you're trying to find an escape route from me.'

'No, it's not like that,' she argued. Was it?

'Then, just sit and enjoy your coffee that you obviously don't need.' He went about adding sugar and cream to his cup. 'Also, I do still prefer milk, but cream isn't that bad, either. You'd be surprised what you can get used to when you have to drink whatever swill they pass off as coffee at a mining camp for weeks at a time.'

'That's right, you have a fancy job title at a mine up in Canada, huh?'

'Grandma Addie's words, I take it?' Branch chuckled, shrugging. 'But, yeah, I guess I do. It's the same place I went to work when ...' He paused and cleared his throat. 'When I left here,' he finished. 'I've just got the education needed to work my way up since then.'

Sheepish, she wondered what he had been about to say the first time. When their lives fell apart? When she told him to leave and never come back?

41

'And now you're an engineer,' she replied. She couldn't bring herself to say it aloud, but she was so proud of him for succeeding.

Branch nodded. 'It's far from glamorous, and I'm gone a lot, but yeah, I've got a good job.'

'And now you've got a house and vehicles, too.' The corner of her mouth twitched, but Kait was sad for him. What it must be like to have to sift through all the things in his grandparents' home and try to decide what to do with them, especially now that he was the only one left to do it. What it must be like to have only tangible things in place of an entire family. 'Make any headway?'

An indignant snort was his initial response. 'I found one of my basketball nets in the attic, does that count?'

Whatever Kait had expected, it wasn't that. Laughter burst from her mouth. Thank goodness she hadn't had a mouthful of coffee. 'I shouldn't be surprised. And is that what you did all day, then, shoot hoops?'

'I said I found the net,' he repeated. 'No ball, though.'

More laughter bubbled up, and she shook her head. 'Can't very well use one without the other, I suppose.'

'It's a mess in there, Kait. I'm serious.' Branch looked uncomfortable having to admit it, and Kait knew why. Grandma Addie had always taken great pride in keeping a tidy and organized home. The house was well lived-in, but everything had a place, and everything was put back in that place when they were done with it. 'I don't remember the attic being that full of stuff, but it's full. Jam-packed. That means that the areas I do remember being full to the brim, like the linen closets and the garage and basement, are even worse than I remember, too.'

She could only imagine the mountain of memories he was going to have to contend with while trying to decide what to do with everything. Having the rest of the month to deal with it sounded feasible, but Kait knew it was going to be difficult. Especially by himself.

'Have you decided what you're going to do?' She couldn't stop the question from passing her lips. 'With the house and whatnot?'

His answer came without hesitation. 'No idea.' Letting out a long breath, he leaned back. 'Sell it, maybe? I don't know, I can't imagine what good it would do for me to keep it.'

And I can't imagine what it would be like if someone other than your family owned it. She would never say it to him, but there was no way she could picture Addie's house being someone else's. 'It can't be that awful to think about actually keeping it, can it?'

Without pinpointing what changed or how, Kait saw Branch's expression transform from a forlorn resignation into a piqued curiosity. His eyebrows didn't raise in askance, and his gaze didn't narrow or widen, but there was a question in his eyes, nonetheless, as he set his mug down. 'It isn't, no,' he replied cautiously. 'But I didn't think there was anyone here who would care whether I did or didn't.'

He didn't think *she* would care, that was what he was really getting at.

'Well, maybe you're wrong.' They were on dangerous ground. The stones at the edge of the cliff she was standing on were chipping away in shards and dust. Soon, she would have no choice but to admit to him – and to herself – that she was over the moon about having him back in town. A lot of people in town would be thrilled, even if Branch didn't realize it. It had taken years for him to return, and Kait wasn't sure she was ready to give him up again at the end of the month.

The cliff hadn't given way yet, however. Kait swallowed hard. 'Take it one step at a time,' she said, hoping to get the conversation back into a safer territory. 'Focus on sorting through things, one room at a time. Keep what you want and need to keep, and donate whatever you're willing to part with. But don't stress over it. Worst-case scenario, you don't finish by the end of December and you have to come back.'

'Yeah,' he said slowly. 'Worst-case scenario.' Those dark eyes that Kait used to get lost in when she was eighteen squinted as he stared at her, like he was trying to see her more clearly, trying to understand what she wasn't saying out loud. 'Better be careful with your advice, Davenport, or I might be forced to recruit your help purely based on your enthusiasm.'

His taunting manner caused Kait to raise her hands. 'Hey, sounds better than the standing plans I have with a set of toddler twins,' she laughed.

Branch's mouth gaped. 'Toddler … twins?'

'Janna's two boys,' Kait chuckled. 'Not mine.' She laughed even harder at the relief that washed over him. 'I live with her, to help her out.'

Branch let out a heavy breath, pressing his hands against the table. 'I really thought I was missing a vital piece of information there for a second.'

'Oh, please,' Kait snickered, waving a hand. 'The only sordid history I've got is you.'

It was the first time she had mentioned their past and put a humorous spin on it. Ever. The joke at his expense might have caught him off guard, but as Branch took in her faint smirk, he recognized it for what it really was – the beginnings of a truce.

'Touché.' He leaned in closer, crossing his arms in front of him. 'So, does that mean you're in?'

'In what?'

'Help me,' he requested softly. 'With sorting through Grandma Addie's house.'

Kait's head snapped back as though she had been slapped. 'You can't be serious.'

'Why not? You just said it sounds like more fun than hanging out with Janna's kids, and you knew Grandma Addie better than almost anyone. She loved you.'

She held her breath. She wasn't the only one who'd loved Kait back then. 'I … don't think that's a good idea.'

'Maybe not,' Branch said, 'but I would still love it if you'd give it a chance. Besides, if it turns out bad, I'll be gone in a month.'

That's what I'm afraid of.

Zach was right about her. Maybe it was her nature to want to see the good in everyone. And maybe she was a nurturer, always wanting to help. But that wasn't what this was about. Branch Sterling had no one left in Port Landon. Was some of that his own doing? Sure. But in the wake of his grandmother's passing, there was no one left he felt close to.

No one except her. And it was Christmas-time. No one should spend Christmas alone.

'As friends.' It wasn't a question, and she thankfully was able to get it out without it sounding like one.

Branch's hands came up in mock surrender. 'Friends.'

In what might have been her biggest lapse of judgment since falling in love with him during their teenage years in the first place, Kait nodded. 'I'm only agreeing to this because the idea of a break from the twins with terrible-twos sounds like a fairytale right now.'

Branch's eyes lit up, rivalling the twinkling lights on the Christmas tree. 'I don't care why you're doing it, Kaitie, just that you are.'

Something fluttered wildly in her belly seeing that kind of anticipation in his eyes. Hearing that kind of wistful reassurance in his voice as he said her name. It was a recipe for disaster, and yet Kait was looking forward to it. But her eagerness was only due to the temporary break from the mundane routine her life had become. It had nothing to do with what she felt for Branch Sterling.

Then, or now.

Chapter 6

Branch

Branch awoke the next morning with multiple folks' voices ringing in his ears.

He heard Jason suggesting that Kait had forgiven him so perhaps it was time to forgive himself. He heard Kait's pretty voice saying it was good to see him while nodding her agreement to seeing him again. And, amid those voices was Grandma Addie, loud and clear.

You kids are so young to be capable of lovin' each other that deep. His grandmother had spoken those words so many times over the course of his life he had lost count, both during his and Kait's courtship and long after its demise.

Not once had she ever said they were too young to feel that way, or too naive in their belief that it was real. Grandma Addie knew better. She had run off and married Grandpa Duke at the tender age of seventeen. She knew a thing or two about real, lifelong love.

She also never changed that statement to past tense after Kait ended things with him following the accident. Love didn't end just because we told it to. Just because we wanted it to, or needed it to.

46

This morning, as Branch climbed out of the double bed in his childhood bedroom, those words were catapulting through his brain on an endless loop. That was when he knew for certain.

The love he harbored for Kait Davenport wasn't some separate entity he had left behind when he escaped Port Landon, and it wasn't something the last eleven years had chipped away at until only dust remained. What he felt for her was still very much real, and very much a part of him.

It was also still very much a part of Kait. The war he saw raging within that green gaze when he first walked into the diner proved she was struggling with it, too. And as much as knowing some part of her still loved him elated Branch, it also fueled sadness at knowing they had wasted so much precious time. He found solace in the realization that neither distance nor years had been strong enough to weaken their bond, however.

He had been determined to see her, then. Kait had given him permission the day before to visit the diner again, and it had taken him all day to do the laundry and cleaning needed to have a tidy bedroom to sleep in, taking care to avoid delving too deeply into the stuff still piled in his closet and dressers. He knew he would find mementos of who he and Kait had once been together in a battered shoebox in the bottom of his closet. Old pictures, folded notes, the burned CDs they used to make for each other of their favorite songs, the concert tickets from the time they snuck into Detroit to see Our Lady Peace's live show and got grounded for weeks … it was all there, all saved so he could remember.

Like he could ever forget.

He hadn't been prepared to face that shoebox, and he didn't have time to give it the time and attention it deserved, anyway. He made sure all the mandatory chores of the day were accomplished before he allowed himself the break needed to make good on his promise to see her again. It took him just as long to work up the courage.

He hadn't expected her to be on a break, by herself. Or sitting alone in that booth with worn vinyl seats and a marred melamine table, coffee cup squeezed between her hands.

And he certainly hadn't expected her to agree to partner up with him and take on the organization of his grandparents' Victorian home. Kait's words were clear despite the tremor she spoke them with; she didn't think it was a good idea. And yet, there had been no denying the glint of joy that reflected in her eyes. Whether that was from being able to spend time with him, or merely being able to have a conversation with someone who wasn't a toddler, a family member, or a paying customer awaiting her to serve their food, he didn't care.

Because Kait was willing to share her time with him, despite everything. And by the time he laid his head down again that night, Grandma Addie's words whispered through his mind once more. Present tense. *You kids are so young to be capable of lovin' each other that deep.*

Age had nothing to do with it. Neither did capability. Kait Davenport had been his first love. His only love. And that love remained, still deep and still real. He was smiling when sleep pulled him into slumber.

Snow drifted in softly floating flecks, somersaulting lazily in the late morning air. A gray cloak veiled the sky, but the accumulated snow that covered everything gave the illusion of a brighter day than it truly was. Or maybe the brightness was seen through Branch's eyes only, tinting everything he saw with more vividness and sparkle.

He refused to let today go to waste, and his renewed vitality aided him in not only dusting and mopping the entire main floor of the massive house, but he also cleaned the inside of the windows by hand, wiping the dirt and dust from the panes and sills to let the natural light in, unobstructed. By the time his stomach was growling for sustenance, he was convinced there was nothing he couldn't do within the walls of his grandparents' home. This place would be gleaming again by the time he was done with it.

Can I really, truly be done with it? Just thinking about letting the house go hit him like a punch to the gut.

He needed food. Then, maybe he could curb the life-changing questions that threatened to diminish his new-found organizational groove. Desperate for fifteen minutes without having to witness the disarray around him, he headed for the door. Kait might have said she wasn't scheduled at the diner today, but Port Landon's downtown beckoned to him like an old friend. Main Street held everything a person could need in a pinch, including hot coffee and a quick bite to eat. He would take his moment of reprieve there.

Swinging the door open, work boots tied and jacket zipped up, he jumped back. 'Son of a—'

'Whoa!' Jason's hand was still outstretched, ready to knock.

'Jay, I didn't expect you to be standing there.' Branch was far too used to spending his time alone.

Jason was bundled up just as warmly, a gray wool toque pulled down over his ears and a thick black coat and matching gloves covering his upper body. 'So much for a friendly greeting,' he breathed out, the air puffing out in a white fog in front of him. 'Where are you headed like the place is on fire?'

'Downtown. I need a break and something to eat. You in?'

'My truck's already running and warm. I'll drive.'

The blue Dodge sat idling in the driveway, and after locking the front door behind him, Branch hopped in. The blast of warm air from the dashboard vents was welcomed despite his short trek from the house to the vehicle. 'What brings you by?'

Jason headed toward Main Street, fiddling with the dials to make the fans blow the heat at them in more furious gusts. 'Thought you might need some help, and I was off work today.'

'Appreciate it. You working in town?'

Jason offered him a sideways glance. 'I own the old Robinson's Auto. It's called Forrester's Auto now, though.'

'No way.' First he had suggested his friend still lived with his parents, then he'd failed to ask him about his employment. Branch wasn't doing a very good job as a friend, even an old one. 'Wife and kids I should know about, too, or do the surprises end there?'

Jason's mouth twitched, but his eyes stayed focused out the windshield as he pulled down the visor in front of him to reveal a wallet-sized picture of a brunette little girl with curly pigtails. 'A daughter, Carlie. She's four. But she lives with her mama in North Springs. I see her every second weekend, though.'

'Wow, awesome. She's cute, man.' Even if he hadn't seen Jason's face, he heard the tinge of sadness in his tone. There was a story there, one Branch wasn't sure his friend wanted to get into. They chatted easily on the way, and Branch managed to tell him about Kait's agreement to help him with the house at the perfect moment, able to put off his friend's reply by following his confession with a question of his own. 'Why are we parking here?' The diner was on the other side of the street, yet Jason steered the truck into a spot nowhere near the diner despite the available parking spots all around them.

Jason turned the key, killing the engine. 'You can go to the diner to see Kait to your heart's content, my friend, but if it's good coffee you want, the Portside Coffeehouse is where you want to be.'

'Is that so?' Intrigued, Branch followed his childhood friend inside, vaguely remembering the coffeeshop from when he'd lived here. If his memory served him right, the coffeehouse had only been a new venture in town back then. Or relatively new. He couldn't remember. Probably because his teenage brain had only ever had room for one thing and one thing only. Or, more accurately, one person.

The Portside Coffeehouse was obviously the place to be, even when it was frigid outside. Judging by the number of folks filling up the booths and bistro tables, they thought that the extra effort it took to shovel their way out of their homes to get here was worth it. As Branch took in the trendy brick walls, the smooth instrumental Christmas tunes that floated amongst the patrons' chatter, and the easy, warm atmosphere created by the large electric fireplace with flickering flames on the far side of the room, he hoped it *was* worth it. The place was cool, giving off vibes of comfort and ease. He could get used to this.

'The usual,' Jason said, smiling at the woman behind the counter.

With long auburn hair and a simple pairing of a T-shirt with the coffeehouse's logo on it and jeans, she was pretty in a natural kind of way. The genuine grin she responded with only enhanced her beauty.

'You got it, Jason,' the woman stated. 'And your friend?' It was like the woman never stopped moving, and never stopped smiling. There was no question about it, she loved her job.

Before he could respond, Jason beat him to it. 'Just make it two, Allison. Better keep it simple. Branch, here, is a newbie.'

Allison's hands never stopped moving, but something changed in her eyes as she regarded Branch with a renewed interest. 'Branch, huh? You're Addie's grandson.'

'Yes, ma'am.' Branch nodded. The woman looked to be only a few years older than he was, but he had a funny feeling she knew him better than he knew her. Polite was the way to go.

'My condolences about your grandmother,' she replied. 'This town lost one of the best when we lost her. Christmas won't be the same around here.'

'Thank you.' If Branch was going to start being social around town like this instead of hiding away in the house as he had originally planned, he was going to need to harden himself to the constant mentions and reminders of his grandparents. He gladly took the coffee cup when it was offered, nodding his gratitude.

'My treat.' Jason handed over a five-dollar bill, waving Allison away when she tried to give him change. 'You know better than to try. Tell Chris I said hey, will you?'

'You bet.' She pushed the bill into the cash register. 'Be sure to take your friend to Paige's, too. Give him the full Port Landon culinary-and-caffeine experience.' She tilted her head toward the wall behind her, but her gaze never seemed to stray far from Branch.

'It's like you're reading my mind.' Jason laughed, giving her a wave on his way out.

On the sidewalk, Branch turned to his friend. 'Okay, I don't know Allison, but I'm going to go out on a limb and say she knows me?'

Jason pressed his lips together. 'I don't think you guys have ever formally met, if that's what you're asking, but it's safe to say she might feel like she knows you. She's one of Kait's good friends.'

A low groan escaped from deep in Branch's throat. 'So, she was looking at me like that because she thinks I'm a complete jerk.'

'I am the last man on Earth who will ever try to figure out what a woman thinks,' Jason chuckled, pushing Branch toward the doorway beside the coffeehouse. 'But, heads up, we're about to enter The Cakery, owned by Paige Henley, and she's another one of Kait's friends. All I can promise is that the sugar high will be worth any dirty looks you get.'

Thankfully, no dirty looks came from The Cakery, just a box of homemade sugared doughnuts and an introduction to the brunette that owned the place. Branch couldn't believe how different the bakery looked now, remembering fondly what it was like when he was a kid, back when old Wilhelmina used to own it.

'Paige seems nice,' he said to Jason as he climbed back in the truck, awkwardly and dangerously balancing his paper coffee cup on the bakery box as he did so.

'Easy, man, she's engaged to Dr Cohen from the vet's office.'

'It was a simple observation, nothing more.'

Jason started the truck and got the heater blowing strong again before he pulled out of his parking spot and headed back toward Branch's grandparents' house. 'Ah, right. Sorry, I just assumed you had a type when it came to women.'

Branch furrowed his brows. 'And what type is that?'

'The type where you only want the ones you can't have.'

'Let me guess,' Branch groaned. 'You're not talking about Paige at all.'

Jason didn't take his focus from the road in front of him. 'I'm just saying, there are a lot of other women out there, Branch. Ones that don't come with so much baggage and backstory.'

His words cut through Branch like a serrated knife. He was second-guessing his decision to confide in Jason about Kait's agreement to help him with his grandparents' house. 'You think I need to stay away from Kait.' Branch turned to glare at his friend, the paper cup in his hands burning into the pads of his fingers.

'It's none of my business, I know that. But are you sure it's worth it to dredge up all this stuff from the past when you—'

'When I'm the reason there's stuff to dredge up in the first place?' Branch snapped.

His outburst earned him a sidelong glance, but Jason remained calm. 'Actually, what I was going to say was are you sure it's worth it when you plan on leaving again at the end of the month?' He paused, letting that train of thought sink in. 'I'm not too keen on the idea of either of you getting hurt again. I think you two have been through more than enough.'

'I'm not trying to hurt Kait.' The words came out in a defensive rush before he could stop them. But was Jason right? Was that all his plans to spend time with her were going to do, hurt her all over again? Hurt himself?

'It's never going to be like it was back then, man.' Jason sounded apologetic, and for that, Branch was thankful. Maybe he did understand, at least a little, how badly Branch wanted a second chance to make the past less painful and turn the future into what he and Kait had always hoped it would be.

But his friend couldn't understand, he realized. If he did, he never would have said that, because as much as he believed things were never going to be like they were at eighteen, Jason was wrong.

Because they already were. Kait Davenport once again consumed his mind, and the events of that horrible night were once again front and center in his thoughts from the moment he woke up to the late hour he laid his head down at night. The past and the present had collided. For him, anyway.

Jason steered the truck into the driveway, parking it behind the rental Escape. The engine was still running when he turned to him. 'Be honest,' he said. 'Is there any chance at all that you'd consider staying in Port Landon?'

Whatever response Branch was about to flounder through was interrupted by the crunch of hard-packed snow behind them. Both men turned to watch a BMW pull in behind the truck.

'Who the—'

'You don't want to know,' Jason interjected, staring at the sporty car with its tinted windows like it was the last thing on Earth he ever expected to see.

A second later, they watched the driver open the door and climb out slowly, and Branch's jaw dropped slightly. It *was* the last thing he expected to see.

With wraparound Oakley sunglasses that matched the same glossy black as his BMW, Zach Canton looked better suited for the beach than the sub-zero temperatures of Michigan in December.

'What's he doing here?' Branch's pulse pounded furiously, his heart banging against his ribcage. He hadn't seen the man since the night of the accident. With every thump of his heartbeat, he became more and more confident that eleven years wasn't enough to divide the past from the present. It had taken seconds for Zach to climb out of that car, and that was all it took for then and now to crash into each other, too.

'I don't know,' Jason replied, turning the key to kill the engine, 'But there's two things you've got to do right now, Sterling. The first is to get out of this truck and find out why he's here. My windows aren't tinted, so he can see us. The second thing is to stop your damn whispering. You sound like a moron.'

Branch hadn't realized he'd whispered his question, but his friend's candor snapped him back to reality and had him clearing his throat to compose himself. The truck door seemed heavier somehow as he climbed out into the cold. Then again, maybe it wasn't the weight of the door that seemed heavier, but the weight of his guilt.

'Branch Sterling. Well, if it isn't the man of the hour himself,' Zach shouted, rounding the front of his car to meet Branch at the passenger side. 'The whole town's buzzing about you being back in town.'

Zach's features were harder than Branch remembered, his eyes clouded and shrewd. 'Just got a few things to take care of, Zach, then I think I'll be on my way.' He gave the man a once-over. 'You look like you're doing all right.' He had watched him walk toward him, waiting for an unsightly limp, or maybe an unsteadiness. But Branch saw no tell-tale signs of residual effects from the accident. None that he could see, anyway.

Zach made a show of waving a dismissive hand. 'I'm doing just fine. It'll take more than the backend of a truck to slow me down.'

Bile rose in Branch's throat. Was it just him that found it tactless to mention the accident so nonchalantly, especially after everything it had cost everyone involved?

55

Jason cleared his throat. 'What can we do for you, Canton?' he asked in a clipped tone.

Nah, it definitely wasn't just him.

Hands in the air, Zach smiled. 'I come in peace, boys, I swear it.' The smug tone and obnoxious chuckle that followed gave Branch the feeling that peace was the last thing on his mind, but Jason's constant glances in Branch's direction were getting through loud and clear. *Just keep your mouth shut and hear the guy out.*

'I actually heard you were the executor of Addie and Duke's estate,' Zach continued, nodding his head toward the looming house that stood before him. 'And the owner of this big, beautiful home now. Thought you might be in need of my services sometime soon, so I figured I'd drop this off.' Zach produced a glossy business card seemingly from nowhere, holding it out between his fingers.

For a second time, Branch's jaw went slack. Dumbfounded, he took the card, staring at it as though it was written in hieroglyphics. He knew from the *Port Landon Ledger* that Zach was a realtor, and a pretty successful one at that, but he never would have expected the man to seek him out about his grandparents' house. 'You came here to tell me you want to list my house?' The word *my* tasted like acid on his tongue, but Branch refused to let Zach Canton stand here and forget that it was more than some real estate listing to him.

'I can do you one better than that,' Zach said proudly, obviously untouched by Branch's indignant tone. 'I'll buy it from you. Top dollar, of course.' He flashed a smile that made Branch's insides contort. 'That's money in your pocket, Sterling, and then you – as you put it – can be on your way.'

He stared into the man's sunglasses, wishing he could see his eyes. Did he really mean it as maliciously as Branch was hearing it? Was he really standing here, offering cash in exchange for the only family home he had, just to get him out of town as fast as possible?

'Zach, I—'

'Branch needs time to think about it,' Jason cut in. 'Zach, he's only been here a few days. Give the guy some space while he sorts through his grandparents' belongings, will you?' He admonished the realtor with every word, while managing to ease Branch's mind and calm him down. He was giving him an out. From the conversation, and from the ultimate decision.

Zach shifted his gaze from one man to the other, his sneer never wavering. 'No problem at all. I just wanted to put the offer out there.' He reached out and tapped the business card, still clutched between Branch's icy fingers. 'If you want to talk, you know where to find me.'

Branch and Jason watched as Zach shoved his hands into his jacket pockets and retreated to the driver's side of his car. The door opened with a muted click, and the sounds of a classic rock radio station floated on the frigid air.

'Oh, and Branch?'

'Yeah,' Branch replied absently. He hadn't moved, hadn't looked away.

Zach winked. 'It's good to see you.' He folded himself into the little car and backed out of the driveway. Neither Branch nor Jason spoke a word until the red glow of the tail-lights disappeared around the corner.

Jason looked downright stricken on his friend's behalf. 'What just happened?'

Branch stared at the spot the impractical sports car had been only moments before. 'I don't exactly know,' he replied absently. Then, he turned to face Jason. 'But in response to your earlier question, I might not have a clue what the odds are of me staying in Port Landon just yet, but I think it's safe to say there's a certain somebody who'll do what he can to make sure the odds are even better that I'll leave.'

Chapter 7

Kait

If anyone would have told Kait a week ago that she would be pulling into Addie's driveway at eight-thirty in the evening to spend a few hours with Branch Sterling, she would have told them to give their head a shake. Yet, here she was, striding up to the front door of the house she had spent so much time at as a teenager, with butterflies fluttering wildly in her stomach and anxiety rippling through her veins.

She knocked, tucking the box under her arm snugly to rub her hands together. Snowflakes had begun to fall, but thankfully it was far from a blizzard. With any luck, only a thin layer would have coated her windshield by the time she came back out and she wouldn't have to scrape away too much ice and snow.

Tugging the door open, Branch greeted her in a pair of worn jeans and a long-sleeved thermal shirt. His dark hair peeked out from under his signature Lakers hat in untameable sprigs, his eyes smiling just as much as his mouth.

'Come in,' he ushered, stepping back to give her room. 'The temperature's dropping fast out there.'

'Good old winter,' she chuckled as the warmth of the house

wrapped around her. 'You know what it's like, good luck finding nice weather before the middle of April.'

'Still such a lover of the cold, I see.'

Kait let out an indignant snort. 'I keep telling myself there are places where it's sunny and seventy-five.' She shuffled out of her jacket and hung it on the coat rack. She was careful not to comment on the fact that the rack was full of jackets and knitted sweaters, ones that obviously didn't belong to Branch or anyone in their age bracket.

Branch nodded his head toward her feet, where she had set the square box wrapped in Santa Clause wrapping paper on the floor while she situated her boots on the mat. 'What have you got there?'

Kait held it out as she stood to her full height, about seven inches shorter than the man in front of her, grinning. 'I saw it during my errands downtown today and thought of you. A, uh, housewarming gift of sorts.'

Wearing an uneasy expression, he turned the wrapped cube in his hands like he didn't quite know what to do with it. 'You bought me a gift.'

'Stop analyzing it and just open the box, Branch.' Kait followed her outburst with an unsteady laugh. She didn't need him thinking about what the gesture meant; she was doing that enough for the both of them.

Like a child, Branch unwrapped the package frantically, making Kait wonder when the last time he received a present was. As the paper fell to the floor and its contents registered in his brain, Branch's face lit up. Yeah, he was definitely still a kid at heart.

'You bought me a basketball?' He stared at the ball in wonder, like it was the golden key to happiness.

Kait laughed. 'Like I said before, you can't very well use the hoop without the basketball.'

'Kait, I don't know what to say,' he replied. 'This is awesome. Thank you.'

59

'Don't mention it.' She was fighting the urge to laugh harder, too enthralled by his excitement over a random item she found on clearance at the gift shop downtown – or the 'everything' shop, as it had been affectionately coined by Port Landon's residents. It was just a basketball, but she could see it in his eyes. It wasn't.

'I have half a mind to give up on organization and go set up a court in the driveway instead.'

She pointed a finger. 'Not a chance. You wanted help, and I just fended off Janna's scrutiny in order to come here and do just that. Where do we start?'

Showing up at eight-thirty hadn't been her idea, but she'd had to wait till Janna got home from her shift at the diner before she could leave. Having managed to get both toddlers to sleep before their mother's arrival, the idea of beginning a daunting project like sorting through a house of old memories wasn't exactly high on Kait's list after an already exhausting day.

But seeing Branch was. And after being subjected to Janna's abundance of questions and overzealous opinions as to how bad of an idea this truly was, Kait had managed to make it out the door virtually unscathed. There was a part of her that wanted to be here, helping Branch, and not even Janna's pessimism and concerns could douse that want. Even if there was a part of her that was fully aware she should run screaming in the opposite direction.

'I was just going through some stuff in one of the linen closets.' He waved her toward the opened doors on the other side of the living room. 'You want something to drink? There's soda and orange juice in the fridge.'

'Orange juice?' Kait contorted her face as she bypassed him and headed straight for the fridge. 'Never thought I'd see the day when you had something in your fridge that was actually some-what good for you. On purpose.' She grabbed a can of soda and cracked it open. It was going to take sugar and a whole lot of jokes to get through this, but she was determined to do it without mentioning the past. Surely they could be friends. They were adults. With new lives and orange juice in the fridge. They could be friends.

Branch headed back toward the linen closet, pushing a pile of threadbare green and yellow sheets further from the doorway. 'Got used to having it every morning while at work,' he explained. 'It isn't half bad and it makes me feel like I'm, I don't know, responsible or something.'

Kait burst out laughing, setting her soda on the dining room table before joining him at the closet door. 'If all it takes is orange juice to feel like a responsible adult, then I know what I've been doing wrong all these years.' She pointed at the pile of green and yellow sheets. 'Is that the discard pile, or the pile of stuff you're keeping in case it comes in style again?'

'If that comes in style again, I don't want to be *in* style.'

'Glad to hear it,' she said with a grin. 'You have a box or plastic bag I can pack it in?'

'Under the sink.'

Kait went about bagging up the sheets and pillowcases they would donate to Goodwill, figuring the sooner some of this stuff was out of sight the easier it would be on Branch. Having to sift through all the things to get rid of was a difficult enough task on its own, without having to look at the piles of it afterward.

'You're a responsible adult.'

Kait's head snapped up at the sound of Branch's voice. She had been lulled into a soothing silence, placing items in the bag as he handed them to her. 'Excuse me?'

A crooked smile played on his lips. 'You have to be. I don't know anyone else who's so intent to look after everyone that they live with their sister and babysit her kids and work all the time just to make things easier on someone else. Janna's lucky to have you.'

Kait's gut twisted, her cheeks flaming at the compliment. 'Janna

61

deserves someone to give her a break,' she replied, shrugging. 'If it's got to be me, then so be it.'

Branch held up a flannel sheet set of baby blue and white flowers, cringing so hard that Kait pressed her lips together to suppress another laugh.

'I take it the boys' father isn't in the picture?' He handed the sheets to her.

No judgment, no pretenses. Janna had never liked Branch, for no other reason than because she had never trusted his unabashed devotion to Kait, a devotion that belied his young age. Kait didn't think anyone would ever be good enough for her in Janna's eyes, but her older sister had been particularly adamant in her opinion that Branch would never measure up. He undoubtedly knew her detest had only grown over the years. Yet, his question was void of any negativity. Kait missed that about him – his desire to know, and his ability to remain impartial unless it involved him.

'He left her when he found out she was carrying twins.' Kait's eyes stayed down, fixed on the basket of miscellaneous household items on the bottom shelf of the closet. 'He wasn't thrilled when he found out she was pregnant, but finding out there were two babies was more than he was willing to handle, I guess.'

Branch sighed. 'Janna deserves so much better than that. So do those boys.'

There it was, the aching in her chest as her heart swelled. No ill will toward someone he knew didn't like him. Branch understood that Janna deserved better than the hand she'd been dealt, purely because everyone deserved better than to be deserted by someone who was supposed to love them and their unborn children.

'Janna and the kids do all right,' she replied, tying the plastic bag up. 'We've got a system. When she works at the diner, I stay with the kids, and vice versa. On the off chance we get paired up on the same shift, we switch with somebody or we hope and pray

Mom's in a grandmother kind of mood. Pass me that basket. I'll sort through it.'

Branch's jaw had tightened, but he nodded and slid the basket over. He knew the hands-off approach her mother had always taken in their own upbringing, preferring the so-called nightlife over the mundane days she usually slept through. Jameson whiskey was her favorite companion, but if given ample notice, Marsha Davenport was able to sober up and actually be kind of fun for the sake of her grandchildren. That didn't mean Kait and Janna didn't rush home from work on those days to get the boys back in their sight, though.

'So, your mom hasn't changed much, either, then.'

'Some things never change.'

He turned and locked his gaze with hers. 'I keep hearing that a lot lately.'

'That's because it's true.' Each word was spoken without so much as an eye blink. It took everything in her to tear her gaze away and focus on the basket. She threw a decrepit box of mothballs into the trash, then sorted out the lightbulbs and spools of thick string that had been tossed haphazardly into the wicker basket.

'You know what I think will never change?' He pulled what looked like a never-opened comforter with a paint stroke motif from one of the middle shelves, still in the bag with a price sticker on it. 'My hatred for pastel colors. Get this thing out of here.'

She wrapped her arms around the zipped clear bag containing the folded blanket, laughing once more. 'Duly noted.' Glancing from the two bags of discarded linens to the partially empty shelves in front of him, Kait raised her eyebrows. 'Branch, you haven't kept a thing.'

'That's because none of this stuff even reminds me of Grandma Addie. Everything in here is probably older than I am, and frankly, I don't remember Grandma Addie ever opening this closet, let alone rummaging through it to find something she actually wanted.'

'Me neither,' Kait agreed. Crouching down, she reached to grab another huge plastic bag from the roll. 'You know what that means.' She gripped the bag on both sides and held it outward, waiting.

Branch looked from her to the bag then back again. 'You know what, you're right. Grandma Addie only ever used the linens from the hallway closet upstairs. These were just extras.' He stood up to his full height and proceeded to push every old blanket and sheet set into the bag until all the shelves in the closet were bare.

Kait tied the bags up and dusted off her hands. 'Or extra extras.' Her mouth twitched. 'She was nothing if not prepared.'

'You got that right.' Branch wiped a hand over the empty shelf as though confirming it was, in fact, bare, then closed the door. 'Well, that's progress, I'd say.'

'Baby steps.' She pulled the plastic bags together into a pile. 'If you want, I can drop these off at the donation depot on my way to work tomorrow morning.'

'Saves me from having the chance to second-guess my decision to get rid of them,' he replied. 'I'll take them out to the trunk of your car.'

Kait never questioned how hard it must be for Branch to have to get rid of things in his grandparents' house, but his comment confirmed he was struggling with it even more than he was letting on. Her heart ached for him, unable to imagine being forced to decide what stayed and what was given away, like some things mattered and others didn't. That was the problem, though, wasn't it? Now, with his only family members gone, everything in that house was all he had left. Everything mattered, in some way.

Outside, the snowflakes had multiplied, being shaken from the blackened sky with more vigor. They fell gently, though, in no hurry to freefall to the ground. The outside light came on, triggered by their motion on the front step, and Branch carried two bags while Kait wrestled with one. The trunk of her old Ford Focus went from empty to piled full in seconds.

Branch pushed the trunk closed, leaning on it with his elbows until it latched. 'Would you look at this? Not even a breeze, and the snowflakes are big enough they look fake.'

'It's snow, Branch. Christmas-card snow, but just snow, none-theless.'

He leaned against her car, watching it float lazily around them. 'Christmas-card snow, I like that. Even if you don't.'

'Sunny and seventy-five, remember?'

Humor reflected in his eyes as he stood there. Both of them had slipped their jackets on but failed to zip them up, and the golden light stretching across the snowy pavement cast dark shadows against the vehicles and shrubs. Kait was still trying to decide if the glint that shone back at her in his gaze was a figment of the light fixture's glow or something more devious when Branch pushed away from the car and held up a finger.

'I'll be right back,' he hollered over his shoulder. 'Stay here.'

Taking the front steps two at a time, he disappeared into the house, leaving her with only the drifting snowflakes to keep her company. Had the man not taken her aversion to cold seriously? A minute later, the front door opened again and an orange basket-ball bounced down the steps ahead of Branch, who was carrying the battered backboard in his hands, struggling to get it through the doorway.

'What are you doing?' Kait shouted. 'You're going to fall down those steps and break your neck.'

'Do me a favor and go catch the basketball that's rolling down the driveway. I'll handle the rest.'

Kait muttered to herself the entire way down the snowy driveway. She knew that playful look in his eye – Branch was in one of his fun-loving moods. She didn't blame him for it. If the tables were turned, she would want to relieve some of the stress in her shoulders after making a little leeway in the daunting task of organizing an entire house. Seeing this side of him was only making it harder on herself, though.

Why was she so hell-bent on being here, on doing this to herself?

She plucked the ball from the end of the driveway and made her way back to the dimly lit pavement in front of the garage. Branch must have had no trouble finding a ladder amongst Grandpa Duke's stuff in the garage, because he had it unfolded and was perched halfway up, hanging the backboard on the rusted metal base that remained on the eave after all this time.

'Branch, it's freezing out here and it's freaking snowing.' She rolled the ball in his direction.

'I've noticed,' he laughed, climbing back down and moving the ladder out of the way. He stopped the ball with his foot. 'But it's Christmas-card snow. We can't just go back inside.'

'Sure we can.'

Branch scooped up the ball and tossed it toward Kait. 'Three points and we can go back in the house.'

Catching the ball in both hands, Kait blinked back the snow-flakes falling onto her eyelashes as she furrowed her brows, watching, skeptical, as Branch pulled the snow shovel from the side of the house and cleared off a square patch of the driveway. 'You want to play basketball. In the snow.'

'Come on, it'll be fun,' he insisted.

'It'll be cold.'

Laughing, Branch leaned the shovel up against the garage door. 'Come on, Davenport, give it a shot.' He took his defensive stance in front of her, his eyes glinting with a playful mischievousness she hadn't witnessed in years.

How much she missed that stare hit her like a tidal wave. She didn't want to fall into his gaze and remember him as the high school sweetheart she once naively believed would be her husband. She wanted to – no, *needed* to – remember that he was neither of those things. Who he truly was, was the man who had hurt her. Lied to and betrayed her.

But it was hard to conjure up the anger she harbored for him when he was looking at her like that, ready to be the man she remembered loving and cherishing so long ago, like time had just rewound itself and placed them back in his grandparents' driveway, facing each other with all their love and hopes and dreams between them. In that moment, Kait wanted to be that doe-eyed, lovestruck teenager once again, instead of the shadow of the woman she had once planned to become.

So, she bent her knees, locked eyes with Branch, and let the faintest glimmer of a smile tug at the corner of her mouth as she pushed the ball outward. It fell in a perfect arc, bouncing loudly off the rim and echoing throughout their little square of wintry wonderland.

'Admit it, that would've been pretty cool if it had gone in,' she chuckled.

'This ain't horseshoes,' he snickered, dribbling the ball as he spoke. 'Almost doesn't count.'

Kait dove toward him, her arms out wide to stop his layup. The ball sailed upward, clanging off the rim again, and Kait laughed as she scurried to grab it. She pivoted, one way, then the other, but Branch blocked her shot easily.

'Get out of my way!' she laughed, circling him to get out from under his flailing hands. She took another shot. It went wide, bouncing off the backboard.

'Aw, you can do better than that,' Branch heckled, stretching out for the ball.

Kait practically scaled him, clutching the ball once she got a hold of it. 'Not with your big, stupid arms in the way!' she yelled, unable to stop laughing. 'Get out of the way, Sterling!'

'Make me, Davenport!'

She got a few steps away from him, dribbling the ball awkwardly, before Branch was covering her again. She could feel him at her back, see his hands in her peripheral vision. She twisted and took another shot just as Branch, a moment too late, wrapped his arms around her middle and tried to foul it. Kait squealed, wriggling against his hold as they watched the ball swish through the hoop.

'Nothing but net!' Kait's arms flailed in celebration. 'Take that!'

He lowered her to her feet, but when she turned around to face him, it wasn't defeat etched on his face. Kait would know, because suddenly his face was so close to hers that she had to angle her chin upward to see him fully.

'Good game.' His words were but a breath on the soft flesh of her lips, caressing across her skin as they came out in hazy puffs as the warm and cold air collided. It only fueled the fire lit inside her as she took in the shadow of his facial hair, the contour of his angular jaw.

This was anything but a game, she could see that now. But if it was, Kait wasn't sure whether she wanted to win or lose.

She took a reluctant step back. 'I should go.' Weakness. That was all she could hear clinging to every syllable that fell from her mouth. All she could see now was the moonlight that shone down on their makeshift court making the snowflakes glow as they floated in the crisp air, and all she could hear was the heaviness of Branch's breath in time with the pounding of her own heart. She never stood a chance.

'Kaitie,' Branch whispered, and she gasped. She couldn't ever remember hearing that kind of weakness from his mouth, either. 'Come back. Tomorrow night. Please.'

His broken sentence gutted her. 'I can't. I work,' she explained painfully. 'Janna will—'

'The next night, then,' he countered, his eyes never leaving hers. 'Please.'

She told herself it wasn't about the heat in his dark gaze or the desperation in his tone. She told herself that what Janna thought of her decisions didn't matter. She told herself this was just temporary, two old friends coming together to sort through the remnants of a tragedy.

And as Kait nodded and headed back to her car, she wondered if having to tell herself that was the greatest tragedy of all.

Because there was nothing temporary about her connection to Branch Sterling. The last ten painful years proved that. She feared the next ten years of lying to herself would be just as unkind.

69

Chapter 8

Branch

The darkness looms, but the shrieks of laughter and shouting advise of the night's rollicking festivities. Music thumps, bodies sway, and the scent of liquor and beer lingers in the air. I haven't touched a drop, but every breath is permeated by it.

So many people. But not the one person I want to be here. So much desire to escape. So much annoyance. Not toward her, though. Never toward her.

I need to go.

The truck's engine rumbles and I feel the heaviness of her head on my shoulder, leaning in. Too close, too out of it. She mumbles something incoherent as her lips touch my shoulder, but all I can hear are his *words, demanding to know where she is. Demanding to know where the woman I adore is. I push her gently back toward the passenger seat, away from me.*

I need to go.

I throw the old truck in gear, and at the same second, bright and blinding, a flash of something explodes in my vision from somewhere. In my haste, I tramp down on the accelerator to force the truck to screech into movement, my mind reeling with my need to get away and my veins pumping with an electric adrenaline.

A jolt backward, hard and fast.

I feel it without seeing it. The sickening thump, followed by screams. From everywhere. Shrill ones carrying from the people on the lawn, guttural ones piercing my mind and stealing my sanity.

There had been nothing behind me, but there was now. Which left nothing ahead for me, either.

Heart banging hard against my ribcage, I clamber out of the truck and see it.

My future being ripped away like it was never mine to hold in the first place.

Branch bolted upright, unable to breathe, unable to see. The room was dark save for the moonlight shining in through the partially opened curtains. His room. In Grandma Addie and Grandpa Duke's house. He was home.

Home. The realization slowed his ragged breathing slightly.

He cursed out loud to himself, his hand dragging through his hair, his skin coated in a sheen of sweat.

It was a dream. A nightmare. Not the first he'd had, and undoubtedly not the last, but a nightmare, nonetheless.

He wished like hell he could tell himself it wasn't real.

Branch spent the next day knee deep in the contents of Grandpa Duke's garage. If he was going to tackle an area of the house alone, it might as well be the one place that wasn't heated. He would save the warm interior of the house for him and Kait to take on together.

Kait. Yeah, he might have technically been by himself, bundled up in his winter jacket and able to see his breath as it came out in even pants, but Kait may as well have been there, beside him, because his mind was definitely with her.

And there was no doubt in his mind that what he still felt for her after all this time was mutual. Kait was struggling with her

71

feelings. He didn't have verbal proof of it, but he felt it with so much conviction that he didn't know how it could be anything but the truth. Branch didn't wish for Kait to struggle, but it made his heart somersault in his chest to know she was conflicted about him. When Branch showed up in town, he knew there was a colossal chance she could still hate his guts. She had told him she never wanted to see him again, and Kait was a woman who said what she meant. Branch wasn't even sure he would have had the courage to seek her out to find out where her opinions lay with regard to him.

But fate, if that's what it was, had done him a solid and pushed him into the diner that day. Branch hadn't had a chance to decide whether or not he wanted to see her, then, just like he didn't have a chance at deciding whether or not he still loved her, either.

Branch's heart still belonged to her, despite time, tragedy, and circumstance.

The way Kait looked at him last night, her bright eyes reflecting the dim golden glow of the outdoor light while fluffy snowflakes melted on her pink-tinged cheeks, he knew she felt a spark between them, too.

That in itself was a miracle, and since it was something he never in a million years thought would happen, it gave Branch a renewed hope that he would have the opportunity to talk about what happened that fateful night and clear the air a bit. With her, and with Zach. He hadn't broached the subject, but Branch doubted anything had changed there, either. Wherever Kait was, Zach probably wasn't far behind. Kait could love Branch back until the moon fell from the sky, but if she didn't believe that the vehicle accident hadn't been the result of some jealous, monstrous rage, then they had no chance to build on that remaining love.

Not for the first time, he felt nauseous thinking about the accident, knowing he had let an immature mix of annoyance and inattention become the catalyst for what occurred that night. But

72

not jealousy. Never jealousy. He'd trusted Kait implicitly, and not even Zach Canton's brazen affections wavered that trust. He felt even sicker knowing he and Kait had gone from the cusp of their life together, hands joined and hearts entwined, to a world where some part of her thought him capable of that kind of malicious act.

To this day, the entire sequence of events confused him, and he had all but given up trying to figure out the whys, whens, and hows of the minutes that led to Zach being behind his pickup truck, his leg fractured, and their lives forever changed.

Rubbing his hands together to create heat, he flexed his fingers to ease the numbness in them, then patted the pocket of his jeans, seeking out the familiar feel of the item tucked into the side of his leather wallet. It was a gesture he did often, sometimes not realizing he was even doing it until the precious metal was in his hand, the significance of it burning into his palm like the red-hot scorching of a cast iron brand. But Branch held onto that ring now just as tightly as he had eleven years ago when he first bought it. It wasn't much, just a simple, thin gold band with a miniscule diamond, but he kept it with him at all times since he'd spent a big chunk of his savings in hope of giving it to Kait at graduation, cherishing it as though it was worth a hundred times its meager cost.

At the time when he'd purchased it at only eighteen years old, the ring had meant everything to him. His one chance to promise Kait Davenport that he would be hers, always and forever.

He had no way of knowing, then, that the love the ring symbolized would cost him everything.

Branch traced the tiny circle, swearing he could feel warmth emanating from it. There were days he had no idea why he kept it, but today, there was no doubt in his mind. All this time, he had kept it because some part of him knew it wasn't over. And he was pretty sure that part was his heart.

There was something seductive about Kait arriving at his house under the blanket of night, giving their evening together a clandestine feel. Like they were being the rebellious teens they had once believed they were, or were going against the grain by dusting the ashes off their burned relationship and clutching to the shred of friendship that remained, no matter what others thought of their choices. Kait's greeting at the front door proved she felt the same.

'Well, hey,' she said. 'We really should stop meeting like this.'

Branch stepped back, motioning her in out of the cold. 'Why, are the neighbors going to start to talk?'

Shuffling out of her coat, she chuckled. 'Like they aren't already.'

Let them talk, he thought. Then, it occurred to him that his opinion wasn't the only one that mattered. 'Does that bother you?'

'Oh, please.' Kait waved her hand dismissively. 'I steeled myself against the gossipmongers a long time ago. Most of the time, folks mean well, even if their opinions are a bit misguided. Besides, if it bothered me, I wouldn't be here.' She didn't give him a chance to comment further. 'So, where are we starting in this big ol' house tonight?' She rubbed her hands together in anticipation.

Branch shook his head. He was thankful she wasn't feeling tortured by being here and having to sort through all the dust and dirt, but he had to admit, he would never understand how some people lived for this sort of thing, sifting through the remnants of days gone by and unearthing the memories and secrets of the past through the tangible memorabilia left behind. Maybe his problem was that he had a personal attachment to the stuff left behind here. It made it harder for him. But it was easier knowing Kait wanted to be here with him, somehow.

'I was thinking we could take on the attic this weekend, maybe, if you're around? I think it would be easier in the daylight since we'd have the light from the windows as well as the light fixtures.'

She narrowed her eyes, and Branch could tell the wheels were turning in that pretty little head of hers. 'Keep talking.'

Her lack of commitment to anything beyond tonight was disheartening, but he tried his best to stamp down the flood of disappointment. 'But, tonight,' he continued, 'we can go through some of the totes and boxes I found piled in the garage. I brought them inside when I couldn't take the cold anymore.'

'You've already tackled the garage?' Kait looked shocked, which made him stop on his way to the fridge to grab a couple bottled waters.

He crossed his arms. 'I can't expect you to be here to help me with all of it.'

'I know.' She shrugged. 'I just … didn't want you to have to do it alone.'

'I appreciate that,' he managed to get out past the sudden thickness in his throat. *More than you know.* 'But I feel better having it done. I managed to box up some of Grandpa Duke's tools to keep, and I set aside some extra parts for the Bronco I found. But mostly there wasn't a lot stored in there.' He stole a glance at the pile of boxes stacked inside the interior door that led to the attached garage. 'Except those.'

'Then let's see what we've got, shall we?'

Kait had the first flaps of the cardboard box pulled up and opened before Branch crossed the room.

'The boxes were pretty light, so I—'

Kait let out a high-pitched squeal, clapping her hands emphatically. 'They're Christmas decorations!' Like an excited child, she leaped over to another box and opened it, too. 'They're all Christmas decorations, Branch!'

He had forgotten how excited she got about the holiday season, the way, even as a teenager, she had jumped at every chance to over-decorate and over-bake and over-do every aspect of Christmas if she got the opportunity. There was no such thing as too much tinsel or sparkle when it came to Kait and her idea of what a magical Christmas should be.

'Well, that explains how little they weighed when I brought

them in,' he said, peering into one of the opened boxes. A large wreath adorning pinecones and frosted holly berries sat on top, waiting to be displayed on the front door. Beneath it, it looked like Santa's workshop had exploded inside. 'Go ahead and take anything you like, Kait. You and Janna can probably—'

'Take them?' Her head snapped up and she stared at him with wide, disbelieving eyes. 'What are you talking about? We're going to put them up!' she exclaimed, waving a hand around.

'There's no need to decorate here.'

'The heck there isn't!' She pulled a huge string of sparkly red tinsel from the box in front of her, carefully coiled and tied with a wire twist. 'I remember Grandma Addie used to string this across the fireplace mantel in little loops. And there should be miniature glass ornaments somewhere in here that hang from each one. Oh, and the blinking mini lights, red and green, they should be in here somewhere, too!'

'Kait.' Branch's hand came down on her wrist, stopping her manic quest for the perfect Christmas color scheme. It was enough to halt her incessant digging, and she stared up at him, this time wearing an expression of puzzlement. 'There's no use in decorating here.'

Her gaze never deviated from his, but something tightened in her jaw. It was slight, but Branch saw it, and somehow the clenching was enough to transform her expression from confusion to outright defiance. 'Why?' she asked. 'Because you're not staying?'

'For starters.' He nodded uneasily. 'We're supposed to be purging this stuff, not recreating one of Grandma Addie's epic holiday adventures.'

'Ah ha!' Kait's hand flew out of the cardboard box so fast he thought she was intent on slapping him. Instead, she pointed an indignant finger in his direction. 'So, you admit Grandma Addie had epic holiday adventures!'

'Easy, Sherlock,' he laughed. She looked adorable when she

was proving a point. A point he wasn't quite sure why she was trying to make. 'The entire town of Port Landon knows Christmas was her time to shine. It was no secret.'

'You're right,' she agreed. 'And last year was the first time that the town, myself included, had to live through the holidays without her home-style brand of Christmas cheer. Do you know what it was like to drive past this beautiful old house and see it in darkness, instead of lit up like some Victorian gingerbread house the way it always was?'

Branch wanted to argue that, yes, he did know. He had lived through the grief and sadness of last Christmas, too. But the truth was he barely remembered any of the details from that time, too overcome with his own pain and loss to think about or realize anything beyond what needed to be done. Funeral arrangements, legal documents, and a black cloud of sorrow. That's what he could recall from last December.

And then he had quietly but hastily left Port Landon, too consumed by his own grieving to think about the fact that others were grieving, too, just in a different way. And maybe this was how Kait dealt with her grief over the loss of the woman who had treated her like family, regardless of whether Branch was there in town or not.

'I'm sorry.' He meant it. 'She really did do Christmas up right, didn't she?' The corner of his mouth lifted as he reached into the box and retrieved one of the pudgy quilted snowmen Grandma Addie had hand sewn herself. Branch knew there would be a set of three of them in that box, each one a few inches taller than the next, and they had been displayed on the entryway table beside the front door every Christmas as long as he could remember. Kait's matching grin said she remembered, too.

'She did. So, why don't we do it up right, one last time? In her honor. You know she would love that.' Kait draped the coil of tinsel around her neck and tossed the end of it over her shoulder like a movie star. Her amusement faltered a moment later. 'Unless you really don't want to. I mean, I understand if it's too—'

'Let's do it.' The words were out of his mouth before Branch could think them through, surprising himself just as much as Kait. But when he saw her smile once more, wide and bright and brimming with delight, he knew why he had agreed.

It had little to do with his desire to deck this house out in holiday cheer the way Grandma Addie had always done it. The truth was it was going to gut him having to rummage through those boxes and put up the festive decorations that his grandmother had so carefully packed away. Her hands had been the last ones to touch them, and she'd had so much love and light in her heart as she had put them up and taken them down. Redecorating from memory – memories he had tried so hard to file away to save himself from the grief of reliving them – was going to take a brutal toll on his heart.

But so would turning down Kait's idea. The glimmer of excitement as she beamed at him now already made his decision worth every ounce of heartache he would endure. He wasn't going to just do this in Grandma Addie's honor, although she would be front and center in his thoughts while he put his plan into motion.

He was going to do it in Kait's honor, too. For the Kait he had let down more than ten years ago. For the Kait he had lost then and somehow managed to find again now, albeit on shaky ground. For the Kait he had loved then and loved just as much as she stood before him today. Branch Sterling had adored two women in his life, so he would do this. For both of them, Grandma Addie and Kait.

'You're serious?' Kait was uncharacteristically still, like she was afraid to move too quickly and spook him.

'I'm serious,' he replied. 'But I've got two conditions.'

Absently, Kait's fingers fumbled with the length of tinsel, making it glitter like a handful of shiny rubies. She said nothing, waiting with arched eyebrows.

'The first,' Branch began, 'is that if we're going to do this, we're going to go all out.'

'Meaning?'

He couldn't believe he was suggesting this, and his stomach twisted as the words fell from his lips. 'Not only do we decorate the way Grandma Addie would want us to, but we also do all the baking and cooking that goes along with it. She never half-did anything, so we can't, either.'

Kait's eyes bulged. 'Branch, your grandmother held a meal for the entire town on Christmas Eve. She prepped and baked for weeks!'

She had every right to question him about it. Kait wasn't exaggerating. Every year on Christmas Eve, Grandma Addie opened the door to anyone and everyone in Port Landon. Food was set out buffet style, and there was more home cooking and homemade desserts than anyone could dream of. It was a meal, but the event was so much more than that. The folks who showed up every year in abundance were those without families of their own to spend the holidays with, folks who didn't have the means to experience an extravagant meal, otherwise. Just thinking about it, Branch could smell the spices in the cider and the smoke of the fire that flickered and danced in the stone fireplace.

'Then I guess we'd better get started sooner rather than later.' His gaze stayed fixed on her, hoping the conviction he conveyed in his voice was stronger than the doubts that plagued his mind. He was crazy to think he could ever spend a day in Grandma Addie's shoes, but he had to try. For Kait.

'You really are serious.' Kait pulled the tinsel from her neck and set it over the edge of the box. She seemed deep in thought, but only for a second. Not long enough to be blatant hesitation, but more like a moment to contemplate what it would mean to her as well if he pulled this off. If *they* pulled this off. When she glanced up, Kait's eyes were firm. 'Screw it, count me in.'

The corner of Branch's mouth curled. 'That was my second condition.'

'That I'm in?'

He nodded. 'Every step of the way.' There was only one thing Branch wanted for Christmas, and it couldn't be bought in a store. He understood better than anyone that the holidays weren't about material things. He also understood what it meant to only have those material things left.

But he still had Kait. She was standing in front of him, somewhere he never believed she would be, and she was making plans that involved him. They were plans for Christmas, a day that would come and go, but it was a start. Time with Kait was the only thing Branch had on his Christmas list, and he would repeat it a hundred times on paper if it meant he got it.

He held out his hand. 'You, me, and Grandma Addie's kind of Christmas. Have we got a deal, Davenport?'

Her throat moved visibly, but as she reached out and shook his hand firmly, there was no mistaking the sparkle in her eyes. 'Deal.'

Chapter 9

Kait

She was crazy for agreeing to this. Certifiably. They both were. And there was no one in Kait's life who seemed to have a problem with telling her so.

Still awake when Kait crept in through the door of their little house after her evening at Branch's, Janna had a throw blanket pulled tightly around her shoulders when she trudged into the kitchen, eyeing her sister warily. Kait heard Janna's footsteps, but she turned away to slide the lock into place, giving herself a moment to compose herself before having to face her older sister. Kait knew what was coming.

'Sneaking in at all hours of the night,' Janna's voice whispered. 'Time really has turned back for you, hasn't it?'

Kait sighed. This was exactly why she had hoped her sister was asleep. At least then she could have saved the lecture until morning. But no, she had probably been staked out on the couch, stewing about what she would say the moment Kait showed up. 'It's hardly called sneaking in when I'm twenty-nine and pay half the rent.' She regretted the words instantly. 'Look, Janna, can we just—'

81

'You remember what Branch did to you, right?' Even in the dimly lit room, illuminated only by the light above the sink, Kait saw the weariness in her sister's features. Somehow, she knew it wasn't all from trying to get the boys to sleep. 'You remember that he cheated on you, and that he hit your best friend with his truck?'

Kait's teeth clenched. She wouldn't necessarily call Zach her best friend now. More like her only friend from her high school days, but she needed to pick her battles and not split hairs. 'I haven't forgotten.'

'Then, what in the blazes are you doing?' Janna asked emphatically. 'The guy's no good, and yet here you are, spending all your spare time with him when—'

'When what, Janna?' Kait tossed her coat over the coat rack inside the doorway and threw her hands up. 'I'm still doing everything I need to do. I'm still going to work on time, and I'm still here with the kids when you need me to be. All I'm doing is helping out an old friend. If the tables were turned, I certainly wouldn't want to be going through the stuff in that big old house by myself.'

'And what about when he leaves?' Janna stood in the doorway, blocking the living room. Kait had nowhere to go. 'Then what?'

'Then I'll just be me again, won't I?' She shrugged her shoulders, giving up the edge in her voice for defeat. 'Then I'll go back to being the woman who just works and babysits and does what's right.'

Janna's head reeled back as though her sister had slapped her. 'You make it sound like that's so bad.'

Shaking her head, Kait turned away and headed for the coffee pot, setting it up for the morning so she wouldn't have to do anything but press the button to start brewing. And so she wouldn't have to be subjected to another second of Janna's intense glare. Things were coming out wrong and she didn't want to insult her sister more than she already had. 'Never mind. I don't want to talk about this. All I'm saying is I've always done what's right, and where's it gotten me? If spending these past few days with Branch has been wrong, then so be it. Because I won't lie, it's been kind of nice. And I won't apologize for that.'

A hollow chuckle escaped Janna's throat, but there was no humor in it. 'Remember that when he leaves and breaks your heart all over again. That's when you will be sorry. Sorry you ever met the guy in the first place.' Janna left the room without another word, floating away with the blanket still draped over her shoulders, like a ghost. The overly opinionated ghost of Christmas past. And present and future, if Janna had her way.

Her older sister's words still haunted her when Kait awoke the next morning and got ready for work. By some miracle, she didn't hear either of the boys murmuring to themselves or showing any signs of being awake, and that meant Janna was hopefully going to get some shut-eye while the opportunity arose. With any luck, Kait could get out the door to go and open the diner this morning without having to have any more heart-to-hearts with her sister until later that night, since Janna worked the evening shift and they would essentially switch places once Kait came home. She wasn't looking for a fight, though. Kait disliked arguing with anyone, but especially Janna. So, she did the only thing she could think of, scribbling a short but sweet note and leaving it beside the coffee pot so she would be sure to see it.

I know you don't agree with me on this one, but have a little faith, okay? Also, Branch and I are holding a Christmas Eve dinner at Grandma Addie's house, in her honor. You and the boys are invited. If you can't have faith, at least have a little Christmas cheer. 'Tis the season.

Love you,
Kait

83

It wasn't the most ideal way to break the ice and tell her about her impromptu Christmas Eve plans with Branch, but Kait preferred to tell her now so Janna had the bulk of the day to let the shock settle before they had to see each other face to face later on. That said, of all the people she knew, Janna could use a little Christmas cheer in her life.

She wasn't sure if the note was a smart move or purely a cowardly one, but Kait set the pen down and left it there, anyway, locking the door behind her on her way out.

The diner was always busy first thing in the morning. It was mostly the coffee crowd, the elderly folks who dragged themselves out of bed before the sun was up and headed toward their designated meeting place to partake in their favorite pastime: Sharing all the news and gossip from the day before, then speculating and embellishing the stories bit by bit to make the plotlines more intriguing. For a small town that relied on routine and boasted a serene atmosphere, Port Landon sure had a lot of small-town soap operas going on if you were talking to the right person.

During the week, however, only a handful of people came in for breakfast. Kait and her coworker, Eve, handled the crowd with ease. As long as there was a pot of coffee brewed and ready to be poured, folks were pretty laid-back as they waited for their food to arrive.

Laid-back was the opposite of what Zach was when the bell above the door announced his arrival and he crossed the restaurant to take up residence at his usual stool near the front counter.

'Morning,' Kait greeted him, grinning as she slid a mug in his direction. 'Coffee?' She already knew the answer. Just another routine in the long line of them that made up her daily life.

'Is he staying?'

Kait frowned and she finally paid attention to her friend's

84

expression. As he shuffled out of his coat, Zach's jaw was tight, his movements jerky as he tossed his jacket onto the stool beside him, his features set into a permanent glower. 'Excuse me?'

'Branch.' He spat the name out as though it left a foul taste in his mouth. 'What's he doing setting up a bunch of light-up snowmen on the front porch of Addie's house if he's leaving in three weeks?'

The realization that Zach was counting down the days until Branch's departure would have rubbed her the wrong way if Kait hadn't been so ecstatic to find out that Branch was out in the early morning sun tending to some of the outdoor Christmas decorations.

Branch was serious. He hadn't woken up this morning and changed his mind about their plans for Christmas Eve. He was really going to take on Grandma Addie's festive tradition. With her.

'Why are you grinning like a fool, Kait?'

She laughed, then. 'Because I can just imagine Branch out there in the snow, wrestling with a four-foot snowman.' She shook her head, wondering what kinds of colorful language he was muttering right about now. 'We made plans,' she explained, wiping down the counter so she wouldn't have to look Zach in the eye. 'We're going to host a Christmas Eve dinner in Grandma Addie's honor. So, Branch must be getting started on the decorating.'

Hands pressed against the counter, Zach stared at her, disbelieving. 'I can't possibly have heard you right.'

'It's a tribute to Addie, Zach. The whole town could use a little festive cheer … you included.' Her mouth quirked up. 'Branch is still only here till the end of the month. That hasn't changed.'

'Not yet,' he replied.

She slammed her fist down hard on the counter between them, but the thump of it was muted by the cloth in her hand. 'Why is everyone so determined to give me a hard time about spending time with Branch?' she hissed. Between Zach and Janna, Kait was sick of hearing about all the bad choices she had made as a teenager, and all the wrong choices they seemed to believe she was destined to repeat once more.

'Because we haven't forgotten,' he said. 'We know what kind of hold he has on you.' Zach's voice was soft, his gaze pleading with her to understand. 'And I don't think eleven years has changed that fact one bit.' He attempted to cover her hand with his, but Kait ripped it out of his reach.

There might have been some truth to his words, but Kait hadn't forgotten, either. She remembered everything, even the things she wished she didn't. But both Zach and Janna, two people who seemed incapable of forgiving or forgetting, were forgetting one crucial thing.

Kait wasn't a teenager anymore. Sure, she couldn't deny that her desire to be near Branch stemmed from feelings his arrival had awakened, emotions she had once thought were dormant for good. But Kait could keep those emotions in check now. She wasn't going to fall head over heels for him the way her teenage counterpart had. Naive, starry-eyed Kait Davenport had left along with Branch when he sprinted for that town limit sign at her command.

'This isn't about what I feel for Branch.' It took everything she had to put forth that sentence, even and confident.

Zach sighed, pushing his coffee mug away, untouched. 'Which proves my point perfectly.'

'How?' she asked, exasperated.

Zach stood, reaching for his coat. 'You just said *feel*, Kait. Present tense.'

She opened her mouth but no sound came out. 'That's not what I—'

'I know you're bound and determined to forget that night, Kait, but you do remember it, don't you?' Zach paused, his fingers clutching the zippered edge of his jacket.

'I know what he did to you,' Kait sighed, defeated. She would never forget that as long as she lived. 'I remember what happened, Zach.'

'I'm talking about what he did to *you*,' he replied. 'I caught him in his truck with Holly Raynard, remember? Right before ...' He let the sentence trail off, but Kait was well aware what came next. Kait hadn't attended the house party being held in celebration of their upcoming graduation, but Branch did. So did Zach. All Kait could think now was that if neither of them had attended that godforsaken party, then none of this would ever have happened. Zach wouldn't have been injured, Branch wouldn't have—

No. She couldn't think about that. To this day, she had barely mentioned Branch's infidelity that night, and only to Janna and Zach. She never spoke of it to Branch's face beyond the moment she found out, and never said the words out loud. Not then, and definitely not now. Because the *what ifs* were potent and venomous, and every time Kait wound up down that caustic rabbit hole, she wound up angry and hurt all over again. Zach had informed her exactly what happened that night: he caught Branch with some girl Kait barely remembered from high school, and when Zach called him on it, jealousy reigned, and Zach paid the price. Branch knew what he had done. He didn't need Kait to throw it in his face.

'Kait, this isn't about the fact that Branch hit me.' Zach's voice pierced her thoughts and she struggled to focus on him. 'It's about the reason he did it,' he added. 'You.'

The air suddenly seemed thinner and inadequate in her lungs.

'There was a time when Branch Sterling would do anything for you,' he continued solemnly. 'Something tells me that hasn't changed. My question to you is, how far would you go for him?'

Zach didn't wait for an answer, tossing a couple of dollar bills on the counter and walking back out into the wintry morning light.

Chapter 10

Branch

Branch was stuck in his own version of Christmas hell.

When he and Kait made their pact the night before, his first thought was that his bittersweet memories of the holiday shenanigans Grandma Addie was so well known for would be his own undoing. As he balanced on the middle rung of the ladder, tangled up in extension cords and growing more frustrated by the second that the hooks on the outdoor lights kept snapping off between his fingers, Branch realized that this, right here, was going to be what truly pushed him over the edge.

Yet, he pressed on. Up and down the ladder he climbed, digging through the boxes to find spare hooks, attaching each light meticulously under the eaves trough, perfectly spaced and even.

It needed to be just right. Branch had never been one to believe in perfection, but he was striving for it every step of the way when it came to the decorations. Grandma Addie had never settled for anything less; she'd spend hours putting together the perfect Christmas centerpiece on the entryway table, moving pinecones and poinsettias this way and that until she was undeniably content with it, something Branch would have thrown together in only a few minutes or not done at all.

But this year, he was doing it. All of it. Anyone who had been to the house during the holidays knew the care and effort that went into the decorating of each of the main rooms as well as the over-the-top scene of decorations that cloaked the exterior of the house in holiday harmony. Every year as long as Branch could remember, his grandmother had decked the halls of the inside and outside of her home with the same festive fervor, and he remembered exactly where each ornament and decoration was supposed to be. Everything had a place, and it was etched into his mind so deeply there was no way he could forget. He would put everything in its rightful place, just as she would have. No blinking or burned out bulbs, no broken hooks, no half-hearted attempts, and no—

Branch's foot slipped and he grappled wildly for the ladder, clutching it like a lifeline. In the process, he tugged on the string of multi-colored lights still tangled between his gloved fingers. With a dramatic domino effect, the first half of the lights that had already been strung up under the eave came snapping off one by one, *pop, pop, pop*, landing unceremoniously in the snow-bank below.

'Sterling, are you trying to break your neck, Christmas-style?'

In his distress, Branch had failed to hear Jason's Dodge rumble into the driveway. The man was jogging awkwardly through the deep snow in the front yard when he turned to face him, fending off the long list of curse words he struggled to swallow down. All that work, all the acrobatics he had pulled off in the process of getting those lights up, down the drain.

'What I was trying to do was make a little leeway, but breaking my neck might be more feasible at this point.' He threw down the cord still clutched in his glove and descended the ladder. 'Not working today?'

Plucking the strings of lights from the snow with his bare fingers, Jason began to re-coil it around his elbow and palm. 'Dad isn't feeling well, and he needed someone to take Mom to one of her specialist appointments in the city.'

'Is there anyone to pick up the slack at the garage while you're away?'

His friend shrugged. 'Benji Carson works as a mechanic alongside me, remember him? But he's only part-time, and I've got a high school student as a helper for us both. Benji wasn't scheduled today, and he wasn't able to come in on short notice, so I had to cancel my appointments for the day. People were pretty good about it, though. Folks know I'm short-staffed, and that my family comes first.'

It wasn't fair, but his comment hit Branch square in the chest. *Family comes first.* Idly, he wondered what came first when someone had no family left. Someone like himself.

'Sounds like you need a hand,' he replied, taking the coiled lights from Jason when he offered them.

'Yeah, well it looks like you need one, too,' he chuckled, squinting in the sunlight as he glanced around at the pile of lawn ornaments near the front door, waiting to be set up. 'What in the world are you doing? If you got a side hustle as Santa's elf, you're pretty miserable at it.'

'Tell me about it.' Branch side-eyed the trio of large plastic snowmen perched on the front step, plugged into a timer and ready to illuminate brightly come dusk. They had been so easy to maneuver into place and get set up. Too easy. In hindsight, it had been the calm before the storm, giving him just enough confidence to think he could handle this on his own. Discarding the string of lights over the front railing to deal with later, that confidence was dwindling fast. 'I think I might have bitten off more than I can chew, Jay.'

'You?' Even with his oil-smudged hat on, Jason's eyebrows arched high on his forehead. 'Can't imagine,' he smirked.

'Enlighten me. Just what have you gotten yourself into this time?'

Inwardly, Branch cringed. Jason was right; it was so like him to take on something over the top and think he could deal with it by himself. He levelled his friend with a neutral stare. 'I've decided to hold Christmas Eve here,' he said. 'Like Grandma Addie would have done if she was still around.'

'No way.' Jason's eyes rounded, but the wide smile that spread across his face was practically childlike. There was no one who didn't understand the magic of his grandmother's Christmas Eve tradition. 'Dude, that's great. What made you decide to do that?'

Branch cleared his throat. 'I, um, made a pact with Kait.'

Instantly, Jason's eyes narrowed. 'Kait?' He crossed his arms, unable to hide his amusement. 'I should've known. Oh, this should be good. And what pact would that be?'

'I agreed to hold the shindig, but only if she and I did it together.'

Jason wasted no time in buckling over, laughing loudly and proudly. It wasn't quite the reaction Branch expected, but he waited him out, anyway, choosing to dig through the cardboard box on the front step for more plastic hooks to pass the time.

'You suckered her into spending more time with you,' Jason snickered once he had mostly recovered.

'I wouldn't go so far as to say I suckered her into it,' Branch replied curtly. 'It didn't take much persuasion, really.'

'Of course it didn't.' Jason reached for the Christmas lights he had slung over the railing, pointing toward the ladder. When Branch didn't respond, neither moving nor looking like he understood the English language, Jason shook his head. 'You do realize she still loves you, right?' Then, he held up his hand. 'Wait, maybe asking if you realize you still love her is the better question.'

Glaring at Jason, he bypassed him, his pockets full of more hooks, trudging through the snow to move the ladder back into position near the corner of the house before stepping up the rungs. 'Trust me, I know I still love her. I don't think I would have offered to do this if I didn't.'

'So, you're past the denial stage. That's a start.' The corners of Jason's mouth curled up. He held the string of lights while Branch, one by one, began to hook them underneath the eave again. It was so much easier to get them into place without gravity pulling the unhooked part of the cord downward while he wrestled to keep his balance and the lights in check. It was also easier with another set of hands, he had to admit. 'You're doing this for Kait, then, is that the deal?'

Branch sighed, letting his arms fall to his sides. 'I'm starting to believe she's the only reason I've ever done anything in my entire life, to be honest.' One look down at the scrutinizing expression of his friend, with his cold hands and calculating gaze, had Branch raising his hands above his head again, getting back to work while he confided the things he hadn't dared to utter before now. 'Don't get me wrong, I want to hold Christmas Eve for Grandma Addie. She deserves that. But there ain't a person in Port Landon who could fill the shoes of that woman, least of all me.' He paused, letting out a long breath to ease the pressure building in his chest. 'But I thought maybe if Kaitie and I did it together, not only would she realize there's still something there between us, maybe we would have half a chance of doing Grandma Addie proud.'

'Sterling, there's not a damn thing you could do that Addie wouldn't have been proud of you for.' He fed a few more feet of the lights upward to him. 'All she ever did was go on and on about your fancy job and how good you've done for yourself.'

'Good Lord, it's not a fancy job,' Branch bit out, stretching out his arm to hook another light into place. 'I work at a mining site, for God sake.'

'You're missing the point.' Jason chuckled. 'Or, maybe that's my point exactly. Your grandmother saw your job as something to be proud of, even if you don't. You're practically thirty, yet you could've colored her a picture and she would have tacked it up on the refrigerator.'

Branch felt his lips curl upward at that. 'Easy, I'm not thirty till the end of the month.'

'Again, missing the point.' Jason stepped closer. 'Move the ladder, will you? You're making me nervous.'

Branch didn't realize how far he had stretched himself over the side of the ladder until he chanced a look down. Yeah, he definitely might break his neck if he wasn't careful. He climbed down the ladder again and moved it a few feet to the left before climbing back up to continue, his mind whirling with everything Jason had said.

'For what it's worth,' his friend piped up from the foot of the ladder, 'I think Addie would be ecstatic that you're hanging out with Kait again. I think she would be insanely happy for both of you.'

Even before Jason verbalized it, Branch had been thinking the same thing. He knew how fond his grandmother had been of Kait, and Kait had been just as close to her. He wondered if, in some roundabout way, he didn't somehow feel closer to Grandma Addie when he was in Kait's presence because of it. There was so much history there, so much Branch would never have to explain or talk about, because Kait already knew everything there was to know about him. She had lived through it alongside him.

Was it that comfort that drew him to her, making him ache to be in her presence the way he did? The thought gnawed at him, but ultimately Branch felt the answer rather than simply knowing it: There was something more to him and Kait than familiarity, and whatever that thing was, it was raw and urgent and real.

'And is that what I am for doing this?' Branch asked, hooking the last red and green lights into place. 'Insane?'

At the base of the ladder, Jason shrugged. 'Possibly, but there's never been a man who loved a woman and wasn't crazy because of it.'

His friend might have meant it as a simple joke, but Branch understood what he was saying on a deeper level. He was right, love made folks crazy. It made them do crazy things, and feel crazy emotions. When it came right down to it, crazy could have easily been synonymous with love. It didn't make Jason's statement any less accurate, though.

Branch stared down at his friend, the man who knew about his tumultuous past and still picked up their friendship where it had left off like they had simply been away at summer camp for the last month, not leading separate lives for the past eleven years. A man who thought he was potentially crazy but was still standing at the bottom of his teetering ladder, ready to hold it steady and do what needed to be done.

'So, I'm crazy,' he confirmed. 'That explains why I'm going to do what I'm going to do, then.'

'Pull off the ultimate Christmas Eve extravaganza with your high school sweetheart?'

The corner of Branch's mouth curled up at the corner. 'That, too,' he replied, wholly committed to doing Grandma Addie's tradition justice. 'But, Jay, I'm going to fix this.' When his friend stared up at him, confused, Branch's smile grew wider. 'I'm going to get Kait back.'

Chapter 11

Kait

It was December ninth. Which meant there were fifteen days until Christmas Eve. It also meant it had been one week since Branch Sterling walked back into Kait's life and turned it upside down.

On the outside, she thought she was dealing with it pretty well, handling her diner shifts and looking after the boys for Janna without so much as a moment's hesitation. Whether it was to Janna's credit or Kait's detriment, her older sister had refrained from mentioning her time with Branch or their plans for Christmas Eve. The silence regarding the subject was welcomed in a way, but Kait couldn't deny, it was a bit unnerving, too. Just because Janna wasn't stating her opinions now, didn't mean she wasn't saving them all up to hurl at her later.

Janna was always going to be opinionated, however, just like Kait was always going to be a sucker for trying to keep the peace. Kait didn't want to argue with her sister, and she certainly didn't want to make waves with Zach. Yet, she had done both, in the name of her ex-boyfriend. Kait might not have known what to feel when it came to Branch, but Zach was right about one thing

– she felt something. Not just back then, but now. And that was the part she wasn't dealing with nearly as well on the inside. She could blame nostalgia and fatigue and shock for the heady combination of emotions battling within her, but they were still emotions, plain and simple.

She had lain in bed the night before, exhausted from her busy day but unable to sleep. How could she close her eyes and drift off into unconsciousness when every time she tried she ended up thinking of Branch's soft, dark eyes, or Janna's warnings, or Branch's comforting voice, or the guilt that was welling up inside her on Zach's behalf, or the memories she had of who she was back then, with Branch, before—

Yeah, she had every right to be exhausted. So much weighed on her mind that it was full to the brim. She didn't know how to let her thoughts recede long enough to shut down and give herself a chance to replenish her energy stores.

So many people in Port Landon had so many beliefs about the accident that tore their three lives apart as they had known it. But that was all they had, speculation and theories, because there were so many unanswered questions about what had really happened. Unfortunately, around here, some folks seemed to be easily persuaded to believe anything as long as it made for a good story later on.

For Kait, though, as well as Zach and Branch, there was no good story. She had pulled the comforter up tighter under her chin, staring out her bedroom window at the pale moon as she thought of all the different versions she'd heard over the years. Hardly anyone could understand that it had merely been an accident. It *had* to be. No malice, no extenuating circumstances, no jealous rage. Just an unfortunate accident. Or, maybe they just didn't want to.

But that was the difference between Kait and some of the folks in their little town. She knew Branch Sterling. Better than anyone. That alone was enough for her to come to her own conclusion;

Branch didn't hit Zach with his truck on purpose. He couldn't, and he wouldn't. It wasn't who he was.

Unfortunately, by the time her shock wore off and she allowed herself to think about the entire thing rationally, Branch was long gone. And he hadn't come back, until now.

Which perhaps was why Kait was so hesitant to bring up that night. Seeing him, talking to him, and realizing how much she missed him … it gutted her to know she had assumed the worst, a temporary blip in that ten-year span when she had allowed herself to be persuaded he was a monster capable of the unthinkable, purely because she hadn't been able to bring herself to ask the hard questions and hear the truth from his mouth.

Guilt swarmed in her stomach at the thought of Zach. He had told her what happened, many times. It was a simple story – he was there at the party and had asked where Kait was, as he had seen Branch with another girl. When Branch left with that other girl, Zach confronted him about his indiscretions, and knowing Zach could blow everything wide open, and that he would, Branch had tried to stop him in a blind rage of jealousy and desperation.

It didn't fit the picture of the man she loved, but the wounds on Kait's heart had been so raw and so excruciating that she took it as the truth. Who was she to argue with a man who had been on the receiving end of Branch's actions, especially when he had been her friend for so long?

But with the years that passed came doubts. Miniscule ones at first as Kait's heart healed, scarred and unrecognizable, then transforming into gaping holes in the story, where she could no longer tell what had really happened and what was speculation that had been added in for good measure. She wanted to believe it wasn't intentional, *needed* to. She wanted to believe that Zach wouldn't lie to her, as well. But if he was right, then her judgment of Branch's character was very, very wrong. And so, the vicious circle of inner conflict continued.

By the time her doubts kicked in, it didn't matter either way.

Branch was gone, banished from town because she had screamed at him to leave, and Zach had recovered. Kait had done what she could to help Zach during his recuperation, knowing his loyalty to her was the underlying reason he ended up with his injuries in the first place, and from there, they had moved on.

Well, maybe Zach was healed, his fractured bone long since mended and callused, but who was going to help Kait to heal?

No one. She couldn't broach the subject with Zach, as he would only accept her questions with indignance and hurt, making her feel even guiltier for not taking his recollection of the events at face value, purely because she had a different view of who Branch was and what he was capable of. And Branch, himself, couldn't help her move beyond this when merely being around him weakened her somehow, making her question herself about who *she* was and what she was capable of.

Could Kait forgive Branch for what had happened, once and for all? Was she capable of putting it all behind her and really, truly moving forward, instead of just spinning her wheels in place? And did she even want to know if there was a different truth to be unearthed about the events of that night?

Kait wasn't sure, but there was one thing she did know as she turned onto her side and squeezed her eyes shut, begging for the reprieve of sleep. She needed to find out.

The list she clutched in her hand was long and detailed. Everything Kait could possibly think of that needed to be done, purchased, and found within the depths of Grandma Addie's house was scribbled on it, to the best of her recollection. The elderly woman had been a creature of habit, and she had gone about putting together her renowned festive event in the same manner every year. People in Port Landon knew what to expect when they entered the front door; pure and wholesome Christmas magic, compliments of an older woman with a heart of gold. Not only did the Christmas decorations get hung and displayed in the same spots annually, but the meal contained the same mouth-watering staples served on the same intricately designed fine china place settings. Kait could see vividly the cut crystal of the massive punchbowl that was also placed on the kitchen counter without fail, with a huge array of goblets and glasses she had collected over the years. It was eclectic, and beautiful, and a warm memory she found comfort in, knowing all the puzzle pieces to turn that memory into a reality once more were stored somewhere within the deepest depths of the house she stood in front of.

Kait knocked, but no answer came. She strained, but no sounds made it through the door. *Odd.*

She knocked again. This time when Branch didn't open it, she turned the handle, the door creaking open easily.

'Branch?' She peeked in. He was here, somewhere. The Escape in the driveway and the newly shoveled front steps proved it.

It was too cold for her to stand out here and freeze. She stepped inside, shutting the door behind her.

Shuffling out of her jacket and boots, Kait left them by the door. Without the wind whistling against her ears outside, she could vaguely hear the melodic sounds of music carrying throughout the house from somewhere, muffled and distant.

'Branch?' she called out again, her sock-clad feet padding silently across the hardwood floors. It didn't go unnoticed that the boards gleamed now. Not only had Branch saved them from the year's worth of dust and dirt that had accumulated, he'd gotten his hands on some polish, by the looks of it. His efforts weren't in vain; the floors looked fabulous.

This time, her shout was answered by a series of thumps coming from above her head, the sound reverberating off the walls and making the chandelier in the dining room shiver.

'I'm up here, Kaitie!'

I wish he would stop calling me that, she thought, hating the way it made her feel a buoyancy she wasn't prepared to identify just yet. She just knew she liked it, the sound of it and the feeling it caused. Maybe a little too much.

Following the heavy footfalls above, muffled by the drywall and insulation between them, she found herself in the middle of the hallway, where the attic hatch had been opened in the ceiling and the ladder was unfolded to touch down onto a strategically placed rug to protect the floor from the rough, weathered wood on the ends of the handrails. Above her, Branch peered down at her from the square hole, barely big enough to allow a grown adult to shimmy through. Hair disheveled and a dark shadow of beard on his lower face, he looked different than the last time she had seen him.

He looked happy. Not just the kind of happy put forth to make others think things were fine, but the genuine, unadulterated kind of happy. It looked good on him. Really good.

'You've got to see this. Come here.' Crouched at the top of the ladder, he held out his hand.

It looked like she didn't have an option.

'Let me guess,' she muttered, taking carefully placed steps up the ladder, 'You found your entire baseball card collection in mint condition from when you were ten, and we can retire on a beach in the Maldives.'

Kait would have missed the next rung completely and lost her footing if it hadn't been for Branch's outstretched hand gripping hers tightly and holding her in place.

We. She'd said we. Like they would take the money and run off together into the sunshine and sand. It took everything in her to swallow down the groan in her throat, but there was no way to conceal the heat flaming up in her cheeks.

'As good as that sounds, this might be even better.' Branch left it at that, helping her up into the attic with slow and steady movements. 'Keep your feet on the floor joists until you get closer to the window. Looks like there's been a leak or something over here and the plywood floor is soft.'

'Ah, another thing to add to our to-do list, I take it?' This time, Kait gasped at her own stupidity. We. Our. Was she ever going to get the message from her brain to her mouth that there was no *we* or *our*? This wasn't her house. It was Branch's. For however long he planned to keep it, anyway. Kait had a place within its walls only until Christmas Eve. After that, the dinner event would be over and Branch would finish packing up what was left here. Then, he would leave, just as he advised her the first day he'd strolled into the diner. He had been honest and forthcoming about that from the beginning, so Kait didn't know why the idea, now, was causing a wave of anguish to flood her belly.

She thought she saw a flicker of something in Branch's eyes – whether it was humor or satisfaction, she wasn't sure – but it could have simply been the streaks of light coming from the window playing tricks on her. A few incandescent light bulbs glowed from the peaked ceilings and rafters, but they were obviously low wattage, and their brightness was obscured by thick dust and cobwebs that draped erratically over their heads.

'I thought you weren't going to take on the attic until after the spare bedrooms downstairs were finished?' she asked, trying to cover up her second slip of the tongue. All around them, totes and boxes were opened, with items that hadn't seen the light of day in decades strewn about the floor. Branch had been up here a while.

He raked his hands through his shaggy hair, only adding to the messiness of it. 'Honestly, I came up here to see if there were any empty plastic totes and ended up getting sidetracked.' Pulling his cellphone out of his back pocket, he winced. 'That was three hours ago.'

Kait chuckled at his surprise. 'You're not the first person to get lost down Memory Lane, and you won't be the last.' She nodded toward the pile of boxes near the corner, cardboard flaps pulled back and lids removed. 'Well, you've got me up here. What did you find that stole the last three hours of your life?'

101

Even in the dim light, Kait watched as his gaze glittered with excitement. Holding up a finger to signal her to wait, he dove for the boxes, stepping over some and around others, mindful of where he put his feet and what was nearby. She had a feeling his caution had more to do with the sentimental value of the contents around him than the integrity of the floor beneath his work boots.

'This.' Branch stood up, gripping a jacket gingerly between his fingers, holding it away from his body as he retraced his steps back to her. It took a moment for recognition to register, but once Kait realized what it truly was, she wasn't sure what was more intriguing, the significance of the jacket or the undeniable pride that radiated off Branch in waves.

'Is that ... an army uniform?' Kait knew it had to be, but as she reached out and ran her fingers along the material – in the dull lighting, she had a hard time deciding if it was a brown color or more of a green – she realized she had never seen something like it in anything but pictures.

'Grandpa Duke's World War II uniform,' he replied, never taking his eyes off it. 'I found it in that battered old trunk underneath the boxes of classic car magazines from twenty-five years ago.'

'If it was near anything to do with classic cars, there's no doubt it was your grandpa's.'

'Exactly.' His mouth quirked up at the corners, but Branch continued, awestruck by the piece of American history in his hands. 'I remember Grandpa Duke telling me about it when I was a kid, showing me what all the different patches and stuff were.' He shifted his hands under the jacket and pointed to some fabric stripes sewn onto the left sleeve cuff. 'I think those stripes are the ones that signify he went overseas, and those ones are the ones awarded for years of service. If I remember correctly, they were only awarded every three years.'

'Grandpa Duke taught you a lot.' There was a wistfulness in

her tone, and Kait's heart ached as it washed over her again that the man was gone, along with his easy demeanor and willingness to teach. It might have been years, and she might not have formally been family, but some people didn't need to be blood relations to be remembered with just as much fondness as the family one was born into.

'Every chance he got,' Branch agreed. His hand brushed over the United States flag insignia on the collar, stopping close to a different one near the shoulder. 'The man was a hero, in more ways than one.'

'He was.' Kait knew he wasn't merely talking about his soldier status. There had been a different kind of war Addie and Duke had been through, and that included losing their only child and unexpectedly raising their grandson. The older couple had done it with grace and finesse and without a moment's hesitation, but somehow Kait wondered if that war didn't still rage on in the form of Branch's guilt and sorrow, half a lifetime later. 'You should try it on.'

'What?'

Kait would have thought he hadn't heard her if his dark eyes hadn't widened, staring at her like she had lost her ever-loving mind. 'It looks like it would fit you,' she explained, smoothing out the garment to show its true size. 'Come on, try it on. Just over your T-shirt.'

'No, it's …' He trailed off.

It's Grandpa Duke's. That was what he had been about to use as his fighting argument, she could see it in his eyes. 'It's yours now, Branch.' She spoke softly, letting her hand fall comfortingly onto his forearm. 'He wanted you to have it. Go on, try it on.'

Slowly, his mortified expression transformed into one Kait couldn't quite read, but she was relieved when Branch began to undo the brass-looking buttons. She wasn't surprised when he turned his back to her as he shuffled cautiously into the jacket, being just as careful to hide his bubbling emotions as he was not to ruin the uniform. Kait let him have his moment, remaining silent and still until he chose to turn around and show her how it looked.

In many ways, it was just a jacket. Just durable fabric and buttons and threads covering a grown man's upper body. But the jacket did something to Branch, transforming him from the casual and calm man she knew into a taller, stronger, and steadier version of himself, somehow. It didn't make sense that the contours of his jaw looked more defined, or that his shoulders became broader, or that Branch carried the air of a man suddenly prepared to take on anything and everything this world wanted to throw at him. But that's what Kait saw as she stared at him. Authority, strength, and loyalty. A man who could, and would, do it all in the name of what mattered most. She was pretty sure that if she could uncover a picture of Grandpa Duke in his uniform more than seven decades ago, the resemblance would be striking.

'It fits you perfectly,' she managed to choke out, unable to look away.

'Yeah, I guess it does.' He smoothed the fabric out, running his hands down his chest before he worked on doing up the line of buttons.

'Isn't there supposed to be a hat or something?' Kait was suddenly scrambling toward the pile of boxes where the jacket had emerged from, following the same obstacle course of a path Branch had earlier. She wasn't aware Branch followed her until he spoke, his voice close behind her.

'There. It was wrapped in the jacket.' He pointed over her shoulder, and Kait stretched out to reach for it, barely able to pinch the visor of it between her fingers. She wiggled them, desperate to gain another inch to reach the hat, then squealed when suddenly Branch's hands were on her hips, holding her steady and giving her that extra bit of length to reach it.

'Pull me up!' she laughed.

He listened, wrenching her back toward him. Kait turned slightly as the momentum propelled her forward, having the wherewithal to hold the hat away from her before it became wedged between their bodies.

One second she'd been dangling over the box of musty memorabilia, the next Kait was staring into the deep-set eyes she knew so well, too well, having long ago memorized every fleck of color in them. Now, only inches away, the poor lighting robbed her of those details, but Kait imagined she could see them, and she focused on that. If she didn't, she would be unable to stop herself from focusing on the ways those eyes were staring back at her, the way she could feel his chest moving under her hand and hear the soft inhale and exhale of his breath.

Too close.

'Try this on.' Her voice betrayed her with every syllable, too high and too breathy, but she placed the hat on top of his disheveled hair, pulling the leather visor down into position over his eyes. The matching leather strap that adorned the front of the hat was worn, its stitching ripped in places, and the brass buttons that held it in place on both sides tarnished, but the indistinguishable greenish-brown color of it matched the jacket, and the large golden emblem attached to the front boasted the same eagle insignia as the buttons, now done up in the middle of Branch's chest.

'You look like this stuff belongs on you, somehow.' Kait didn't even realize the thought had escaped her lips until Branch's eyebrows shot up, shadowed by the visor.

'Maybe I should have enlisted in the military instead of heading up north to that job in Canada.'

'No.' The answer came out forceful, shocking herself as well as him. 'No,' she said again, this time less panicked. 'I don't know if I could have handled that.'

Her confession floated on the air, churning in the space that separated them, a secret that wasn't a secret at all, yet it carried the same surprising weight of something unknown, purely because it wasn't just thought, but spoken aloud.

And as surely as Kait knew she couldn't have handled it, a part of her was just as certain she couldn't handle this, either. Them, their closeness despite the distance. Or was it the distance despite their closeness? Everything about this, now, was contradictory in Kait's mind. The strength she felt that gave way to weakness – or was it weakness transformed into strength? – in his presence was no exception.

Yeah, she definitely couldn't handle this, being here, with him, like this.

The problem was, now that she had experienced it, she couldn't handle *not* being here with him, either.

Chapter 12

Branch

That was close. Too close.

One minute things were playful, juvenile even, with Kait trying desperately to get her hands on the hat just barely out of her reach, laughing like they were still two kids with their entire lives ahead of them. The next thing he knew, his gesture to help had turned into Kait against his chest, her gaze locked with his, her lips so close to his he could feel her breath whispering with his own.

Branch could have kissed her. And he would have if she had stood there one second longer, staring up at him with those hooded eyes that kept deviating down, as painfully aware of the mere inches between their mouths as he was. But he hesitated one beat too many, leaving Kait the chance to lean away and move the conversation back to less shaky ground.

There was no mistaking what he had seen in her expression, brief but blatant. She had thought of it ten times over while they stood there, lost in each other. So, they were on the same page, then, when it came to the obvious unbroken connection that bound them. But the same page wasn't enough. Branch needed to ascertain which paragraph she was on or else he risked the chance of making a grave mistake that could result in losing her for good.

'Your turn.'

Kait's face announced she didn't have a clue what he meant by that, but she let out a long breath the moment he stepped away to push around the contents of one of the boxes behind him.

'Grandpa Duke's uniform isn't all I found up here.' Branch stood up, holding a green and white checkered dress in his hands, wrinkled from years stowed away but in perfect condition.

'Would you look at that,' Kait chuckled, taking it in her hands when he passed it to her. 'This is straight out of the 1940s. It's got to be.'

'Grandma Addie really did keep everything, I think.' He motioned toward her. 'Like I said, your turn. Looks like it would fit you.' It didn't go unnoticed that he was throwing her own words back at her. And he was doing it on purpose, accompanied by a cheeky grin.

'You want me to put this on?' Kait hadn't expected him to turn the tables, but the more Branch watched her, the clearer he realized there was something else bothering her, too. Having just slipped into his grandfather's military uniform, Branch had a pretty good idea what it was.

The same hesitation plagued her that had plagued him. She was unnerved by the thought of donning Grandma Addie's clothes.

'Go on,' he said again, hoping to ease her mind. 'Try it on.'

'Stop using my own words.'

'Then stop wasting time.' He bit his lip, suppressing his amusement. 'Just pull it up over your jeans and T-shirt.'

She looked ready to protest again, but a moment later she turned her back on him, just as he'd done to her, and unzipped the dress, stepping into it and shimmying it up her thighs. When she turned back around, it was pulled into place and she was tugging it tight at the waist.

'I think it'll do up,' she said, stepping toward him and turning away. 'Can you zip me up?'

Branch thanked God for small miracles. If she had been facing him, she would have seen his mouth open and close without any sound coming out. There was nothing suggestive about her remark, yet doing up the zipper of a woman's dress, albeit one worn over jeans and a T-shirt, was an overly familiar gesture. Intimate, in a way.

Maybe he'd seen one too many movies on Netflix. Nah, this was Kait's fault, all those cheesy chick flicks she subjected him to when they were teenagers had rotted his mind. Or maybe he was just too hopeful for a sign of intimacy between them and Branch was willing to see those signs anywhere, regardless of whether they were real or not.

'Branch?'

He was just standing there, like a fool. 'Right, sorry.' He pulled the dress together at the small of her back. It was a bit loose on her, even with her clothes underneath, and the zipper slid up easily. 'All set, milady.'

Kait whirled around, forcing the swaying skirt to take flight into a full-blown twirl. 'It was the 1940s, Branch, not the 1700s.' The laugh that followed was uninhibited, freeing him of the apprehension he had let himself succumb to only moments before.

He shrugged. 'Sounded polite, I thought.' Awestruck, he watched as Kait swayed this way and that, mesmerized by the way the full skirt seemed to float around her as she moved, her wide smile and soft chuckling transforming her into the young Katharine Hepburn he'd seen in those old movies Grandma Addie used to love watching so much. 'So, if not milady, then what does a well-meaning soldier say when he wants to ask a pretty lady to dance?'

Kait could hear the music drifting up through the attic entrance from the Bluetooth speaker he had set up in the kitchen downstairs. He could tell by the way she spun around and swayed in time with the melody, not just moving to see the skirt flail out, but finding the rhythm and allowing it to guide her.

She stopped, her hands still gripping the fabric as she stared at him. A second later, her mouth lifted at one corner. 'He probably just asks her to dance. Why does everything have to be so complicated?'

Why, indeed. Something about the way she asked the question told him it didn't have a thing to do with soldiers or eras gone by. There were so many things in their lives that were complicated, but this wasn't one of them. Branch held out a hand, letting the brass button near his wrist glint in the incandescent light that shone from the bulb above them. 'Will you dance with me, milady?' He was sticking to the joke, purely because it had made her smile the first time he said it.

The second time earned him one that lit up the drab room around them.

'How corny, good sir,' she laughed, slipping her hand into his. 'But, yes, I'd love to.'

The music suddenly seemed louder, somehow, like the joining of their hands and the feel of Kait under his fingertips managed to heighten his senses. In an old-fashioned stance, he pressed his palm into her side with their joined hands held outward, a polite space between his body and hers. But as the song changed, the first chords of a classic love song beginning to float through the air, Branch felt it before he saw it, and suddenly Kait was closer, like the melody wasn't the only thing drifting, like somehow they had been entranced by the lyrics of love and longing. Branch didn't know who made the decision to step in closer, or if it was even a conscious decision at all. He didn't care. All he did care about was the fact that halfway through the second verse, Kait's head rested against his chest, and his hand that had been holding her gingerly by her side now enveloped her, holding her to him like a precious treasure he was petrified to part with. It was how close to the truth that was which petrified him most.

He prayed the song would last forever, refusing to fade at the end and playing again on repeat. Branch didn't know what the song was called, and he had never been one to pay much attention to musicians' names from any genres other than rock and country, but whatever the song was, and whoever the singer was, they were his favorite. Purely because they, together, the singer and their song, had managed to do what he had only dreamed of for the past eleven years. Kait was in his arms, and there was nothing else in the world Branch Sterling had ever wanted more in his entire adult life.

'Kaitie, where have you been for so long?' He whispered the words without forethought, his mouth pressed against her hair, intoxicated by the berry and vanilla scent of her shampoo. The question wasn't one that required an answer, just more of a desperate utterance, a fevered thought that had unconsciously boiled over and slipped from his tongue. Which only made Kait's reply that much more surprising.

'Right here.' Her voice was barely audible, but he felt her jaw move against his chest as she spoke. 'I've been right here.'

'I think I have been, too,' he replied, hugging her tighter. He could no longer hear the music over the pounding of his own heart, the blood rushing in his ears like a dam broke somewhere within him. Maybe it had. And maybe he was right. Maybe this was where he had been for the past decade, right here, holding Kait and inhaling the scent of her shampoo and basking in the warmth that emanated from her as they moved in perfect rhythm.

He might have left Port Landon, but Branch's heart had been here the entire time, with Kait.

They never missed a beat, still dancing to the rhythm of each other instead of the melody, lost somewhere amidst their high emotions and loud heartbeats. And yet, the moment Kait raised her head to reveal her pretty gemstone eyes to him, Branch could see the truth – she'd been right here, with him, the entire time, too.

Eyes locked on his, Kait's gaze said more than her words ever could. Branch couldn't tear himself away, couldn't see anything beyond her natural beauty, couldn't hear anything beyond her shaky breaths mixed with his heart as it attempted to beat out of his chest.

He didn't know when he decided to do it, or if there was ever a conscious thought about it at all. He had a feeling the action had nothing to do with his brain and was led entirely by his heart. Either way, he leaned forward and pressed his lips to hers, soft and tentative and perfect in every way.

The house could have fallen down around them. The song could have changed, and the sun could have refused to shine. Branch wouldn't have noticed any of it, because nothing but kissing Kait mattered, nothing but the fact that she didn't recoil or pull away. They stood there, unmoving, lost in each other as though not a minute had passed since they had been eighteen and head over heels for each other.

He opened his eyes. Everything came rushing back, his senses kicking back into high gear. The music floated into his ears, the dust and cobwebs stringing across his peripheral vision. But Kait was still standing before him, her eyes fixed on him, unblinking, and her arms somehow wrapped around his waist. Neither of them spoke or dared to move, rendered speechless and unable to command their limbs to do anything but hold on to one another for dear life.

'What just happened?' Kait sounded distant. Whether it was her own shell-shocked state that caused it or Branch's inability to focus on anything but the ghostly caress of her lips still lingering on his, he wasn't certain.

'I think,' he replied, his mouth curling upward, 'you just forgave me.'

'Branch, I did that a long time ago.'

It felt good to hear it, but he wondered at what cost that forgiveness had come. 'You'd be the only one, then,' he told her, unable to find the strength to step away and put distance between them. If he was getting to live out the dream of having her in his arms once more, even for a fleeting instance, he wasn't about to let go of that dream until absolutely necessary. 'I don't blame you. For anything that happened afterward. I just want you to know that. I don't blame you for telling me to leave.'

Pain marred Kait's features at the mere mention of that night but he wasn't going to let the subject drop easily. They had spent a few days together now, for countless hours at a time, and yet the subject had never been broached. She had never been one for confrontation or conflict, and Branch knew she would continue to let it be the elephant in the room as long as he allowed for it.

Their kiss changed things. It changed Branch's solemn outlook, and his plans. It was one kiss, but he felt it. The longing. The passion. Kait still loved him, just as he still loved her. And that changed everything.

'I should've heard you out.' Kait let her arms fall to her sides, taking a step back. She was quickly looking a whole lot less certain about this – their proximity and the topic of conversation – and Branch figured she was about two seconds away from wrapping her arms around herself and shutting down completely. 'I should have talked to you,' she continued. 'And listened. I should've just listened.'

'Kaitie, it's in the past.' Branch stepped forward slowly. Her skittish resemblance to a timid deer had him reluctant to move too quickly, fearing she might feel cornered and take off down the attic ladder, but he chanced reaching out for her arms, tortured by her obvious unease. 'We can't change it. Trust me, there are so many things I wish I could. I'd do things differently. Anything to save you from the hurt I put you through. You've got to believe that.'

113

'I do,' she croaked out, appearing stricken by the thought. 'I believe you would change what happened if you could.'

Her unspoken words were just as powerful as the ones that came out of her mouth. She believed he would do it all differently if he could, but Kait was acutely aware of what those kinds of regrets could do to a person given enough time. She had been living with similar regrets for more than ten years as well, and they had eaten away at her in the same unforgiving, gnawing manner his had.

'I would,' Branch assured her. 'I'll never forgive myself for what happened to Zach. I never liked the guy much, but he was your friend. I would never tell you who you can and can't be friends with, not then and not now. And I certainly would never purposely use my truck to …' He couldn't even say it out loud. 'It was an accident, I swear it. That's not the kind of man I am, you've got to know that.'

'I wouldn't be standing here if I thought you were.' Kait's fingers absently raked through her hair, smoothing out her ponytail. It was her tell. Whenever she was nervous, she played with her hair in some fashion. 'And what about Holly?'

For a split second, Branch had no clue who she was talking about. That's how much of a whiplashing change of direction the name was from the subject of the accident. It shouldn't have been, seeing as it was no secret the girl had been in the truck with him that night, but Branch couldn't understand what, after all these years, she had to do with things. 'Holly Raynard?' He hadn't said the name in years, and even now when he thought of her, his mind conjured up an unpleasant image, an intoxicated and practically passed out Holly, her head flopping back onto the headrest of his truck as he folded her into the passenger seat to take her home. 'Kait, I haven't thought about her in a long time, but you're going to have to explain to me what—'

'You know what, don't.' Kait's hands came up in front of her, halting him from gaining any further access to her, distance wise and verbally. 'I've changed my mind. After what just happened, I think we need to leave the reminiscing alone for today.'

There it was, the inevitable shutdown of Kait Davenport. She was leaving him with more questions than answers, but if there was one thing Branch knew about her, she wouldn't be coerced into talking about something if she didn't want to. The conversation was over.

For now.

Besides, the most important factor in her parting statement was the acknowledgment that something *had* just happened. He'd kissed her, soft and sweet. And Kait had kissed him back. To have that occur between them, on top of finally scraping the surface of the unfortunate events that led to their relationship's catastrophic demise, it was a miracle in itself.

They had come together to pay tribute to Grandma Addie, the woman who had instilled the spirit of Christmas in Branch for so many years, who had treated Kait like family right along with anyone else who wanted or needed it. With a little holiday magic and a whole lot of luck, Branch and Kait had a real chance at coming out on the other side of this festive event stronger than ever. Healed.

And together.

Chapter 13

Kait

'The usual, dear.'

Arnold and Jemima Jackson had taken up residence in their regular booth. Nothing had changed. The elderly couple were doing the same thing they did every day, asking for the same order they always requested.

And yet, Kait couldn't remember the particulars of that order. 'Right,' she said, playing it off as a joke. 'Two coffees and ...' She trailed off, hoping to heavens Jemima would chime in and remind her what kind of pie to cut for them. It was one slice, shared between them, she recalled that much, but as for the kind of pie they wanted, it was—

'Lemon meringue,' Arnold piped up, peering at the waitress with a curious gaze. 'With two forks. Are you suffering from Old Timer's, too?'

Jemima clucked her tongue at her husband, swatting his hand. 'For heaven's sake, Arnold, leave the poor woman be.' She turned to Kait. 'That's his term for Alzheimer's, and frankly it's a joke in poor taste. I apologize for my tactless husband. Goodness, we can't expect you to remember everything.'

116

Kait forced a broad smile on her face, waving off her apology. 'No harm done, Jemima. I'll get your coffees and lemon meringue pie.' She cast a jovial glance at Arnold. 'With two forks.'

It was official; she wasn't the only one noticing her inability to concentrate. Leave it to Arnold to be right about one thing, though. Kait was definitely suffering from a condition, but it wasn't Old Timer's, as he had so eloquently put it.

Two days ago, Branch had kissed her and turned her world upside down. It was like that simple kiss had flicked a switch somewhere inside her, making it so that she couldn't think of anything but that moment. So sweet, so comforting.

That kiss had been a decade in the making, not a decade too late as she'd originally thought. It wasn't too late for them. It couldn't be. Kait didn't know how she could feel so much for him if there was no chance left for them to be, well, *them*. Branch and Kait. The way she always thought it would be.

As soon as that thought sparked in her brain, however, it was quickly thwarted by the fact that Branch wasn't staying in Port Landon.

He's got a job in the North and less than twenty days left in town, she silently chastised herself. *You're not part of his escape plan.*

No, she wasn't. Kait was the *reason* for his escape plan. At least, her eighteen-year-old self was. Now, though she couldn't bring herself to admit it out loud, Kait wanted nothing more than to be the reason he decided to stay.

It wasn't the first time the thought had entered her mind. She had no right to ask such a thing of Branch, but it didn't mean she didn't want to, anyway.

Wanting to do something and actually doing it were vastly different things, however. Take her fleeting mention of Holly Raynard, for example. Kait wanted so badly to demand answers from Branch, to scream at him to tell her why he chose one night with a girl from high school over the plans and dreams she and he had promised each other. They had been so close to graduation, only another week or so and they would have been free to—

No. That was why she had stopped Branch from finishing his sentence, too scared of his answer to let him utter it aloud. Once it was out, Kait couldn't undo it. She couldn't put the words back in his mouth and make him swallow them, pretending they had never fallen from his lips. The truth was a dangerous thing, and though she desperately wanted it and needed it, she knew that once she had it, she could never give it back.

So, she had stopped him before he could say anything that might ruin the high she was unable to shake since their kiss. Kait didn't remember the last time things had felt so completely and utterly right in her world, so she had been selfish, committed to holding on to that feeling just a little bit longer.

Now, she was consumed by what she did know, and just as overwhelmed by what she didn't. Everything revolved around Branch somehow, leaving Kait enthralled and wondering how in the world she had managed as long as she had without him to make her feel the way she was feeling now.

Cutting the pie and placing the two cups of coffee onto a plastic tray, Kait delivered it to the Jacksons' table, apologizing again for her 'Old Timer's', offering Arnold a playful grin in hopes that it would ease Jemima's lecture later on. She made it back behind the counter just as she happened to glance toward the windows nearest the entrance.

Her eyes widened. 'Eve, quick! Do me a favor and tell him I'm not in today!' she hissed before ducking behind the wall that separated the waitstaff counter from the kitchen. Seconds later, the bell above the door chimed loudly, announcing Zach's arrival.

She shouldn't be hiding from him, but as Kait pressed her back against the wall and listened to Eve weave a tale about her switching a shift, she didn't feel there was any other way to handle

Zach and his less than subtle hatred of Branch. She didn't begrudge him his reasons for not wanting Branch in his life, but there was no way he would ever understand her reasons for wanting Branch back in hers. And since an elderly man like Arnold Jackson could see there was a mind-numbing haze wrapped around Kait's brain, obscuring her focus and fogging up her mental clarity, she knew Zach would easily pick up on her distracted demeanor as well.

It might not be right to hide from him, but it was easier. At the moment, not much else was plain and simply easy for Kait, so she would take it where she could get it.

'Oh my gosh,' Kait gushed, letting the rich aroma and bold taste of dark roast coffee overwhelm her senses. 'I know I serve up coffee all day at the diner, but I'm telling you, there's no substitute for the kind of caffeine fix found in these four walls.'

The four walls she was referring to happened to house the trendy coffeehouse owned by her good friend Allison. Its comfortable combination of modern, industrial, and a dash of rustic décor, with its brick walls and wooden bar and intricate bistro-style tables, made sure there was something here that would appeal to everyone. If having the best coffee in town didn't get customers in the door, the relaxed ambiance would.

'Glad to hear it.' Allison slid into the booth across from her, donning her signature T-shirt with the coffeehouse's logo on the front despite the fact that it was technically her day off. Her long auburn hair was untied, though, falling down around her shoulders, so that was a clear indication she wasn't in work mode today. 'Although, I've got to say, the way you're hugging that mug and fluttering your eyelashes every time you take a sip, I'm starting to wonder if Paige and I shouldn't leave you two alone for a bit.'

Allison's cousin, Paige Henley, snickered, pressing a hand to her mouth as she set her own mug down. 'Geez, can you at least save the jokes for when I don't have a mouthful of sweet, decadent vanilla latte in my mouth?'

'Good grief, you're just as bad as she is.' Allison pointed at Kait, shaking her head when the two women high-fived from across the table. 'You two act like you've never had decent coffee before.'

Kait grinned. 'Well, you know, it's just so hard to come in here, because in order to get good coffee, we've all got to put up with, well, you.'

'You put up with me for my coffee,' Allison laughed. 'Duly noted. But you'd better be careful. I'm real good at revenge.' She tilted her head toward the booth beside them, where both of Janna's twin boys were sprawled across the vinyl seats, snoring softly. 'I'm liable to spike their sippy cups with espresso.'

There was rarely a shortage of banter when the three women got together. Allison, never one to hold back what she was thinking and always harboring more energy than the other two of them combined, helped to complement the more relaxed personalities of Kait and Paige. Though Allison and her cousin were both a few years older than Kait, the friendship she had discovered within their trio was one she couldn't express her profound appreciation of in words.

She had only met Paige a little more than a year ago, when she moved from New York to take over Port Landon's local bakery, but she and Allison had been friends for more than six years, since a particularly trying day when Kait had walked into the coffeehouse and requested the biggest, boldest, strongest cup of coffee she could get. Whether the tall woman with long auburn locks on the other side of the counter struck up a conversation with her out of amusement or just plain pity, Kait didn't know. But the friendship that bloomed was one for the ages, she was certain of that. Kait didn't think she knew anyone else who would let her bring two rambunctious toddlers into their place of business and help to get them down for a nap, allowing for time to have a real conversation with adults who would hear her out and just let her get some things off her chest.

'You wouldn't.'

Allison gave the twins a sidelong glance, a wry grin on her face. 'You're right. Don't hate me for saying this, but how in the world can they look so angelic as they sleep, when minutes ago they were tearing apart the napkin dispensers and wreaking general havoc on anything in their cute little hurricane path?'

'I know, right!' It felt good to hear someone else with the same conflicted thoughts. She adored Janna's boys, but there were some days she wondered how in the world she wasn't falling asleep while still standing. They were beautiful kids, but they were exhausting, too. 'I'd never say that to Janna, but I hear you,' Kait agreed. 'They're the best nephews in the world, but, boy, do I hear you.'

Kait didn't miss the brief glance that passed between her two friends as they sat across from her. If history was any indication, she was fully aware of what it was about, a conversation that had happened many times in the two years since the boys had been born.

'Look,' she said, hoping to steer the topic in another direction, 'I want to thank you two for dropping everything to come and hang out for a bit. I know you're busy.'

'We're busy?' Allison didn't miss a beat. 'You just got off an eight-hour shift two hours ago, and you showed up here with Double Trouble. You're busy, too, Kait. It's my day off. Paige, you got anywhere better to be?'

The slender brunette offered Kait a reassuring smile. 'I'd just pulled a cake out of the oven when you called. I've got to give it time to cool before I can do anything with it, and I've got a new college student hired to handle the front counter. She knows where to find me, so I'm all yours.'

'There you go, then.' Allison waved a hand, urging Kait to start talking. 'You called the meeting of the wise, girlfriend, so something's up. You've only got until the moment one of those precious little rugrats stirs, so what's going on?'

Kait hadn't been sure if calling an emergency coffee date with her friends was the right move to make, not knowing if she would feel better talking about everything or if she would even know what to say. Now, sitting in front of them as they admitted they had effectively wiped their schedules for her at a moment's notice, she was glad she'd made the call. And so, so thankful for both of them. If they weren't the personification of everything her tiny hometown stood for, she didn't know what was.

She didn't dare pick up her mug, fearful her strength might suddenly give out at any moment. 'Something … happened.'

Another glance was exchanged between Allison and Paige, this time tainted with worry.

'Okay …' Allison drew out the word. 'Are you all right?'

'Yes,' she replied quickly, followed by, 'Well, yes but no.' Flustered, she huffed out a loud sigh. 'I kissed Branch.'

In perfect unison, the jaws of both women across the table from her gaped open, then they stuttered out, 'What?'

'Well, he kissed me, I mean,' Kait corrected. 'But I kissed him back, and I … well, I guess it doesn't really matter who kissed who, does it?'

'No, it really doesn't.' Allison wore a wolfish grin, leaning forward, chin on her hands. 'What does matter is that it's got you all aflutter. Who am I kidding, it's got me all aflutter, too!' Her friend clasped her hands together and bounced up and down in her seat.

There wasn't a woman Kait could think of who loved the idea of love more than Allison. She had always been a hopeless romantic, but seeing as she still considered herself a newlywed after getting married less than a year and a half ago, the milestone had somehow taken that love of romance and turned it into a full-blown passion. So, news like this was going to send her friend into a heart-shaped frenzy despite the fact that she, as well as

Paige, knew the whole sordid story of her tumultuous past with Branch Sterling.

Paige put a hand on Allison's arm, calming her. 'But you're conflicted about it,' she said. 'Because you thought you hated him.'

'Exactly.' Kait fidgeted with her coffee mug. 'Is it wrong if I still love him after everything that's happened?'

'Kait, you can't pick and choose who you love.' Allison paused, choosing her words carefully. 'I think you know that better than anyone.'

She was right. Allison knew all too well about the two-year relationship she had had with Zach. Or, more accurately, attempted. She'd been a sounding board for her during many conversations as Kait tried to convince herself she would eventually feel the same way about him as he felt about her, to no avail. If there was one thing she'd learned from her efforts, it was that love wasn't a choice.

'I wanted to love Zach,' Kait said sheepishly. 'You know I did. I tried to, but I just didn't love him that way.'

'Even after everything,' Paige added in a soft tone. 'Don't you see? The tragedy you went through wasn't enough to force you into loving Zach, because it wasn't enough to make you stop loving Branch, either.'

Covering her face with her hands, she pressed her fingers into her eye sockets, letting out a dramatic groan. 'What am I going to do?'

Kait had managed to put off talking about Branch to her friends since the day she found out he was back in town, only divulging that that, yes, her high school sweetheart was in Port Landon, and, no, she didn't want to hash out what that meant to her. Snippets of the truth had come out through brief text messages and fleeting meetups while each of the women were occupied with living their own lives. But now, having her two most trusted confidantes in front of her, ready and waiting to listen and help in any way they could, Kait just wanted answers.

She didn't want to have to overanalyze every aspect of her past any more, and she certainly didn't relish the idea of trying to figure out what the heck to do now that the past had caught up with the present. She yearned for someone to tell her what the right thing to do was, because right and wrong when it came to her feelings for Branch seemed to be a blurred line.

'What do you want to do?' Paige asked encouragingly, a soft smile highlighting her features.

Another groan threatened to bubble up in her throat. To Kait, Paige's question sounded a whole lot like, *We can't make that decision for you.* She lowered her hands, pressing them into the table edge. 'I know that both Janna and Zach—'

'Whoa, wait a minute.' Allison held her hands up, shaking her head vehemently. 'We know, we know … Janna hates Branch because he broke your heart, and Zach hates his guts because, well—'

'Because Branch accidentally hit him with his truck,' Kait finished for her.

'Keep telling yourself that.' Allison rolled her eyes. 'That might be part of it, but not the whole reason. That man hates Branch because he has the one thing Zach never will.'

Kait arched a brow. 'And that is?'

'You.'

A lump formed in her throat as her friend's words settled between them, heavy and tangible. She wasn't sure anyone had ever voiced the suggestion out loud about Zach's jealousy where she was concerned, but Kait had to agree with Allison, albeit reluctantly. Zach had been directing disdain in Branch's direction long before the accident. 'Had,' she corrected. 'You said Branch has me. He *had* me.'

Allison didn't even try to hide her amusement. 'Yeah, right. Keep telling yourself that, too.'

Her gaze flitted from Allison to Paige and back again, but Kait saw the same glimmer in their eyes. They weren't buying her half-hearted detachment for a second. 'Are you sure you can't tell me what to do? I'm driving myself crazy.'

Allison's smile faded, and she pushed her coffee cup away, giving herself room. 'You have to decide what you want. It's that hard and that simple.' She paused to cast a quick glance at Paige, who gave a sympathetic nod of approval. 'Don't think about Janna, and don't think about Zach. In the end, it can't be their happiness that dictates how you handle this. At the risk of being crass, look where that way of thinking has gotten you so far.'

'I don't sacrifice my own happiness so others can have theirs.'

Allison opened her mouth, but Paige reached out and covered her mouth before she could speak. 'I'm pretty sure Allison is about to tell you to keep telling yourself *that*, too. You know, in her charming, sarcastic tone.'

She chuckled at Paige's warning as Allison batted away her cousin's hand.

'Precisely, my dear Paige. And while I didn't exactly say you sacrificed your own happiness for others, you hit the nail on the head. That's exactly what you do, and you know it. Kait, things went awry when you were eighteen, and what did you do? You stayed here in town, played nurse to the man who was injured by your ex's mistake, and even put yourself through two years of a relationship with him despite knowing you didn't love him.'

Kait opened her mouth to protest, but Allison wasn't done.

'After that,' she continued, 'You moved in with Janna after her own relationship went south, putting up with the on-again, off-again shenanigans between them because you didn't want Janna to feel like she had no one else to turn to. When she got pregnant with the boys, it sealed both your fates. That jerk she was with took off, leaving her with two more mouths to feed and a chip on her shoulder the size of Texas. I don't blame Janna for that, by the way, that's not what I'm saying. But that whole situation left you with something, too.'

'What?' Kait wasn't sure how she felt about having the last

eleven years of her life summed up so quickly. Or so accurately.

Allison's gaze connected with hers. 'It left you with someone else to look after,' she replied tenderly. 'Someone else to focus on. Kait, you've spent the last decade looking after everybody else, running yourself ragged in the process, just so you didn't have to think about the broken heart you never quite got over.'

She desperately wanted to slam her fists on the table and tell Allison she was wrong. That she didn't have a clue what she was talking about. But having it laid out before her, from the mouth of a good friend, the impact of her words hit her with the force of a tsunami.

'Allison—'

'You want to know what I think?' Allison leaned back, pausing to give Kait a moment to compose herself. 'I think you've got a second chance here. I know a horrible thing happened and it ripped you and Branch apart. But that was a long time ago. You two were just kids. Besides, you've said it yourself that you've always had unanswered questions. I'm a firm believer that everything happens for a reason, and I find it hard to ignore that everything seems to have come full circle. You still love him, and he still loves you. You can ask all the questions you want, but I think, in the end, that's really everything you need to know.' She shrugged, like it was the easiest decision to make in the world. 'You wouldn't be playing Christmas elf with him and helping with Addie's house if there wasn't still something there. You owe it to yourself, Kait. Take that second chance.'

'Just like that.' Kait didn't understand how she had walked through the front door of the coffeehouse with the weight of the world on her shoulders, and somehow her friend had succeeded in summing it up and making it sound like the answers she needed had been there all along. All she'd had to do was actively seek them out.

'Just like that,' Paige repeated, leaning forward on her elbows.

'Besides, I saw this Branch fellow you're so conflicted about. He's handsome, Kait, I'll give you that one.'

It was Kait's turn to let her mouth gape. 'When did you see Branch?'

'The same day I did,' Allison replied, grinning. 'Jay Forrester brought him by for coffee, then I sent him over to the bakery. Not just for doughnuts, either. I wanted Paige to get an eyeful of the infamous man she'd only ever heard about. You know, for just this type of occasion.'

'You knew I'd end up calling you both for emergency girl-talk.' She didn't know whether to be affronted that they hadn't said anything before now, or elated that her friends knew her so well.

'Darn straight.' Allison looked mighty pleased with herself. 'And I'm going to have to agree with Paige on this one. Branch Sterling has got some rugged good looks going on.' Waggling her eyebrows, Allison chuckled when Kait waved a hand, dismissing her and the suggestive gleam in her eyes.

'You're right.' Kait threw up her hands, defeated. 'I should just give up now and fall head over heels, madly in love with him,' she laughed playfully.

'From what I hear, you already are.'

All three women's heads swiveled at the sound of the raspy voice. Immediately, Kait regretted blurting out the words she had just said, even if they were spoken in jest.

Sonya Ritter stood at the head of the table, clad in a black T-shirt that matched Allison's and a Cheshire cat grin.

'Oh, Kait,' Sonya continued, sounding like she pitied her, 'everyone who's somebody in Port Landon knows the unfortunate story of the dreadful circumstances that sent that Sterling boy packing. It's no secret.'

'Gee, thanks, Sonya.' Kait bit the words out, though there was a hint of sadness in them as well. She was never going to outrun the past, and she knew that, but Kait was a bit surprised to hear Sonya, Port Landon's resident matchmaker, say something negative without throwing her own dash of positivity into the mix. Sonya loved to meddle – lived for it, really – but she did it for a good reason always expecting the best possible result when it came to the matters of love. Usually. 'Tell me something I don't know.'

Being Allison's only full-time employee, Sonya probably had a list of a gazillion things she should be doing, yet the older woman looked in no hurry to head back behind the ordering counter, and Allison had a faint cheeky grin on her face. She was in no hurry to send Sonya away, eager to hear what the town's beloved matriarch had to say about Kait's off-the-cuff comment. The older woman's opinions about love and her seemingly magical ability to bring two people together were legendary in their tiny town.

'Well,' Sonya replied, hands on her hips, 'what I don't think you know is that, not only does everyone know how the story began—' She sent a fleeting glance toward Allison and Paige, something passing silently between them that Kait couldn't read. '—but we also know how the story's going to end.'

'The story did end,' Kait argued, watching as the older woman's bob haircut barely moved as she tilted her head curiously. 'More than ten years ago.'

Sonya, in typical fashion, allowed her slow, knowing grin to speak for itself, letting a silence ensue that became thick with tension. Kait could feel it, the realization washing over her that her friends and Port Landon's mother hen knew something she didn't.

Sonya moved so slowly, so rhythmically, it was as though Kait's gaze couldn't follow her movements. She was just suddenly there, leaning down, close to her face, the scent of espresso and caramel syrup wafting from her in comforting waves.

'I knew that boy's grandmother,' Sonya whispered. 'Even better than you did. Addie told me things, dear.'

'Like … like what?' It made sense that she and Addie talked, but it never occurred to her that Branch's grandmother might have had things to say about Kait. About that night. Or that she might have voiced them to a friend. Grandma Addie just wasn't the gossiping kind.

Sonya didn't speak for a moment, but when she did, her words were clear and concise. 'Addie knew, just like I do, just like everyone does, that eventually that boy would come back to town. And when he did, he would bring the remnants of his bruised and battered heart with him.'

The air was thicker now, it had to be. Kait couldn't take in an adequate breath. 'Why?' It was an odd question, but all she could muster.

'Because his story isn't over, dear.' Sonya said it like it was the most obvious thing in the world. 'And neither is yours. You want to know how I know?'

Kait wanted to scream *Yes!*, but the dizziness she felt, the proverbial precipice she was standing on, made it impossible to formulate a coherent sentence. She nodded.

Sonya stood up straighter, and the fog surrounding Kait seemed to lift and dissipate along with her. 'Because you two aren't together, where you belong,' she replied simply. 'Yet.' With that, Sonya offered her up a wink and walked away without another word.

129

Chapter 14

Branch

When Branch took the time away from work and made the solid plan to come back to Port Landon for an entire month to do what needed to be done with his grandparents' house, he knew it would be hard. Really hard. He never expected anything less.

But he didn't expect this.

Sure, he figured there was a chance he could run into Kait. Port Landon was only so big, after all. But it had taken less than two full days to come face to face with her.

It took just as long for him to fall smack dab back in love with her, too.

Many times, Branch had wondered what it would be like to see her again; how the conversation would go. In every scenario he came up with, she put him in his place, telling him he had a boat load of audacity showing up here now, or she ignored him completely like he didn't exist at all.

But she didn't, which proved two things.

She was still in town, and she was still Kaitie.

His Kaitie.

He didn't have a clue what to do about it, though.

Well, it wasn't that he didn't know, it's just that Branch's thoughts on the matter weren't the only ones he needed to consider. He wanted to believe her thoughts resembled his own.

They weren't over. Maybe they never had been. And that thought both gutted him and exhilarated him simultaneously. So much time wasted, but so much brightness that lay ahead.

In theory, anyway. He had spent the past eleven years living to work, his job permitting him the reprieve from having to face his hometown and the backlash he was so sure would come. Working in northern Canada at a remote mining location, his schedule offered him a two-weeks-on, two-weeks-off lifestyle. He would board a plane and head into the job site in Alberta, staying at the on-site lodging camp and working twelve-hour shifts for thirteen consecutive days. On the fourteenth day, he boarded that same plane and headed back home, a term he used loosely for the closet-like studio apartment he rented in Grand Rapids, furnished by the landlord and only an eight-minute drive from the international airport in decent traffic. He lived there when he wasn't working, sure, but it wasn't home to him.

During his allotted two weeks away from work, Branch usually spent the first few days sleeping, exhausted from the previous stint of workdays and desperate for a good three nights' rest in a bed that was more than a simple cot. Once his fatigue lifted and he felt more like himself, however, Branch never quite knew what to do with himself. If he didn't steal away for a few days to visit his grandparents, he didn't have much else he could call a social life. He didn't have friends to hang out with, had no garage to tinker in, and he certainly didn't date.

Branch Sterling, for all intents and purposes, had become a recluse at the ripe old age of twenty-nine. It hadn't really bothered him before now, though. Maybe that was because he tried not to think about it, resigned to the life he led and working himself to the bone to keep his body and his mind occupied when he could, but the likelier reasoning was her. Kait. His reason for everything.

There was a difference between wishing, hoping, and praying for another chance to prove to Kait that he was the kind of stand-up man she had once believed he was, and having a real chance at obtaining that second chance. Until he held her against him, danced slowly, and kissed her tenderly, that was all he had really held on to – hope. Just was a sliver, a meager one that had become more frayed and brittle with each year that passed.

But he had held on to it, nonetheless. Now, Branch wasn't just fueled by his hope, he was fortified by hers. Kait hoped, wished, and prayed for the same thing.

That realization in itself was enough to have Branch rethinking everything. It should have been simple; stay on course, stay driven, and stick to the solitude he had come to expect. Then, leave his hometown.

Except, this *was* his hometown. The only home he really remembered. He knew the cliché; people spent their entire teenage years waiting for the chance to get out, only to find themselves looking for every chance they could to see the lights of their hometown once they had grown up. Maybe he was a walking cliché, but for a man who had no family left, no friends, and no real roots, he had managed to walk back into Port Landon and unearth a house he could call his own, a long-time friend who welcomed him home without hesitation, and his first love.

It sounded like home to him.

Now, with Kait's pretty face and alluring eyes never far from the forefront of his mind, Branch was seeing his hometown in a different light, through the logical, rational eyes of a man about to turn thirty. He wasn't a wild-eyed teenager anymore, and neither was Kait. She had stayed in Port Landon, growing and gaining her strength within the town instead of without. She had been front row and centre in the aftermath of the accident but she stayed, nonetheless.

For the first time, he wondered if he had been wrong about his hometown's reaction to his mistakes. He wondered if Jason was right, that he'd been so keen on hating himself for it that he hadn't realized he was the only one. That the community had never been out to exile him the way he'd exiled himself. The town was still here, reminding him he was one of their own. Kait was still here, too, which made Branch wonder if maybe, just maybe, he could stay as well.

The notion was momentarily debilitating. As he went about pulling the last three-foot plastic candlestick in line with the others that lined both sides of the driveway, he realized how easy it could be. The house that loomed over him, though dated and in need of a little TLC, was his. So were the contents inside. It was daunting and gut-wrenching, but a pure and simple fact. Grandma Addie and Grandpa Duke had left everything they had to him in their will, and that made him the proud owner of 14 Crescent Street. He had a home, Grandpa Duke's Bronco, Grandma Addie's old Buick, and everything he needed to turn the house and property into a home. A real home. *His* home.

All he needed was Kait. And truth be told, now that Branch had witnessed a fleeting glimpse of what it could be like to hold Kait's hand and take on whatever life wanted to throw at them, he wasn't certain he had it in him to walk away from her for a second, final time.

His lack of roots weighed heavily on him as he struggled with the candlestick, attaching its electrical cord to the other one four feet away. Tonight, all eight of them would light up the driveway like it was a path to Santa Claus's home at the North Pole. Well, if he owned a Victorian home with an attached garage, that is.

He just got the last of the cords plugged in when the sound of tires crunching on ice and snow announced a vehicle pulling into the driveway. Thinking it was Jason, Branch didn't turn immediately. That was his first mistake, seeing as he might have had time to compose himself if he had taken the opportunity to glance over his shoulder.

'That's an awful lot of Christmas decorations.'

Branch, still crouched near the outdoor electrical outlet, sprang to his feet. 'Zach,' he said, surprised. 'Sorry, I thought you were someone else.'

His Oakley sunglasses reflected Branch's shocked expression. In his crisp khakis and his leather shoes, Zach looked comfortable, professional, and unfazed. It only increased Branch's discomfort.

'Let me guess, Kait?'

It wasn't so much the mention of her name that set Branch on edge, but the smug way Zach sneered it. Like there was a joke he was missing, somehow. 'Actually, no,' he replied, fighting to keep his tone neutral. 'Not until tonight, anyway.' It was the truth, but the insinuation had Zach's jaw just as clenched as his was. 'I thought you were Jay, to be honest,' he added as an afterthought. 'Jay Forrester.' Things needed to be civil between them. He was Kait's friend, after all.

'Right.' He couldn't see Zach's eyes, but his head swiveled one way, then the next, his hands shoved in his pockets as he assessed the exterior of the house. 'Look, I was just driving by and saw you outside. Thought I would stop and see if you've given my offer any more thought. Although, I've got to say, this is quite the festive scene you've put together in the front yard, especially for a man who says he's only in town until the end of the month.'

Branch couldn't be sure, but hidden under all his questions and calm inflection, he thought he heard a veiled threat. At the very least, Zach was doubting Branch's word, and that was enough to raise his hackles. 'I'm sure you've heard that Kait and I are going to hold a dinner here on Christmas Eve in Grandma Addie's honor. So, I'm decorating the way my grandmother would have, Zach, nothing more.' He thought of adding that he didn't have to explain himself, but he managed to swallow down the defensive words.

'And my offer?' Zach was persistent, that's for sure.

Branch, however, had no choice but to be honest. 'I haven't given it much thought. I've been kind of busy.'

'So I've heard.'

Branch didn't have to guess. He knew that comment was about Kait, not the dinner or the house. 'Zach, if you've got something to say—'

'Trust me, I doubt you want to hear it.'

'What I'm doubting are your reasons for wanting to buy my grandparents' house.'

Branch adjusted the ballcap on his head, giving himself a moment to rein in the defiance in his voice. 'If this has something to do with the accident, you know I'll never be able to apologize to you enough about what—'

'You're going to do the same thing to her now that you did back then,' Zach interjected. To his credit, there was no malice in his tone, just a matter-of-factness that stopped Branch in his tracks. 'You're going to hurt Kait.'

Of course, this was about Kait. It was always about Kait, for both of them.

'I'm not here to hurt her,' he stated, his eyes flaring hot with conviction. 'I won't ever hurt her again.'

'You weren't at that party to hurt her, either,' Zach reminded him. 'And look how well that turned out.'

It was a twist of the knife, one that had been piercing his soul for ten long years. The accuracy of Zach's summation sliced through Branch, and his hand came up to press against his chest, as though checking for a wound.

'You want to buy my grandparents' house, purely so I'll leave town.' The realization washed over him, tunneling his vision and thinning out the air he tried to take in. 'So I'll leave Kait.'

'She means a lot to me,' Zach replied. 'I'll give you whatever you're asking for it, plus ten percent. It's worth every penny to make sure she doesn't get hurt again.'

Was he shocked, or impressed? Branch couldn't figure out what he felt knowing Zach would pay whatever it took to get him out of town and away from his long-time friend. As quickly as his emotions whirled, it took only a heartbeat for him to choose his response. Really, there was no choice at all.

'The house isn't for sale.'

'Excuse me?' Whatever Zach expected from their conversation, it wasn't that. He pulled his sunglasses off, staring at him with a confused, narrowed gaze. It was the first glimpse of his eyes Branch had witnessed since the accident a decade ago. His gaze was gray as steel and just as hard.

Branch shook his head. 'I'm not selling it.' No amount of money would ever be enough to make him walk away from his second chance with Kait. That chance might be slim, but it was a chance, nonetheless. He owed it to himself – to them, and the lovestruck teenagers they had once been – to try. Besides, it was his grandparents' place, and in a roundabout way, that made him feel like they were the ones offering him the second chance. He liked that idea.

'If you're not selling, then what *are* you doing?'

Again, Zach wasn't just talking about the house. The worst thing Branch probably could have done was laugh, but it was out before he could stop it. Pulling his hat off to rake his hands through his hair, he placed it back on his head, invigorated by having made one, albeit impulsive, decision. 'I honestly don't know. But I can tell you what I'm not doing. I'm not hurting Kait,' he said, emphasizing *not* for good measure. 'And I'm not leaving.'

The realtor stood before him, still as stone. Branch couldn't pinpoint what changed, but he swore something did, as though a fire had just erupted somewhere he couldn't see. 'You have my card if you change your mind.'

As Branch watched him walk back to his BMW, he wondered what a shrewd man like Zach Canton was capable of in the name of love. Whatever the answer was, he had a feeling he would find out soon enough.

'Door's open!'

Branch would have met Kait at the door if he hadn't been flat on his back, buried underneath the ancient limbs of an artificial Christmas tree. It was a miracle he had even heard the knocking on the door at all with the amount of pine sprigs and cobwebs that surrounded his head like a dome.

Forty minutes ago, he'd tugged three dilapidated cardboard boxes out of the attic, down the rickety set of stairs, and into the living room. Each one was clearly marked in black permanent marker, but Branch knew what those boxes held. Grandpa Duke had always been so meticulous about putting the old artificial tree away, neatly tying the removable limbs into bunches according to size with string, making sure nothing was bent before it was stored away for another year. Grandma Addie was the designated holder of each bunch while he tied it and carefully tucked it in the box. When he passed away, the role as keeper of the Christmas tree had been handed down to Branch. Grandma Addie always waited for him, letting Branch be the one to unpack the tree before Christmas – sometimes, it was down to the wire on Christmas Eve night – and helping him as he carefully stowed it away, even tying the knots of string the same way Grandpa Duke had.

Loneliness had seldom been on his radar since he arrived back in Port Landon, but the moment he unpacked the artificial tree, there was no denying that's what he felt. Something wasn't right about putting up a tree – that tree, in particular – without his grandparents by his side. It was the first time he had ever tried to do it alone.

Branch didn't think he'd ever been so happy to hear Kait's footsteps in the front foyer.

'You sounded like you were speaking through—' Kait rounded

the corner, her hair tossed up in a messy bun and her eyes rounding as recognition took over. 'We're putting up the Christmas tree?'

Branch slid out from under it just in time to see her fist pump the air and do a little gleeful dance. Sitting up, knees bent in front of him, his mouth curved into a grin. 'After that, how can I say no?'

'I walked in expecting to have to find out what's in the basement of this place. Trust me, putting up the tree sounds much better.'

Branch took a glance at his handiwork, thinking the tree looked pretty good considering it was older than he was. Wiping the dust from his hands, he stood. 'The tree's already up, all we've got to do is decorate it.'

'Now you're speaking my language,' Kait replied, rubbing her hands together excitedly.

Kait and her love of Christmas. He wasn't sure he would ever tire of seeing how excited it made her. Children might anticipate Christmas morning, but Kait Davenport got butterflies from preparing for it.

'There's a box at the foot of the attic stairs. It's got the ornaments in it.' He pointed his thumb over his shoulder. 'You grab that, and I'll grab snacks. We'll make an event out of it.'

Something passed over Kait's face but Branch didn't wait around to give her a chance to turn him down. He wanted her to remember all the good things about their time together, and he wanted her to enjoy her time while she helped him pull off this Christmas caper. It didn't go unnoticed that she showed up promptly when she said she would, after working, after babysitting, and no doubt after having to hear her friends' and family's opinions of him.

He wanted her to know he appreciated every second she gave him.

By the time Branch made his way back into the living room,

Kait had the box of ornaments on the floor, cardboard flaps opened wide, and a glittery array of baubles laid out on the carpet and couch cushions, sorting them, by the looks of it, according to color. Tinsel draped over the arm of the couch, and strings of lights set off to the side of the box, Kait was prepared to tackle that tree and turn it into a holiday masterpiece.

'I was just going to put 'em on the tree as I grabbed them out of the box.'

The comment got the reaction he was expecting. Kait fixed him with a horrified stare.

'You don't just put them on, Branch. Well, unless it's the tree at the diner. Then I just put them on willy-nilly. You know, just to drive Janna bonkers.' She grinned, then waved a hand, dismissing the idea. 'But this one's a work of art.' She shook her head, obviously saddened by his lack of knowledge on the topic. 'For that, I'd tell you to leave and come back when I'm done, but it's your house. That would be rude.' A faint smirk played on her lips.

'Rude, but warranted, by the sounds of it.' He set the tray down on the coffee table beside her. 'Maybe that'll make up for my Christmas indiscretions.'

Branch took a step back and watched. Waited. He'd had to make a special trip out to the grocery store, then the convenience store when he couldn't find what he was looking for, but the search had been worth it. As soon as Kait turned toward the tray, he could visibly see the moment the memory registered in her mind.

'Oh, you remembered!' She plucked the plastic package of cinnamon bear candies from the tray with one hand, tipping the bottle of Mountain Dew with the other, as though she had to read the label to confirm what it was. 'These are still my favorites.'

There was nothing special about the candy or soda, but together they signified a night during their teenage years that Branch would never forget. Kait hadn't either, obviously.

'It's been barely two weeks since I got here, but I've had time to notice that some things haven't really changed, even if we have,' Branch explained. 'I was hoping this was one of them.'

She continued to stare at the bottle, holding the cap between her fingers. 'I don't think I've ever bought cinnamon bears and Mountain Dew together since,' she chuckled, turning to him. 'But there's nothing better.'

Branch swallowed past the lump in his throat. She was something. *This* was something. 'Rip them open, then. We've got a tree to decorate.'

Kait did, and they fell into an easy silence. Branch poured Mountain Dew into glass tumblers, and Kait got to work, strategically stringing the lights around the tree, then the tinsel strands. Branch did his best not to intervene, but as he watched her, her expression determined and wheels turning, he became more and more convinced she was calculating the distance between each light and piece of garland she added. She had a head full of holiday equations, and the final result would be the perfectly accessorized tree.

No wonder she wouldn't just let him put the glass ornaments on. There was a plan. A strategic sequence of actions. It was on the tip of his tongue to jovially ask if she needed graph paper or a ruler or something in order to get all the bulbs hung just right, but Kait spoke first.

'We were just kids that night.' She kept her focus on the shiny crimson ornament in her hand. 'Obviously, or we wouldn't have been sitting out there eating cinnamon bear candies and drinking Mountain Dew.'

She didn't laugh outright, but he heard the upward curl of her lips. Branch continued to pull the last remaining bulbs from the box, his expression stoic, but inside he was elated.

She was thinking. About them. Who they were, and what they had become. Who they could be. Good.

'I don't know, we're almost thirty now and still eating and drinking them, so maybe it's a grown-up thing to do.'

She cast him a narrowed glance. 'Easy with the thirty comments,' she replied wryly, turning back to the tree. 'I'm just saying, we were so young. Yet, we still seemed to think we had all the answers.'

If Branch closed his eyes, he swore he could still smell the damp vegetation around them, hear the crickets and the frogs and their night-time interlude. They'd had less than a month till graduation, so many dreams, and so many hopes. But it was the promises Kait was thinking of now. The ones he had made to her. They ones they had made together.

'I meant every word, Kaitie.' Branch's hands stilled. He couldn't function with such a vivid memory rearing up and striking him with vehement vengeance. 'Those answers still apply.'

A tense quietness ensued, and Branch let it ring out, the silence as deafening as a torrential storm. He ached to go to her, to use words to remind her, but he could see the truth – he didn't need to. She was there, in the darkness, caught up in the memory just as irrevocably as he was.

'I haven't been there since, but we used to go out to that old house all the time. The old Hansel and Gretel House.' She whispered the town's name for the rundown homestead ruins affectionately. It was just a weather-beaten cottage in the middle of the woods, abandoned and forgotten by everyone except the teenagers who needed a place to escape from the small town they thought they despised. But it was the place Branch and Kait had often run to, trudging through the trees to sit on the dilapidated front step that threatened to cave in at any possible moment and hold each other, arms tangled as they whispered about the future they were going to have together. 'Everyone went there.'

'But that night, it was just us,' Branch added carefully. 'Just us and our cinnamon bears and Mountain Dew.'

A choked sound erupted from Kait's throat, laughter mixed with pain. 'And our dreams,' she said. 'My gosh, Branch, you said that after graduation it was going to be you and me, always. You said we were so close to our own forever …' She trailed off, swallowing hard. 'That night, you said you were going to—'

'I know.' Every synapse in his brain was firing only one signal straight through him: *Go to her. Now, you fool.* But Branch knew if he wrapped his arms around her and hugged her to him, she would fall apart. The waver in her voice warned him of it. Hell, they both would. The gold ring was burning a hole through his wallet, letting its presence be known.

But he needed Kait to remember. He needed her to stay with him in the memory.

'I did,' he whispered, holding out his hand. Branch couldn't bring himself to leave her there, so close yet so far away from him. Not when she was remembering so crystal clear the moment he had sat there, her body tucked into his, under the darkness of night at the Hansel and Gretel House and told her in a voice barely above a whisper that he was going to marry her someday, if she would let him.

She remembered every word. So did he.

'I didn't expect a thing when I came back to Port Landon.' He let out a long breath when she entangled her fingers in his and squeezed tightly. 'But this, right now, you and I … Kaitie, I wouldn't change this for the world.'

An electric-like snap and crackle buzzed through him where his fingers touched hers.

'Me neither.' The way her chest deflated as she pushed out the words, he wondered how long she had been wanting to say them aloud. He stepped closer, clasping her hand tighter, letting the electricity between them spark brighter.

'It's been more than a decade, and yet there's been no one else since. There is no one else for me. And there's no one else for you, either.' It was presumptuous, bordering on cocky, and—

'There was, though,' Kait squeaked out.

—and wrong, evidently.

'Was,' she repeated, emphasizing it. 'A long time ago. About a year after the accident, I tried to date again. It was a futile effort, but I didn't want to feel like I felt, then.'

Her anguish was so close to bringing him to his knees it was painful. Painful to feel, and painful to watch. He didn't let go of her hand, though the room seemed to spin with her confession. 'It's okay,' he told her softly. 'You deserved to be happy. Loved.'

But Kait shook her head vehemently, tears brimming her eyes. 'Not when I didn't love him back.'

'Who?'

Her glassy gaze met his, and she looked downright stricken to have to even say his name out loud. 'Zach.'

Suddenly, it all made sense. Zach Canton had disliked Branch before the accident because he stood in the way of his friendship blossoming into a romantic relationship with the woman he pined for as long as he could remember. But Branch had been thrown out of the picture by that night's events, paving a clear path for Zach to make his way into Kait's heart.

And yet, Zach had become Kait's boyfriend and ultimately lost her. Branch wasn't a betting man, but if he was, he would bet everything he owned that, even with Branch long gone, Zach couldn't compete with the ghost of Branch and Kait's love. No amount of distance or time or tragedy could erase the memory of that, Branch realized that now.

He almost felt sympathy for Zach, a man who only wanted to love someone whom he couldn't force to love him back.

Almost.

143

Chapter 15

Kait

Something was happening. A shift, a push toward the edge of something strong and inexplicably real despite its lack of definition. Something involving the remnants of an evening Kait still recalled vividly … hushed promises and pretty words floating on the scent of cinnamon candy and sugary soda …

And she had to ruin it by being brutally honest.

A tender moment with the man she never thought she would see again let alone fall back in love with, and she had to go and mention Zach Canton.

'It's okay,' Branch repeated, giving her hand a soft squeeze. 'You've done nothing wrong.'

Then why does it feel like that? A defeated sigh escaped her lips. 'Maybe not, but you had a right to know.'

'It doesn't change a thing,' he replied without hesitation. 'Not to me.' He reached into the box and pulled out a tiny glass teddy bear ornament. A cardinal sat nestled in its paws. Branch held it out to Kait. 'More than ten years have passed since those promises were made. You had every right to move on.'

'I didn't do that very well, now, did I?' Kait held the ornament between her fingers, scrutinizing it so she didn't have to look him in the eye. Admitting failure had never been one of her strong suits, always being the one to forge on until things worked out the way she wanted them to. But there was no other way to see it – she had failed miserably when it came to moving on from Branch.

'You tried,' he assured her, setting the box back down. 'Which is more than I can say for myself.'

Kait thought about making up some outlandish encouraging anecdote, saying she was sure he'd tried in his own way. But Branch Sterling had never been a man who ran away from a fight, or put himself first before those he loved. Yet, he had hightailed it out of Port Landon and returned only because of his beloved grandparents. He'd run, used work as an excuse to stay away, and had come back now, without his family to hide behind. She couldn't lie to him. She wouldn't.

'You know,' she said instead, turning the ornament slowly in her hand, 'cardinals are supposedly messengers from heaven. They show up when you need them most.'

'Is that right?' Branch reached out and ran a finger across the smooth glass of the bear's head. 'You think Grandma Addie's trying to send me a message?'

'I think it's an awful coincidence that you pulled that out of the box and gave it to me, seeing as I knew what cardinals symbolized and you didn't.'

The smile that formed on Branch's lips sent goosebumps across her skin. 'It wasn't a coincidence I pulled it out of the box, Kaitie.'

'What do you mean?' Confused settled in, furrowing her eyebrows.

Branch pointed at the ornament. 'That was Grandma Addie's favorite ornament. She was the one to put it on the tree every Christmas. That thing's been passed down for at least three generations that I know of.' His grin grew wider. 'It's not a Christmas ornament, per se, but Grandma Addie hung it up every year, anyway, because of what it signified to her.'

Kait stared at it, the bear suddenly feeling warm in her clammy hands. 'What does it signify?'

Branch reached out and closed his hand over hers, the ornament wedged between them. 'Grandma Addie always told me that ornament was magic. It brought people together. People who were meant to be together, that is.' He paused, his dark eyes locking with hers. 'It was passed down to her the day before she met Grandpa Duke.'

Kait's mouth opened but no sound came out. The ornament felt heavy as lead in her palm, and Branch's hand enveloping hers was burning her up from the inside out. 'I … I don't know what's happening right now, Branch.'

He stepped in, close enough that their clasped hands touched his chest. 'Me neither, but I want to be here, so I can find out. So *we* can find out.'

The walls could have crumbled down around them; Kait wouldn't have noticed. She was too enthralled with the words that had fallen from his lips, and what they meant.

Branch wanted to stay. Here. 'You're serious?'

'I've got promises to make good on.'

Eventually, Kait was sure she would have a million questions as to how exactly it was going to work, where they went from here. But, right now, she didn't care about the logistics. The only thing she cared about was the man in front of her, holding her hand, telling her he wanted to stay in Port Landon. With her.

'Okay.' She sounded dazed even to her own ears.

Branch chuckled. 'Okay.' He released her hand. 'Go put the ornament on the tree.'

'Are you sure?' She didn't want to take a family tradition from him if he wanted the honor of hanging it up himself.

'Grandma Addie gave me a house, a new beginning, and a path straight back to you. I'm going to go out on a limb and agree with you; finding that ornament today was no coincidence. Go on.'

She was pretty sure her heart was about to beat out of her chest as she turned and stepped forward, slipping the gold string onto the pine branch, watching as the red and green lights behind it illuminated the bear's shiny contours.

From behind, Branch's arms slipped around her, and he rested his chin on her shoulder, gazing at the ornament with her. 'That's perfect, Kaitie.'

'It is.' Not just the ornament, but the moment itself. Her very own Christmas miracle. Her head tilted against his, she smiled. A genuine one.

'For what it's worth, I agree with you about the cardinal, too,' Branch whispered.

'You think she's trying to send you a message?'

'I think she already did, it just took me a little longer to sit down and listen,' he laughed, hugging her tighter. 'But, message received, Grandma Addie. Loud and clear.'

All the late nights and early mornings were starting to catch up with Kait. She thought she'd been a billboard for fatigue before, her most alluring dream being twelve hours of uninterrupted sleep under the thick downy comforters of her own bed, but she had bypassed the definition of fatigue completely and headed straight to pure and utter exhaustion.

She had no one to blame but herself, and truth be told, even with her heavy-lidded eyes and foggy brain, she didn't regret all the time she was awake lately. She would do it all again, in the exact same way, if it meant she felt the way she did right now. Because underneath that excessive tiredness was a sense of accomplishment, a swell of pride …

And a pulse of anticipation.

It had been so long since Kait had been excited about something. She couldn't recall the last time she woke up with anything but a need just to make it through the day unscathed by life itself. She was all about survival, for her and for her family. Existence. Being there, showing up, and doing what she could to make it through the next twenty-four hours, knowing the only thing she needed to do after that was wake up and do it all over again.

I've got promises to make good on, he had said. Yesterday, Branch had made his choice – he wanted to stay in Port Landon. He was choosing to see his grandparents' estate as a gift rather than a burden or a reminder of what he had lost. It was his now, and he wanted to keep it. He wanted to try. Not run, like last time, but try.

Kait was going crazy. She had to be. Who else would remember all the things that happened when they were younger, be painfully aware that he had been gone from her life for ten long years, and then welcome him home with open arms like he'd done her a favor by coming back?

She would blame the daze she was walking around in for her lack of judgment, but Kait knew it wasn't just because of her exhaustion lowering her guard.

It was hard to judge someone when you loved them. Wasn't that the definition of unconditional, after all? There was a time when she had tried to hate him – she had certainly wanted to – but there was no denying the truth.

Kait's love for Branch had always been stronger than her hate, even when she couldn't admit it to herself. There was no way to hide it anymore. As time passed, the mention of his name had faded, going from the main topic of everyone's coffee chatter to barely spoken at all, which made it easier to ignore. Time itself had allowed her wounds to scar over, the sting less acute.

Once he showed up in town, however, in front of her, time might as well have rewound itself. Her feelings for him were there, as though she was eighteen again. The only difference was that the sting wasn't just less acute. It was gone, along with the hatred she had once clung to so desperately.

Yet, her love for him remained, despite everything. Allison and Paige were right; she couldn't ignore that.

Even if a select few people wanted her to.

It being her sister's day off, Kait expected to see Janna the moment she dragged her weary body through the door of their shared house. The morning shift had been surprisingly busy at The Port. The part she didn't see coming was when Janna met her at the door and spoke up over the loud babbling of toddler conversation going on in the living room.

'Can we talk?'

Kait didn't even have her boots off yet. She suppressed the groan rising in her throat. When were her sister and Zach going to get the hint that she wasn't going to partake in an intervention? She didn't want it, and she was willing to accept whatever consequences came of her actions. Why wasn't that enough?

'Sure, what's up?' Goodness, she needed to learn to handle confrontation better. It had been days, though, since her older sister had uttered more than trivial small talk her way, obviously upset by Kait's blatant dismissal of her worries where Branch was concerned, so it was good to know she hadn't written her off completely.

Janna pushed away from the doorway, nodding toward the living room. Regardless of how serious their conversation might be, nothing was more crucial than being sure not to leave two overly curious toddlers unattended.

Kait followed her silently, wishing she could disappear upstairs and shower. She was sure she smelled like an oversized French fry. The old glider rocking chair she settled into smelled like tomato sauce, a by-product of one of those few incidents when she and Janna had somehow let the boys out of their sight for a fraction of a second, so she didn't figure it mattered much.

'If this is about Branch ...' She really didn't care to argue again.

Janna chose a spot on the floor beside the twins, where

they were building a wavering tower of plastic blocks, leaning dangerously to one side.

'This isn't about Branch,' she assured her. 'It's about you.'

'Me?'

Janna pushed one of the blocks into position, preventing the tower from falling and the tears that were sure to come with it. 'I try so hard to do what's right, Kait. So hard.'

Kait hadn't expected that. She leaned forward, her eyebrows furrowed. 'I know that. Where's this coming from?'

Janna didn't make eye contact. 'I've tried so hard to do what's right,' she repeated, 'But I guess I never stopped to think if what was right for me was right for you, too.'

Maybe it was her tiredness, or it could have been her muddled thoughts, but Kait didn't understand. 'What are you talking about, Janna?'

'When things went bad with Dorion, and when these two little guys were born ...' She raised her head. 'I didn't ask you to stay in town. Or to move in and help me the way you did. The way you still do.'

'I never said you did.' Guilt was forming in Kait's stomach, strong and caustic.

'I know,' she agreed. 'But even though I didn't ask, you did it, anyway. You took charge of the situation like you were the big sister, not me. Like you always do. I didn't ask, but I expected it from you, just the same.'

'Janna—'

'No, let me finish.' She held up a hand. 'I never fought you on it because I needed the help. I needed someone to help me through this, and as usual, that someone was you. Coming to the rescue and acting like we're the same person, somehow – that's you in a nutshell.'

Silence ensued. Kait didn't have a leg to stand on when it came to that argument, and she knew it.

'I didn't want you to make the same mistakes I did,' Janna

continued. 'You'd already had your heart broken once, and it killed me to watch you hurt that bad. I took your help when you offered it because I needed you, but I also let you move in and everything because I thought I was protecting you.'

If it wasn't for the formidable tower building going on the middle of the living room floor, Kait was sure she would have been able to hear a pin drop. 'Protect me from what?' She choked the words out, her throat thick with emotion. Her older sister wasn't a heart-to-heart kind of woman. She obviously had things she needed to get out.

Janna chuckled hollowly. 'I wish I knew, now. But I've held on to you so tight since the accident, been so vocal about the things you do and the people you're with, I think I've managed to isolate you from everything and everyone around you but me.'

'That's not true.' Elbows on her thighs, Kait stared at her with pleading eyes. 'I'm here because I want to be.'

'What you want is to be with Branch Sterling, Kait.' Janna's eyes were full of concern, but they never wavered. 'And I want you to know that I might not like it, might not like *him*, but I won't be the one to stand in your way of that. I don't ever want you to think you have to make a choice.'

A single, hot tear trailed down Kait's cheek and she wiped it away hastily. 'Oh my gosh, Janna,' she whispered. She didn't know what to think, what to say. The whole speech was so unexpected and so, well, un-Janna-like, Kait was reeling.

'I wanted to prevent you from making mistakes,' her older sister sniffed, 'But I think I prevented you from really living in the process, too. I'm sorry, Kit Kat.'

The sound of her childhood nickname on Janna's lips threw her into an all-out crying fest. She dove forward and wrapped her arms around her sister, stunning the two toddlers beside them into silence.

'What I have or haven't done in life isn't your fault,' Kait cried into her hair, refusing to let go. 'I don't regret a second of it, and you shouldn't, either. I've been right where I wanted to be, beside you, with these two rugrats.'

As if on cue, two sets of grubby hands pushed up against her side, and she pulled away to find both boys, arms spread wide, trying their darnedest to be involved in a four-way group hug.

'Come here, you two.' She scooped one boy up, while Janna hugged the other against her chest, crying openly now.

'You didn't make any mistakes, Janna.'

Through her tears, Janna's head turned, confused. 'Yeah, right.'

'It wasn't a mistake you made to love Dorion the way you did,' she continued. 'Loving someone isn't a mistake. Ever.'

'I'm going to have to say I disagree with you on that one, sister dearest.'

Kait knew she would, but it was her turn to stand on the podium and let her speech be known. 'Go ahead,' she said, pointing between them at the two small faces peering back at her. 'But look at these boys. No, you definitely didn't make a mistake. I think everything happens for a reason, and just because things didn't work out the way you wanted doesn't mean it was wrong, or a mistake.'

Janna tapped one boy on the nose, making him grin. 'You're not just talking about Dorion.'

Kait let out a long breath. 'Branch isn't the fly-by-night teenager you think you remember. He's not an eighteen-year-old with a skewed view of the world. He's different, now. Mature. And you should hear his ideas about the things he wants to do to fix up Duke and Addie's house. He wants to stay, Janna.' She hadn't said the words aloud yet, still trying to let them sink in. But now that they were out, it made the corners of her mouth turn upward. 'Branch wants to stay in Port Landon.'

'You really believe he will?' There she was, the skeptical Janna she knew and adored.

'I do,' she replied without hesitation. 'I believe him, and I love him. I don't think I ever stopped.'

Her sister stared at her long and hard. It could have been seconds or minutes that passed, it was hard to tell. 'Kait, a stranger off the street could've told you that.'

Oh. So much for it being a surprising revelation, then. 'He's different, Janna,' she assured her once more. 'I'm telling you, things are going to be different this time.'

'I hope so, because I don't want to have to track him down if he leaves you in the broken mess you were in last time.' Her eyes said she was pessimistic at best, but Janna's mouth had the faintest curl to it.

It was the closest thing to her blessing Kait was going to get. Still, it meant more to her than she could ever say.

Chapter 16

Branch

Branch had heard Grandma Addie say it time and time again, in a variety of different ways. *Time flies ... don't be in a hurry to grow up ... time goes by in the blink of an eye ...* He had always listened to her when she reminded him of it, but he'd never truly witnessed the truth of her anecdotes until now. Then again, maybe it wasn't so much a matter of experiencing it for the first time as it was actually paying attention to each day as it passed and feeling the clock tick by a little faster as the month drew to a close.

How in the world there were only twelve full days left in December, he had no idea. The fact that it meant there were only five days left until Christmas Eve was even more unthinkable. Five more days to pull off the dinner he hoped would do his grandmother's memory justice.

It was only five days, and he didn't feel prepared, but Branch was confident his efforts wouldn't be in vain. He had Kait by his side, after all. Nothing could go wrong when her hand was in his.

He hadn't seen her since the evening he'd wrapped his arms

154

around her in front of the partially decorated Christmas tree and softly advised her that he wanted a second chance. Everything else – the house, the vehicles, all the tangible things that surrounded him – were his if he wanted them, no questions asked. Kait Davenport's heart wasn't something so simply obtained, or kept.

But it was the only thing Branch wanted, needed, and was choosing not to live without.

Okay. It was only one word, tossed around in routine conversation like it meant nothing. But when Branch suggested he could stay here in Port Landon and make good on the promises he made all those years ago, Kait's response consisted of only that word.

In that context, it meant everything.

Her schedule at the diner and Branch's insistence that she didn't have to help him with absolutely every aspect of cleaning and sorting and purging that went on within the walls of 14 Crescent Street meant he hadn't laid eyes on her since then. But every time he caught sight of the artificial tree perched in the window, or the leftover cinnamon bear candies on the kitchen counter, or even the attic ladder that led to the spot where he had kissed her so tenderly a matter of days ago, Branch thought of her so clearly that he could have conjured her image up from thin air. She wasn't there, but she was still with him.

With mere days left before the big event, Kait insisted on being with him when he tackled the daunting task of shopping for all the groceries needed to pull the event off. Branch wasn't going to say no to any time with her, no matter how trivial that time might seem. If there was one thing he had learned in the last few years; no time spent together with the ones you loved was ever meaningless.

The parking lot was packed. He circled the entire lot twice before managing to secure a spot, one that was about as far from the entrance as he could get. He looked around at the people milling about, permanent smiles on their faces despite the hectic time of year, then realized how ridiculous he was being.

There he was, gawking around the packed parking lot at all the vehicles, and there were undoubtedly twenty similar Ford Focus cars there, maybe more. Every time he had seen Kait's car, it had been well into the evening. He knew the car was an older model, and a dark color. Hardly distinguishing features around these parts. Pulling his phone out of his jacket pocket, he pressed a few buttons, preparing to text her and let her know he was there.

'Boo!'

Branch turned just as Kait latched on to his coat sleeve, laughing.

'Scared you, right?'

'Petrified me,' he chuckled. 'Where are you parked? I was just about to text you.'

She pointed clear across to the other side of the lot. 'Between that monster truck wannabe and the black van. You can't see it from here.'

'Then how'd you see me?'

Kait made circles with her thumbs and fingers, staring up at him through her pretend eyeglasses. 'Eagle eyes.' She laughed again.

'Someone's in a good mood,' he teased, shoving his phone back in his pocket as they headed toward the front entrance. Kait hooked her arm through his, and suddenly he was in a pretty good mood himself.

'It's my day off, Branch. No diner, no kids, and no timeline. Just you, me, and a grocery store with frantic customers I don't have to serve food to. Sounds pretty great to me.'

It was his turn to laugh. He held the door open for her, and the scent of freshly baked bread wafted out into the frosty air. His rumbling stomach told him strolling past the bakery and remaining empty-handed might be a futile mission. 'If you would've let me pick you up, you wouldn't have even had to scrape the ice off your car. *Then* it would've been a perfect day off.'

Her mouth curled in amusement, but Kait's eyes narrowed. 'You know why I wanted to drive myself.'

'Does Janna even know where you are right now?'

'She does,' Kait replied, pulling a shopping cart from the row inside the door. 'That doesn't mean I want to flaunt you around in front of her, giving her a chance to corner you.'

He reached out and took the cart from her, purposely placing his hand over hers on the handle. 'You don't want to flaunt *us* around, you mean?' He knew what she meant, but couldn't help poking fun at her for her dramatic choice of words. 'So, that means you don't want me to hold your hand in public? Or you don't want me to put my arm around you as we stroll down the aisle of canned goods? Maybe you don't want me to kiss your cheek as we buy bread at the bakery counter—'

'Enough!' she hissed jovially, turning her hand palm up under his to squeeze it tightly before gently pulling away. 'My plight to get Janna to come around to the idea of having you here is going to be slow but steady, I'm afraid, but she will come around. We've just got to give her time, Branch.'

'Your plight?' He blew out a breath. 'Damn, that sounds serious. Good thing we've got nothing but time, Kaitie.' He nudged her playfully out of the way, pushing the cart toward the first aisle.

She fished the crumpled list from her purse. They had been working on it for days, adding things here and there as they thought of them. 'She'll get used to it,' Kait continued. 'She's already warming to the idea—'

'Kait.' He reached out and touched her arm, slowing her steps and making her head raise. 'You don't have to convince me that your family will eventually like me, okay? I know Janna, remember?

She'll either like me someday or she won't. I can't change how she feels about me. Just like I can't change how I feel about you.' He offered her what he hoped was an encouraging smile. 'It's you I want to be with. If I've got you, then we'll figure everything else out as we go along. Okay?'

'Okay,' she replied.

There was that word again. So simple, yet filled with more meaning than four letters should be able to contain. A long breath signaled her relief, but Branch saw the war that battled behind her eyes. She was always so worried about everyone but herself. Surely she had to know he would never come between her and her sister? He also needed to get through to her that her sister's opinions, however harsh, held no weight in his decision to stay. He had made up his mind.

But it was Kait's day off, a day to rest and relax. Albeit, they had a list of things to buy the length of his arm, but that didn't mean he needed to use this time to talk about heavy, life-changing topics. They had time for the open declarations and logistics later. Right now …

'Let's start checking things off that list.'

What she needed was something to occupy her mind from the ever-whirling thoughts he could practically see tumbling around inside her head. Kait was a planner, always had been. Crossing things off lists was as good a place to start as any when it came to distraction.

Her curt nod announced she was just as ready to get down to business. Holding up the list, she addressed him with a renewed determination in her eyes. 'I've rewritten our list in order of where it is in the store, meaning we shouldn't have to run back and forth, up and down the aisles, and we have less chance of forgetting something.'

'Why am I not surprised?' He headed straight for the bakery counter, drawn to the decadent scent of warm bread like a moth to a flame.

Kait followed a step behind, consulting the strip of paper in her hand like it held the answers to the meaning of life. 'So, from the bakery section we need sweet rolls and—'

'No, we don't,' he interjected.

Kait glared at him, holding out the list once again as proof. 'Yes, we do,' she argued. 'I doubt Paige has time at The Cakery to make them; she's busy as all get out this time of year. And I know we're technically supposed to be using Grandma Addie's recipes and making them ourselves, but unless you've become a gourmet chef since I last saw you, I don't think either of us has the skills or the time to pull all this off, Branch. I'm sorry.'

'Don't be. I meant to tell you, there's been sweet rolls and a whole slew of other baked goods in the freezer downstairs since yesterday morning.'

'You baked sweet rolls?'

She looked so downright shocked that Branch wished he could have told her it was his doing, just so he could bask in the pride of knowing he had surprised her. 'Nah,' he chuckled. 'I guess Jay told his mom about our Christmas Eve plans. Once she caught wind of that, he says she rallied her friends up and they did as much baking as they could. She wanted to help us out, and she did her best to make some of the items that Grandma Addie used to make, doing it all from memory.'

Stunned, Kait gaped at him. 'That's incredible.'

'That's what I said when Jay backed his truck into the driveway yesterday and hauled it all into the freezer.'

If she was surprised by the gesture now, he wished she could have seen his reaction then. Branch had been floored. He still was. Port Landon had struck again, an outpouring of affection from the residents within it, looking out for their own. It was just the Port Landon way.

'So, we have enough baking, if we include the cookies and tarts The Port is donating, plus the gumdrop cakes I made.' In true Kait Davenport fashion, she plucked a ballpoint pen out of the deepest depths of her purse and stroked off a bunch of items on the list.

Branch's expression mirrored the one she had worn only moments ago. 'You made gumdrop cake? I haven't had that stuff in years.'

Grandma Addie's specialty had always been fruitcake, a sweet and potent mix of candied fruit and nuts smothered in a rich brown sugar sauce, and Branch had always eaten more than his fair share of it every year, much to his grandmother's amusement. But gumdrop cake ... now that was Kait's specialty. Growing up, she hadn't been an avid baker, but there was a year in the beginning of their teenage relationship when she had wanted to do something special for Christmas. Wanted something to call her own tradition. Hours of scouring the old, dusty cookbooks in her parents' kitchen unveiled an old handwritten recipe card tucked in the inside cover of a vintage cookbook. It was assumed the recipe was her grandmother's, since neither of them could ever recall Kait's mom baking anything from scratch, but that, to his knowledge, had never been confirmed. What was confirmed was how delicious that gumdrop cake recipe turned out to be.

'It might be the only thing I know how to make,' she snickered, 'but I make it well. So, yeah, I've got four loaves of it in the freezer at my place.'

'So, yeah, that's three for me and one for Christmas Eve, right?'

'In your dreams, Sterling.' She motioned in the opposite direction of the bakery section. 'That might be a few things off the list, but there's still a gazillion others. Better get pushing that cart.'

And push the cart, he did. As Kait scratched one item after another off their list, he continued to pull cans and jars and boxes from the shelves as she rhymed them off. They fell into an easy routine, an effective one that seemed comfortable despite the hustling and bustling of people around them. Sporadically, folks greeted Kait as they passed by, and there were even a few surprised hellos and shocked expressions directed at him. Branch wasn't sure whether their surprise was from his presence in town, or his presence with Kait. People were polite, though, and he was thankful for it. He was growing tired of being fearful someone was going to bring up the past and ruin their fun outing.

'Looks like you know pretty much everyone,' he teased after an elderly man and his wife patted Kait's arm on their way by and bid her a good day.

She gave him an *Oh please!* expression as she pointed at the different kinds of cheeses for him to grab from the cooler shelf. 'All these people know you, too. They just don't recognize you, or they aren't paying much attention, not expecting to see you here.'

'Here,' he repeated, grabbing wedges of Havarti, Monterey Jack, and old cheddar, planning to cut them up and fan them out on a serving tray with an assortment of pickles, the same way Grandma Addie used to. Presentation was everything. 'With you, you mean.'

'I didn't mean …' She trailed off, resigned to the truth, just as he was. 'Well, maybe that, too.'

Branch let the conversation dwindle, but his mind was alive with cluttered thoughts. About his hometown. About living here. About Kait. She had seemed so sure of him as they stood in front of the Christmas tree a few nights ago, showing no hesitation on her part about his decision to stay. It was true, he hadn't asked her if she wanted him to stay, and he wasn't sure if he had outright said the words that he was, in fact, not leaving on the thirty-first, but he thought she understood him. Assumed she did.

Okay. They had both said it, sealing their pact to move on, hand in hand.

At least, he thought that's what happened. Now, as he let the memory tumble over and over in his mind, Branch was starting to believe things weren't left as clear cut as he had thought they were.

161

The shopping cart was heaped high by the time they reached the cereal aisle, but only one other person was there so he turned into it. 'Let's go down this one, first.'

Kait checked her trusty list. 'I don't think we need anything—'

'A man's got to eat,' he advised. 'Even if it is Lucky Charms.'

'Kids' food,' she laughed, following closely behind.

'Don't knock how good a bowl of marshmallows and sugar-laden three-leaf clovers can be.' He feigned a serious glance in her direction. 'It's grownup food, through and through.'

'Whatever you say.' She held up her hands in mock surrender, stepping back.

The other customer in the aisle wheeled his cart around the corner, and Branch used the moment to reach for her, pulling gently on her puffy jacket, now partway unzipped, to close the gap between them.

'What are you doing?' she chuckled, but her eyes betrayed her, darting from one end of the aisle to the other.

'Making myself loud and clear.' He ran his thumb across her cheek, overcome by a wave of satisfaction when Kait took in a sharp breath, her eyelashes fluttering with his touch. 'I want to be with you, Kaitie.'

'I know.' A featherlight whisper from her lips, an answer Branch felt as well as heard.

'I want to be sure that's what you want, too, though.' He held her there, cupping her face in his hands, afraid to look away and miss something, anything that might indicate how she was truly feeling right now.

'It is,' she said on a sigh. 'More than you know.'

'I might know more on that topic than you think.' One corner of his mouth lifted, elation buzzing in his veins. She wanted him, just as much as he wanted her. There was nothing more important to him than that. 'So, we're on the same page, then. That's half the battle. I can't stand here and tell you I know exactly how we're going to pull this off, seeing as I still have a job that keeps me away for weeks at a time—'

'I'm not asking you to quit your job for me.' She had recovered somewhat, her gaze steadier. 'We just have a lot to work out.'

'And we will work it out, I promise.' He vowed to do whatever it took to make this work, and making that vow was his first step. 'I know no one in this town ever expected me to come back here, Kait. I know what they think of me—'

'You're wrong about what people think of you,' she interjected. 'People here still love you. Just look at what Jay's mom and her loyal baking troops did, which only proves my point. You're still a part of this community.' Her gaze stayed fixed on him. 'I think you're harder on yourself about what happened than anyone else in Port Landon ever was, Branch. Save for me and my family.' She swallowed, hard. 'And Zach.'

'Rightfully so,' he replied. 'What I did turned this little town upside down.'

'No, it turned *you* upside down,' she corrected. 'It tormented you, made you think everything and everyone was against you because of it, even when that wasn't true. Around here, some folks like to talk, that's true. But a lot more prefer to help their neighbors. Folks care about each other here, and they protect each other. Maybe you were just too young back then to realize that the whole community was like an extended family, not just the people in your grandparents' house. After the accident, your wellbeing mattered to everyone, too, Branch, not just Zach's.'

'The only people who mattered were either disappointed in me or disgusted by me, Kait.' The second the statement was out, he regretted it.

She didn't hesitate. 'I wasn't fair to you, in a lot of ways. But you weren't fair to me, either.' Her eyes blazed, so much tumultuous emotion in them that he wasn't sure if she was about to pull away from him or break down and cry. 'I can't change the past.'

He needed to veer the conversation onto steadier ground. Make himself crystal clear. 'That makes two of us,' he replied quickly. Confusion niggled at him, about part of what she said, but he needed to pick his battles. The past was the battle he hoped to end with this conversation. If it had to be done in the middle of the cereal aisle, so be it. 'Just like we can't change what Janna thinks, or what anyone else thinks, for that matter. But we can change how we go forward, and I want to go forward with you.' He took a deep breath, then let it out. 'Ignore everything and everyone else, Kaitie. We can hide if you want, but let me love you, the way I always have. The way you deserve. Please.'

He didn't think he could get any clearer than that. He loved her, and he didn't deny it. He wouldn't. Anyone, even in an overcrowded grocery store, could see that she was the only one there in his eyes.

Let me love you, he chanted silently, watching her gaze search his expression for something he couldn't define. *Because I already do, and I don't know how I'd ever stop.*

'Okay.'

Her voice was so quiet, and her mouth barely moved, so he wasn't sure he had heard her correctly. 'Okay?'

A faint grin appeared. 'Okay,' she said again. 'It's crazy and it's unexpected and surreal, but I'm all in, Branch.'

He felt even more alive than he had the other night in front of the Christmas tree. This time, there was no room for misinterpretation. They were doing this. Really doing this.

He reached out and grabbed a box of Lucky Charms from the shelf. 'Hide with me for a second.'

'What?'

He didn't elaborate. Instead, Branch held the cereal box up in front of them, preventing any prying eyes from witnessing their tryst, then he kissed her, soft and warm and full of promise.

Kait chuckled against his lips, her eyes fluttering back open. 'Well, aren't you two lovebirds a sight for sore eyes?'

Instantly, the floating feeling and euphoria was shattered. Branch jerked the cereal box down, his expression a mirror image of Kait's horrified one.

'Zach.' She sounded breathless, and Branch suspected it wasn't merely from the effects of their kiss.

The man held up his hands, a shrewd and wicked grin marring his features. 'Don't stop on my account,' he quipped. 'I'm just passing through.'

'Zach, I—'

'Kait, you look traumatized,' her friend snickered. 'It's fine, really. It was inevitable, really, wasn't it? You two have always been each other's kryptonite.'

Branch waited for some condescending remark that she was Zach's kryptonite as well, if the past was any indication, but only a white-hot glare followed.

He couldn't stand to see Kait looking so uncomfortable, like she had done something wrong. Like *they* were wrong. 'Look, Zach, I know you—'

'Wrong again, Sterling,' Zach shot back, a malicious laugh mixed in with his words. 'You don't know me, and you don't know what you've put me through. What you've put her through.' His hand flailed out of his pocket to point an incriminating finger toward Kait. 'There's only one good thing about this that I can see.'

Neither Branch nor Kait had the will to question him further. Instead, they stood there, still as stone, waiting.

Their silence only heightened Zach's amusement. He continued down the aisle, passing by them as he left. On his way, he leaned in toward Kait, whispering just loud enough for Branch to hear. 'This won't last,' he said. 'Because, Kait, history repeats itself. Remember that.'

Chapter 17

Kait

Kait was unnerved to be caught red-handed by Zach in the middle of a playful kiss with Branch. And yet, to be there, in the middle of such a mundane place as a grocery store, amidst the folks she had known her entire life, feeling so lighthearted and joyful in the company of the man she'd never stopped loving, was a heady mix of petrifying and exhilarating at the same time. It was as though she felt every emotion simultaneously, and yet she didn't have a clue how to feel about Zach's inopportune timing.

She did know how she felt about Branch, though, and that was what mattered. Because she now, without a doubt, knew how he felt, too. There was a smidgen of guilt that coated the edges of her happiness, only because she had made him feel like he had to reassure her of his stance in the first place. Maybe she shouldn't have mentioned Janna, and perhaps she had been wrong to make it sound like she wanted to hide from the watchful eyes of Port Landon, but if they were going to do this, take a chance and be together, Kait needed a safe place to confide her worries and her thoughts. Not only because they were plentiful on any given day, but because she would go mad if she didn't get them off her chest.

She had always considered Branch her safe place. Judging by the easy way he calmed her fears, he still was. And if he didn't care what others thought, if he was willing to steel himself and take on whatever came next, she needed to find strength in that, because she knew all too well that she had never been the one to let others' opinions roll off her back.

As conflicted as she was about where she stood with Zach after his impromptu appearance, Kait left the grocery store with a renewed sense of self. Branch had brought up the past, the fact that those who had mattered to him at the time of the accident had harbored disdain for him after it, and she had taken the opportunity to stand up for herself. She knew he was referring to her, and as much as it hurt to hear it, he was right. She had been completely and utterly wrecked by that night. In the immediate aftermath, so hurt and so broken by what he'd done, she couldn't even look him in the eye.

Eleven years later, she wouldn't apologize for that. It was how she had felt then. And she took ownership of her actions. So, no, she wouldn't say sorry for hating what he had done to her. To her friend.

But she would forgive him. Time played a strong factor in alleviating her heartache, there was no doubt. But she was different now, and so was he. She believed that with all of her being.

That's why Zach's parting words haunted her. *History repeats itself. Remember that.*

Couldn't he see that all she did was remember? The wounds on her heart had long since closed over, but scars remained, mostly because of the memories she had never been capable of letting fade into the recesses of her mind. She remembered it all. Getting the phone call, the flashing red and white ambulance lights. The images still seared into her brain.

She remembered. That was why Kait was so determined to prove him wrong. The history in question was part of their past, and she was going to do everything in her power to let it stay there.

Port Landon's gossip veins were wide open and flowing. It had been a simple trip to the grocery store to get the food items needed for Christmas Eve, an attempt to avoid last-minute shopping in case there was something they couldn't find right away and needed to search out elsewhere. The responsible, mature thing to do, planning ahead and being prepared.

In the eyes of their small town, however, they may as well have snuck out to the old water tower and spray-painted *Branch loves Kait* in neon colors. Folks had seen them together, and that was enough to deduce that they had fallen right back into each other's arms, still the same crazy kids they had been a decade earlier.

Okay, so it wasn't a far stretch from the truth in some ways, but they didn't know that. The moment Kait arrived at the diner the following morning, though, she quickly realized that the town's coffee-drinking crowd did know something. The way they watched her as she refilled their coffee mugs, all eyes on her and glittering with smugness, smiles dancing on their lips as they grew silent with her approach.

They knew. She knew they knew. The hushed whispers and nudges as the day wore on only confirmed it. So did her coworker Eve's blatant questioning.

'So, you went and got yourself a man, did you?'

At twenty-five, Eve Sawyer was almost five years younger than Kait, but she harbored the luxury of having moved to Port Landon only two years ago from a small farming community in Wisconsin Kait had never heard of. That meant people around here only knew what Eve wanted them to know about her. To her credit, she had managed to keep her private life, well, private. Kait, knowing too well what kind of detrimental effects small-town gossip could have, had never tried to pry much information from the black-haired girl. She knew three things for sure; Eve had a love of red lipstick, regardless of how it clashed with the lavender hue of their uniforms, she had once mentioned that Port Landon was a bustling metropolis in comparison to the tiny town she was raised in, and she was nice. Genuinely nice. To everyone, regardless of whether she knew them or what she heard about them. Kait admired her for that.

Obviously, she was blunt, too.

'That's the buzz around town, is it?' Kait was a little impressed by her coworker's frankness, especially seeing as no one else had had the guts yet to mention so much as Branch's name to her face. But that didn't mean she was going to tell the whole sordid story to Eve, either. She kept her head down, calculating the tab for one of her tables.

Out of the corner of her eye, Eve waved a hand. 'Something about a sighting at the grocery store, your arms linked with his, lost in his take-me-away eyes – okay, I made that last part up, but honestly, who are you, J.Lo? People are talking about you like they're about to sell your picture to the paparazzi.'

Kait almost choked on a laugh. Turning, she faced the younger woman, hoping her skepticism was evident. 'Surely it can't be that bad. I went to the grocery store with an old friend.'

'With an old boyfriend.'

'Fine, an old boyfriend.' She tossed the pen down. 'It's not as scandalous as people are making it out to be.'

'No?' One of Eve's perfectly manicured eyebrows arched high. 'So, this doesn't have something to do with Mr Heart Eyes that comes in here every day to make sure you're still here, single, and ready to mingle?'

'What?' Her skepticism transformed into full-fledged bewilderment. 'Mr Heart Eyes? Are you talking about Zach?'

Eve rolled her eyes. 'Who else? He's in here every day, without fail. I know, I know, you're friends. But if that guy had a chance, he'd snatch you up, take you home, and love you forever like a cute stray puppy.'

169

'That's kind of a creepy analogy.'

'But accurate.' She pointed a finger at her, the red varnish on her nail glinting in the fluorescent lighting. 'You didn't answer the question.'

'What question?' It was getting hard to keep up with the conversation, and Kait had work to do. Tables to tend to. Topics to avoid.

'Does the paparazzi sighting have anything to do with him?'

'No,' she snapped. 'Well, yes, we saw him at the store, but, no, it's not Zach everybody's rambling on about. I was there with Branch.'

'Branch,' Eve mimicked, testing out the name on her tongue. 'That's the high school boyfriend you had, right?' She snapped her fingers, putting it all together. 'Ah, he was the guy here last week, huh? Tall, ruggedly handsome. Wow, I thought he hit your friend with a truck or something? Cheated on you with some bimbo?'

Kait stared at her coworker, mouth open. All she could do was thank the heavens above that the woman had the decency to keep her voice down. 'How in the world do you know all that?'

Eve shrugged. 'Janna and I talk.'

'About my poor choices in life?' She always wondered what Janna was like with other employees at The Port. She had no friends, per se, at least no one she hung out with or visited. After Dorion left, Janna had been content to socially distance herself from everyone, and that hadn't changed in the first two years of the twins' life. She withdrew from everything and everyone after her heartbreaking ordeal, and though she had always been warier of people than Kait was, she had gone from wary to outright distrusting. Of everyone, anyone. At least that's what Kait had thought. It turned out she'd been confiding in Eve, talking about things Kait never expected, so who knew how deep those conversations got.

Another shrug. 'About a lot of things,' Eve replied.

170

Okay, Eve knew more than she ever expected. A lot more. That didn't mean she had to stand here and fill in any of the details Janna might have kept to herself. 'As interesting and cryptic as that sounds, I've got some customers to look after. The long and short of it is that I was at the grocery store with Branch buying food, can you imagine?' She feigned sarcastic shock, pressing her hand to her chest as she gasped. 'We saw half the town there, as you can already surmise, including Zach. It's not the outrageous story everyone's making it out to be.'

'Maybe not yet, but I've got a sinking suspicion that might change right about … now.' Eve smirked, her gaze flitting past Kait's shoulder toward the door. The bell clanged loudly, and Kait whirled around to see what she was talking about.

Or rather, who.

Zach entered the diner, pushing his sunglasses up on top of his head. A groan emitted from her throat, causing a wave of guilt to wash through her. He was her friend, her good friend, the one who had stuck by her. She should be ashamed of herself for being less than enthused to see him, knowing he would eventually make his way here, as he always did, because he cared about her, as he always had.

'Hey,' she greeted him, accompanied by a small wave. 'Let me just get these bills delivered to my tables, then I should be able to chat for a few minutes.' It was the most nonchalant version of *We need to talk* she could come up with. Kait didn't give him a chance to protest, grabbing a couple of check holders in one hand, the calculated bills in the other, and rushing hastily toward the tables she was serving, thankful they were in the opposite direction of Zach and her coworker.

She needed to compose herself. He was the only one who had witnessed their kiss – the first and only real public display of affection they had allowed the world – and now it was making Kait feel like she had somehow betrayed Zach by doing it. Rationally, she knew it wasn't the case, and she knew loving

171

Branch the way she did wasn't wrong. It couldn't be. If it was, then she would never understand how love was such an unjust and cruel emotion, and how it was so unfair to be able to feel it in the first place.

She needed to make Zach understand. They were friends, had been as long as she could remember. She knew what he'd been through, and lived through the tragedy alongside him. Her pain might not have been physical, then, as his was, but she had endured pain like she'd never experienced before. And she prayed she never would again.

But something deep inside her was breaking ground in the parched foundation of her resolve, bringing Kait a sense of renewal and regrowth. Love had bloomed once again for her, something she thought she would never have again, and for that reason alone – the sheer need inside her to feel that much at all – she was desperate to grasp the second chance she had been given and hold on to it with all her might.

She needed to be the one to make Zach understand. He didn't need to like Branch, and she doubted he would ever give his blessing, but Kait needed to talk to him, face to face, and be honest with him. She owed her friend that much.

She slipped the bills into the vinyl folders and dropped them off at their respective tables, asking if they wanted top-ups on their drinks or needed anything more. Satisfied that her customers were taken care of, Kait made her way back to the front counter, where Zach had already taken up residence at his usual stool, hunched forward on his elbows. When he turned, however, his expression was anything but the easygoing one he usually wore during his trips into The Port to see her.

'Are you all right?' She already knew the answer but she asked anyway, curious what Zach would openly divulge. He was troubled by something, that was obvious, but she wasn't sure he would offer up the whole story here, with prying eyes and perked-up ears sitting only a few tables away.

'Never better,' he muttered. 'Are you?'

She found his question odd despite the lack of emotion in his voice. 'Of course,' she replied carefully. She caught herself before she followed it up with *Why wouldn't I be?* If Zach was hurt by what he'd witnessed yesterday at the grocery store, Kait wanted to tread lightly, fearful of sounding defensive toward him. 'I think we need to talk, Zach.'

'I think you're right,' he replied, accepting the cup of coffee she poured him with a grateful nod.

'About Branch.'

He scoffed. 'Right again.'

She knew what he was going to say. She shouldn't be with Branch. She shouldn't be doing this to herself. To him. She and Zach were supposed to be friends, and friends didn't rekindle romances with men who had caused other friends so much pain and heartache. He was going to ask her if she had really, truly forgotten everything they had been through, or if she was just so starved for attention and enamored by the man that she would let the past fade into the background like it never happened at all.

These were all things she had lain in bed at night thinking about, swirling around in her mind and keeping her awake. Somehow, Kait had managed to move past all the negativity and find a sense of peace in the second chance she had found. Now, all she had to do was help Zach find a little peace, too.

'We've been through so much together, you and I,' she began, tucking her notepad and pen into the front pocket of her apron. 'The last thing I want is for you to be angry with me.'

She stood across from him, her hands on the counter as she idly fidgeted with her fingers, giving him her full attention. Zach took the opportunity to reach for her hand, his gaze downcast.

'I'm not angry with you. I don't even think that's possible.' He looked up, the brief glimpse of a sad smile on his lips.

She returned that smile, hoping hers was more encouraging.

'That makes me feel a little bit better, I think, but there's still something bothering you. And we've got to talk about it in order to work through it.'

He shook his head. 'You don't understand,' he insisted. 'I'm not angry with you, Kait. I'm sad, and I'm hurting. Not angry.'

A sigh fell from her lips. 'But, Zach, I don't want you to be any of those things. I know there's so much history between all of us that it makes it hard to see anything beyond that, but I really want there to be a chance we can all move on. I'm not saying you and Branch need to be best buddies, and I'm not saying that we can all just forget all the painful things that happened. But I think we need to at least forgive each other.'

'You want me to forgive him for what happened that night.' It wasn't a question, and she was grateful he had the decency to refer to that night in a roundabout way. Zach knew how each mention of his injuries sliced through her like a hot knife.

'I wish that could happen someday,' she admitted, though she thought it was unlikely to occur. 'But I would settle for you forgiving me.'

His head snapped back as though she had slapped him. 'Forgive you? For what?'

She swallowed, her hand turning in his to give it a sincere squeeze. 'For not being who you need me to be.' It was something she should have said a long time ago. Sure, she had apologized profusely after the accident, and she'd said how sorry she was when they had tried to be more than friends and failed, but Kait wasn't certain she had ever bluntly stated how she had failed him through both of those debacles. 'Years ago, we tried to push the boundaries of our friendship into something more than it was, and as much as I wanted to be that for you, I couldn't. I know how much it hurt you, and I wish things could be different in many ways, but they can't.'

She wasn't sure if she was making things better or worse with her convoluted explanation, but when she took a pause for breath and Zach didn't interrupt, Kait forged on. 'Which is why I'm hoping you'll forgive me now, because the truth is, I don't think we can control who we love. I know how you feel about Branch, but I know how I feel about him, too. I can't stop it, despite the events that happened all those years ago. I know what he did, and I still love him. I don't know what that says about me, but I do know I never expected to be standing here with a second chance to make things work with him. So, I need you to forgive me, because I still love him, and because I'm ready to take that chance with him.'

Zach's hand didn't jerk away from hers as Kait feared, and he didn't push away from the counter or storm out of the diner. Her confession hung between them like a thick veil, and she let him have the moment of silence that followed to choose his reply. She owed him that much.

A long breath sounded as he stared down at their linked hands. 'You're right, Kait, we can't control who we love.'

Her weary nod matched his defeated expression. 'I know,' she whispered softly.

'I know my feelings for you are unrequited, and I'll never blame you for that. The only thing I wish is that you loved someone who loved you the same way you love them. Someone who deserves it. Deserves you.'

Even after everything she had put him through, he was still only worried about her own wellbeing. He really was a good friend to her. 'I appreciate that more than you'll ever know, but I do believe Branch loves me, Zach. As hard as that is for you to hear, I know he does.'

'I wish that were true.'

His pessimism raised her hackles, but she fought to push down the annoyance rearing up inside her. 'Zach—'

'Kait, I'm trying to tell you something,' he interjected. 'I don't know what he's been telling you—'

'Zach!' She hissed out his name, desperate to keep her voice down but just as adamant about getting through to him. 'Come on, I'm begging you to stop questioning his motives. Every time you do, you question me, too. You realize that, right? What is so wrong about Branch deciding to stay here in Port Landon to try and get his life back? *Our* life back?'

Chagrined, Zach pulled his hand away from hers and slipped it inside his half-zipped jacket. 'That's what I'm trying to tell you,' he replied, tossing a stack of papers in front of her, held together with a silver paperclip. 'He's not staying.'

'Excuse me?' She felt as though her stomach had plummeted. 'Of course he is.'

'Then where's he living?' He turned the papers around in her direction so she could see the typed font for herself. 'I've met with him twice already. This is the purchase agreement he had me put together. His grandparents' house is being sold to me in order to ensure a quick sale. I'll resell it for a profit.'

Kait gawked at the contract in front of her, not bothering to flip through the pages. The top page showed Branch's full name in bold letters, along with the address and lot number of the house on Crescent Street.

'This isn't happening,' she whispered.

'I'm sorry, Kait,' Zach replied, 'But it is.'

There was no way to pretend that the truth wasn't there in front of her this time, spelled out in black and white letters.

Branch had lied to her again.

A hollow ache crept into her bones as the realization washed over her. More lies from him. More gullibility from her.

He was selling his grandparents' home, the one he had sworn only the day before was going to be his, so they could be together. Kait swallowed down her tears. She hoped the profit was worth it. Because while he might have gained money from his decision, he had ultimately lost her heart.

Chapter 18

Branch

If the arrival of the hectic Christmas season could be depicted in an image, then the state of Grandma Addie's kitchen was a good place for an accurate representation. It wasn't just the abundance of décor that surrounded him or the Christmas tree in the bay window, but the wrapping-paper tubes leaning against the staircase, the mix of boxes, jars, and cans of food littering the countertops, the freezer full to capacity with donations from Jason's mother and her friends, and the array of small, colorful, handmade toys he purchased on a whim from a charity who had set up a vendor table inside the doorway of the grocery store. He had no doubt that some folks would bring their children to the house on Christmas Eve. At least there would be something for them to enjoy beyond the food.

Branch hadn't really taken in how much the house's main floor had changed since he began to clean and sort and organize almost three weeks ago. Not until he'd had to clutter up his progress with all the things needed to pull off the holiday dinner. Gone were the cobwebs that had strung from the corners of each room and window ledge. The thick coating of dust that had given everything a hazy quality had disappeared, revealing the intricate moldings of the doorway trim and the surprisingly shiny gleam of the natural hardwood floors despite the scuffs and nicks that no amount of elbow grease would ever take away. *They give it character*, his grandmother would have said.

Grandpa Duke and Grandma Addie's house was huge, old, and showing signs of wear, but the attention he had shown it had served the place well. It looked good, and Branch felt good for it.

He could only imagine what it was capable of looking like once he put a few months of effort into it, or years, instead of mere weeks. A swell of pride rose in him, knowing he was more than capable of restoring this house to its former glory.

He hoped his grandparents would have been just as proud.

The more Branch thought about it, the more confident he was that he was making the right decision. He might have had himself convinced that his hometown as a collective whole, had turned against him, but it took Kait saying it bluntly for Branch to consider that it was more likely he was the one who had turned against himself.

It tormented you, made you think everything and everyone was against you, even when that wasn't true.

She was right. It was hard to see anyone else in a comforting or optimistic light when all he could see through his own eyes was his own terrible, unforgivable mistake.

The accident could have been so, so much worse; he knew that. Thankfully, though, it hadn't been. Zach didn't like him, and Branch didn't begrudge him that, but the man had healed and recuperated. He was also extremely successful if his newspaper ads and number of real estate signs were any indication. Zach Canton had done well for himself, and Branch was glad for it.

He didn't need him to forgive him for what happened that night, Branch just needed to forgive himself.

More of Kait's spoken words were sinking into his brain as well.

I wasn't fair to you, but you weren't fair to me, either.

What did she mean by that? Because he left? Because he had gone to the party without her in the first place? The accident itself involved only him and Zach, so he didn't see how he had been unfair unless she was referring to his departure following it. It was an odd choice of words.

But once again, she was right. They couldn't change the past, only move forward from it and learn from their mistakes. Branch's plans included doing exactly that.

He did the best he could to straighten things up and make the house as tidy as possible under the circumstances. The main floor was where the Christmas Eve festivities would take place, and there was nothing more he could do in those rooms right now. He was as ready as he would ever be.

The spare bedroom down the hall hadn't been touched yet, however. He intended to close the door to all the rooms save for the kitchen, dining room, living room, and bathroom, as well as turn on the heat in the attached garage, now empty and devoid of anything that made it look like a storage area, and set up extra tables and chairs in there for the Port Landoners to stretch out and be comfortable during their dinner. It looked like the spare bedroom was where he was spending his evening. He could sort through the dresser and closet tonight and be completely done with the organization of every room on this floor. It would feel good.

At least, he thought it would. Branch needed to remind himself that everything didn't need to be done by the end of the month anymore, let alone today.

He wasn't leaving. Well, he was, because he had to go back to work in January, but he wasn't leaving for good. Two weeks of work, then he would be back. It wasn't an ideal situation, but it would all work out.

He had no more reasons to run from this place, and every reason to stay.

Branch rummaged through the conglomerate of cans, jars, and boxes on the counter to find the bag of remaining cinnamon bears, snatching it up and taking it with him as he trudged toward the hallway.

Most of the lights were off in the house, only the one over the kitchen sink and a lamp in the living room casting a soft yellow glow to illuminate his path. Nine o'clock at night and he already had the house shut down for the evening. If this was a sign of what his impending thirtieth birthday brought with it, Branch wasn't sure how he felt about his prospects for a social life.

The dimness and surrounding quiet made the knock on the front door sound louder than it truly was, as though each bang reverberated off the walls and shook the foundation beneath his feet.

Maybe he was getting dramatic in his old age, too.

Branch opened the door, and suddenly the only foundation that was shook was the one on which his contentment was built, and the only drama he felt deep in his bones was in the stare that was fixed on him, unblinking and searing with the uncontrollable blaze of an inferno.

'Kaitie?' He hadn't been expecting her to stop by, knowing she had to work and then had to watch the boys for a few hours for Janna. 'What are—'

'How many times have you seen Zach?' Each word was ammunition, blasting from her mouth in a quick, sharp sequence.

'Zach?' Put on the spot, he struggled to catch up. 'At the grocery story, I guess, and—'

'Here?' she finished for him. 'How many times did you see him here, Branch?'

Confusion reigned. All he could comprehend was Kait's blatant fury and that something was happening. Something he didn't understand. 'Twice, I think. Kait, what's—'

'You think?' A scoff escaped her lips. 'Don't you know?'

'Fine, okay, he was here twice.' It hadn't occurred to him that perhaps he should have told her about Zach's unexpected appearances, but it hadn't seemed important. Until now. Now, it was obviously very important. He just couldn't figure out why. 'What's this about?'

'I want a yes or a no, Branch. Did you meet with Zach twice without telling me?' She didn't blink, didn't move.

Didn't he just answer that? He opened his mouth to argue, but feared he might only make things worse. 'Yes,' he said simply, despite having about a hundred *buts* he wanted to add to the end of the sentence.

Her throat moved, but Kait stayed where she was, a pillar of unnerving seriousness. 'Did you and him talk about selling this house?' She held up a warning finger. 'Yes or no.'

'Yes,' he replied. 'Technically. But I wasn't—' *Keeping it from you. Thinking about going through with it*. More explanations he didn't give her, because she wasn't capable of hearing him clearly, too infuriated by a situation he couldn't piece together.

'Don't talk to me about what you weren't,' Kait snapped. 'I *know* what you weren't. You weren't going to tell me everything. You weren't going to follow through on all your promises. And you weren't the man I thought you were.' She shook her head. 'You still aren't.'

She might as well have punched him in the stomach. 'Kaitie …'

'Don't.' She held up a hand, blinking fast to keep the tears glistening on the edge of her eyelids at bay. 'Don't do that. Don't stand here and call me that, not while I was so close to making the same mistakes again. My gosh, Zach was right. History repeats itself.'

'No.' He muttered a curse word under his breath. 'Kait, that's not what this is. I wasn't purposely keeping anything from you, I just didn't think it was worth mentioning.'

Whatever she thought the right answer was, it wasn't that. 'Worth mentioning? Branch, we're supposed to be in this

181

together!' She raked her hands over her ponytail. 'And here you are, saying one thing and doing another. Sounds oddly familiar.'

'Kait, you're not listening to me.'

'You're right,' she agreed. 'I'm not. And I won't, not anymore.' She was still in the doorway, the front door swung wide and letting the frigid December air permeate the house's cozy interior. The cold air was nothing in comparison to the icy stare she pinned him with. 'I believed you,' she choked out. 'I believed *in* you.' The emotion she was trying so hard to hold in was flooding out of her in the form of tears, splashing onto her cheeks. A thickness in her throat gave her voice a strangled quality. 'But I've been here before, and I should have known better. Go home, Branch. Wherever you came from, wherever you've been these past eleven years, go back there.'

'Kait, no ...' He reached out for her, desperate to comprehend what was happening. She flinched and stepped away, holding her hands up to prevent him from getting any closer.

'Leave me alone, Branch.'

Distraught, he begged her to listen to him. 'Kait, just let me explain—'

'No, I'm done listening to your words.' She hugged her arms around her middle, her breath puffing out in hazy short bursts where the warm air collided with the cold. 'Because that's all they are ... words. Empty ones.' She paused, giving him another stricken glare. 'I think that's the only thing I don't understand, why you ever made promises to me in the first place.' Another step back, another step away from him. 'You and I both know you were bound to break them.'

He stood in the doorway and watched her go back to her car, still running and waiting for her in the driveway. He could have screamed her name, pleaded with her to wait, but Branch was so gutted by her parting words he didn't know what he would have said if she turned around.

Leave me alone, Branch. Go home.

He didn't know how he was supposed to do that when the woman he called home had just climbed into her car and driven away, the glowing tail-lights taunting him as she disappeared out of sight.

Chapter 19

Kait

History repeats itself.

In Kait's eyes, that's exactly what this was – a repeat of her past, of their past. Zach had warned her, Janna had warned her, and yet here she was, finding out Branch kept the truth from her and made her believe in things that would never transpire.

Why? That was what she wanted to know more than anything. If he wanted to sell his grandparents' place and leave Port Landon, if that was his original plan, why play with her emotions the way he did? Why be so cruel, making her walk through those rooms and trudge through that attic thinking he was going to turn that old house into a home? Thinking Branch wanted to build a life with her?

In hindsight, she knew he had been trying to give her those answers. Kait despised the way he brought out the irrational part of her, the way her emotions rose up and cut off her ability to be the level-headed woman she was. She felt so much, and hurt so deeply. Faced with his lies, her ability to handle normal, reasonable conversation was robbed by her own subconscious desperation to protect herself from him and his betrayal. Without realizing it in the moment, she regressed into the teenage version of herself, willing to sacrifice the truth for the sake of having to hear one more pretty lie from his mouth.

Damn him.

No, damn yourself, she chastised herself. *You knew better.*

It had all sounded so wonderful. So perfect. So exactly how she dreamed it would be if the accident had never happened and Branch hadn't strayed. If Zach had never been hurt, and her heart had never been broken.

Except the accident did happen, and people were hurt and hearts were broken and perfect didn't exist.

She had been a fool to think otherwise. Even in the bright light of morning, she could see that she had been too willing, too eager to rekindle what they lost and believe what he said. But she had believed Branch, and that was why her chest constricted so tightly every time she thought about it. The way he acted, the things he said … the more Kait replayed it all in her mind, the more she felt that his plans to stay here and give their relationship a second chance just made more sense to her than lying about it all and selling the house out from under her nose. It was a small town, Branch had to know she was bound to hear about it. Especially when her friend was the realtor.

But there was no arguing with a document. Black ink on white paper with Branch's name on it – the proof couldn't get much more concrete than that. And he admitted to meeting with Zach twice, as well as keeping it from her.

She would never understand what he planned to gain from any of it. It would never make sense.

But it didn't have to make sense to hurt her. Even as she sat in the kitchen of her little house, feeding mushy cereal to the only two boys who would never break her heart, she would never forgive Branch for doing this to her. She would never forgive herself for letting him.

'Don't ever lie to Auntie, okay?' She offered up another spoonful of mush, much to one of the twin's delight. 'It seems Auntie has a thing for loving boys who lie to her.'

That was probably the worst part of it. She loved a man who had lied to her once, then she willingly allowed him the chance to do it a second time. But nothing was worse than the fact that she still loved him.

I still love him, lies and all.

Kait would never forgive herself for that, either.

It should have been a day she anticipated. She should have been a bundle of nerves over the minute details of the event she had so painstakingly planned with Branch. She should have been so excited to see all her hard work and ideas come to fruition in such a festive and beautiful way.

Instead, Kait dreaded today. Because if it was really, truly December twenty-third, then that meant tomorrow was Christmas Eve. And that meant the holiday dinner at Grandma Addie's house wasn't going to be the beginning of the life she thought she was starting alongside Branch. Now, it was just a bleak reminder of her gullibility and desperation. She didn't need any more reminders.

Upset enough by what happened, she hadn't been brave enough to tell Janna about Branch's lies. Knowing Janna, she wouldn't be able to bite her tongue and suppress the *I told you so* she'd been chomping at the bit to get out since the beginning of the month, and Kait couldn't bear to hear that at the moment. The fact that her older sister was right only made it harder to take. But as she shuffled into her coat, heading to the diner for the morning shift, her luck of being able to occupy herself enough to avoid being cornered by Janna ran out. They were sisters, and Kait knew she could read her like an open book, even when she didn't want her to. Kait could do the same to her.

186

'What happened?' Janna held one of the twins in her arms, propped on her hip as she stood near the counter, nursing a cup of coffee that was undoubtedly cold by now.

'Nothing.'

'Liar.'

Kait really didn't want to get into this right now. Not ever, if she had the choice. 'You were right about Branch,' she said simply. 'He's selling his grandparents' house.'

'Damn,' Janna muttered under her breath. She gave the toddler in her arms a sideways glance, cringing at her own language. 'You didn't know, obviously.'

'He made me think he was keeping it. That he was going to live there and we'd …' She didn't know how to finish that sentence anymore.

'Live happily ever after?'

To Kait's surprise, her sister didn't sound condescending. In fact, her down-drawn mouth and glossy eyes spoke of a sadness she could relate to. If there was anyone who knew what it was like to be let down by someone who claimed to love you, it was Janna.

'Something like that.' She gave a noncommittal shrug, reaching for her purse.

'I'm sorry, Kait.'

Janna's apology dragged her attention away from her escape, and she gave her sister her full attention. Being sorry was a long way from pointing out the warnings she had so blatantly ignored, as she'd expected.

'I know I haven't kept my mouth shut about my feelings regarding him, but I'm sorry it didn't turn out the way you wanted it to.'

It was just another fairytale that had turned into a nightmare for the Davenport sisters. 'Thanks, Janna.' She turned and headed for the door.

'If it means anything, I didn't want to be right.'

187

She sighed. It did, it meant everything. 'I didn't want you to be, either.'

'I guess it's better you found out now, rather than later,' Janna continued. 'How *did* you find out?'

Her desire to retreat to the complete silence of her car was immense, but Kait couldn't be rude. First, her sister knew the diner schedule; Kait was heading into work more than half an hour earlier than needed. Second, Janna was being supportive, and she wanted to hold on to that as long as she could. 'Zach's the realtor he's selling to. Turns out they've met a few times. He showed me the contract.'

Janna's forehead crinkled in bewilderment. 'Then why didn't Zach tell you about it before now? He could have saved you a lot of pain, too, I'd think.'

She stared at her sister as the question settled in between them. Focused on Branch and his lies of omission, she hadn't really given much thought to Zach's role in the situation.

She was now.

Janna was right again, and Kait had a sinking feeling that the answer to her question meant everything, too.

A few days ago, Kait saw the spirit of Christmas everywhere she looked, from the banners on Main Street's lamp-posts that boasted *Happy Holidays!* to the glint in passersby eyes as they bustled about with their paper shopping bags and barely contained anticipation.

Now, her own Christmas cheer had been replaced by a thick veil of pessimism, and no amount of multi-colored lights or holly berry wreaths or promises of Christmas morning delight was going to permeate it.

Christmas miracles were for people whose hearts were still in one piece.

She parked her car behind the diner, thankful there were designated spots for staff there. It was early, most shops hadn't even officially opened yet, but both sides of the downtown street were lined with vehicles. There were two things Port Landon took seriously: shopping local, and Christmas. Put those two things together and you ended up with a very crowded Main Street.

The winter air bit at her cheeks as she slung her purse over her shoulder and made her way out onto the street. There was a back door available for staff, but Kait disliked using it, not keen on the idea of having to walk through the busy kitchen to get to the staff lockers where she deposited her belongings each shift.

The front door seemed farther today, though, thanks to the icy wind, and she kept her head down, chin tucked inside the collar of her coat as she made a beeline for the door without looking around. A second later, she wished she had.

'Kait.'

She whirled around, hearing her name despite the voice being unidentifiable against the wind's relentless blowing. Hands in her pockets to shield her bare fingers, she froze. Not from the chill, but from the sight of him.

Her eyes met his, then she turned around, intent on leaving him on the sidewalk, alone. Where he deserved to be, as far as she was concerned.

'Kait, wait,' Branch called out. 'Please!'

Her chest tightened as she spun back toward him. 'I have to go to work, Branch, and I have nothing left to say to you.' She didn't want to give him the chance to upset her any more than she already was.

He jogged the last few steps to close the gap between them. 'I get that, I do. But if you won't talk, at least listen to what I have to say. Please.'

His cheeks, marred with a couple days' worth of beard growth, were pink from the cold. Warmth was in his dark eyes, though. It could have been forty below zero, and those eyes still would have harbored more radiant comfort than Kait would ever see in the gaze of another person.

His hold on her made her ill.

'Give me two minutes,' he pleaded, his hands up as though bargaining with a skittish animal he thought might bolt at any given moment. 'I just want to figure out where the hell we went wrong.'

Wait, was he implying she had done something to make this whole thing go awry as well? The final thread of her wavering calmness snapped. 'Where *we* went wrong?' Kait's eyes widened, unable to believe what she was hearing. 'This is about where *you* went wrong, and my closest guess is that it has something to do with the fact that nothing's changed. You're still the same man you always were, and I was dumb enough to think you'd changed. So, yeah, I guess maybe we both went wrong, all right, but it was in very different directions.'

'Kait, I didn't lie to you,' he insisted. 'I'm not selling my grand-parents' house, if that's what—'

She let out an indignant scoff. 'Why not now? Don't botch the deal with Zach on my account.'

'I'm not botching anything—'

'Except us,' she spat. 'Purely because you'll never learn. It's not that hard to be honest with someone, Branch. Obviously, for you, it is, but not for everyone. I will never understand why you didn't feel you could tell me about meeting with Zach, and I will never, ever understand why you would make up all those lies about you and me being together, about us having a life together—'

'Those weren't lies, Kait!'

'The hell they weren't,' she fired back, the smoldering inferno inside her erupting into furious flames. She couldn't even feel the cold around her now. She was immune to it, armored by her own rage. If anything, she was burning up from the inside out. She had more to say to him than she'd thought.

The flames must have been evident in her eyes because when he spoke again, his tone was softer, less desperate and more imploring. 'Kaitie, I love you,' he said. 'Those three words aren't enough to describe what I feel for you. You've got to give me a chance to explain—'

'I don't have to do anything,' she corrected him sharply. 'That's the part you don't understand.' She could feel the impending emotional upheaval, beginning in her belly and flooding up into her throat. Soon, the tears would come. In a bid to regain control once more, she shook her head, hoping to fight back the burning she felt in her eyes. 'You can love someone to the moon and back, but sometimes you've got to let them go. That's what I'm doing, letting you go. And if you love me like you say you do, you'll do us both a favor and let me go, too.'

He stared at her, shell-shocked. 'I can't do that.'

She pulled her hands from her pockets, holding them up. 'What you can and can't do, or will and won't do, is no longer my concern, Branch.' There was no hiding the pain in her voice, as much as she wished she could hold it in and hide it away from him. 'I'm letting you go, once and for all.'

Kait couldn't handle one more heartfelt plea from him. He had said it, those three little words consecutively. It was the first time she heard those words from him in over a decade. But no freedom accompanied the emotional statement like she had spent the past decade believing it would, only a raging river of tears and heartbreak. She refused to let the madness go on any longer, turning away from him and escaping into the sanctuary of the diner.

'Kait! Damn it, Kait, wait!' Branch followed her inside. His persistence got the best of him, however, and as he reached out, desperate to keep her there, Kait rounded on him, slapping his hand away.

'Branch, enough!' Not only was she distraught that he had followed her into her place of employment, she was shocked by his unwillingness to do as she asked. But if he didn't care about the round-eyed audience watching their entire spectacle with morbid fascination, neither did she.

'I let you make a fool out of me once, Branch Sterling.' She enunciated each word, hurling it at him like ammunition, making sure each one hit its mark. 'I saw the pictures on Zach's phone, and I know what you did. I believed your lies, and all it got me was a boy pretending to be a man.'

To his credit, he stayed silent, but his mouth slightly gaped and his eyes were fixed on her. She had never been one to air her dirty laundry to the world, but she had Branch's attention, so her outburst was at least having some effect.

'You should've known back then that I would find out. It's a small town, secrets aren't secret forever. But you didn't learn your lesson.' Kait let out an indignant scoff. 'Well, guess what? I found out the things you didn't want me to know, all over again. I saw the proof, Branch, right there in black and white. Which makes us both idiots – you, for thinking I wouldn't find out, and me, for letting you make a fool of me once more, and for ever believing a word that came out of your mouth.'

As if on cue, a sob bubbled up and Kait had to clasp her hand over her mouth to swallow it back down. Barely holding herself together, she watched Branch stand before her, confused, shocked, lost. It wasn't until his gaze focused on a point behind her that she turned to see both Eve and Gerry, the cook, standing near the front counter, ready to jump in as backup if she needed them. She wasn't sure they had ever heard her raise her voice before.

But she didn't need them. She didn't need anyone, not anymore. She couldn't and wouldn't put herself through that kind of pain again.

'Goodbye, Branch.' She passed by her coworkers on her way into the back room, barely making it there before her tears began to fall.

Chapter 20

Branch

Whatever he expected from his appearance outside The Port, it wasn't that.

Branch allowed Kait's anger to continuously erupt in front of him for two reasons. The first one was that she needed an outlet. Even from his vantage point down the sidewalk, he saw the weary lines on her face and the hooded sadness in her eyes. She would spontaneously combust if she held that amount of fury inside her for much longer.

The second reason he let her wrath continue was not only because he was shocked into a speechless stupor by the words spurting from her mouth, but because, in those mere minutes, Branch found out more than he ever would have during normal conversation.

More than he had found out in eleven years.

And now that he had given himself time to think about what she said, Branch was the one who felt ridiculous. He didn't understand how he hadn't figured it all out before now.

It was all starting to come together in his head, though. He didn't care about the fact that a couple of coffee drinkers and a few of Kait's coworkers had seen him get ripped apart by her verbal onslaught. They would be the talk of the town for a few days, then the gossiping crowd would move on to something more entertaining. What Branch cared about was the truth, and he was closer to it now than he had ever been.

Years ago, he had made a mistake that cost him the life he and Kait had dreamed of, believing the catalyst had been his reckless actions that resulted in the injury of her friend, an event that he felt certain had been misinterpreted as the consequence of one man's jealous rage. *His* jealous rage.

Fast forward a decade, and he was about to lose his only chance at holding on to her again, because of lies and deceit.

Except those lies weren't coming from Branch's mouth, and the only jealousy that had resulted in reckless actions was from someone else.

Zach.

He was the common denominator in both equations, then and now. Deep in his gut, Branch always suspected Zach would do whatever it took to win Kait's heart and remove him from the picture, but now he had confirmation.

I saw the pictures on Zach's phone, and I know what you did.

He had no idea what pictures she was talking about, but considering the context and the fact they were on Zach's phone, Branch was sure he had found the concrete piece of the puzzle he'd been missing. The pictures she spoke of so venomously were an integral part of the reason she'd screamed at him to leave Port Landon that night. Branch, however, had been so shaken and such a complete mess that he hadn't stopped to question Kait's anger. He had just accidentally hit her friend with his truck while trying to get—

Holly.

And what about Holly? Kait had referred to her the night he kissed her in the attic. It was the first time he had heard Holly Raynard's name in years, and at the time it blindsided him. Even at the time of the accident, he'd barely known her, but he had known her enough to want to make sure she got home safely. In a town as small as theirs, everyone knew everyone in some way. Holly had been drunk out of her mind that night, and he'd had to pretty much drag her to his truck, but that was where his connection with her began and ended.

Not in Kait's eyes, obviously.

Branch pulled his rented Escape in front of the door of Forrester's Auto. The garage had three bays and looked identical to his memories of the building when he was a kid, back when it was still owned by the Robinsons. The only difference was the huge Forrester's Auto sign above the doors, in vibrant green and white, not faded by years of the sun beating down on it the way the old Robinson's sign had looked. A Christmas wreath hung on the door into the office, lit up with green and red lights, and a familiar Dodge truck was parked at the side of the building.

'Thank God,' he muttered under his breath. Climbing out of the vehicle, Branch was met by the curious eyes of his friend as the door opened up and his head peeked out.

'Sterling, I forgot you were driving one of those.' Jason stepped out into the cold, clad in a pair of stained work pants that were probably cleaner than they looked and a T-shirt with a flannel shirt over it. 'Not sure I'll ever get used to you driving an SUV, to be honest. Isn't that like one step away from a minivan?'

Branch ignored the joke. 'The night of the accident, did you ever hear anything about some pictures?'

Jason's face grew serious. 'What?'

'Pictures,' he repeated more urgently. 'Have there been rumors about pictures from that night?'

'It's a little early, and that was a long time ago, so you're going to have to explain yourself a little better. Preferably inside, where the heat's on.' He waved him inside.

Branch followed him into a cluttered office, the heat blasting from the electric heater beside the battered desk – well, he assumed there was a desk somewhere under the pile of papers and pens

195

and Post-it notes. Amidst the mess, Jason located his abandoned travel mug and took a drink.

'Now, what's this about pictures?' he asked, his forehead wrinkled in confusion. 'Who would want to take pictures of that?'

'Not of the accident,' Branch explained, shuddering at the thought. He took a seat in one of the two chairs nearest the door, presumably for customers to use while they waited for their vehicles. 'I just came from The Port, where Kait lost it on me. I think she thinks I'm trying to sell my grandparents' house without her finding out.'

Jason's eyebrows drew down. 'Are you trying to sell it?'

'No! I told her a few days ago I'd made the decision to stay in Port Landon. I said I planned on fixing the place up. On being with her.'

His friend let out a low whistle, a faint grin on his lips. 'So, why doesn't she believe you, then?'

'For the same reason I think she thinks I cheated on her with Holly Raynard at the graduation party that night,' he stated, a bad taste forming in his mouth at even having to say the words aloud. 'I think Zach lied to her.'

'Whoa, wait a second.' Jason was struggling to wrap his head around it all, and Branch gave him the time he needed. He could relate to the breakneck speed of information being thrown at him. 'There isn't a person in this town, then or now, who'd believe you would cheat on Kait, man.'

Something sparked in his chest – pride. It felt good to hear that his sense of honor was noticed and appreciated by people other than himself. 'But maybe they would be swayed if there were pictures that made it look like I was.'

'You think Canton took pictures of you and Holly, then showed them to Kait.' It wasn't a question, and Jason's features were tight and grave.

'It's the only explanation I can come up with. She mentioned pictures on Zach's phone today, and she asked me about Holly one afternoon when she was at the house. Why else would she do that? I haven't seen Holly Raynard since that night, and as far as I know she doesn't even live here anymore.'

'Last I heard, she was trying her luck in Nashville,' Jason replied absently, his mind obviously elsewhere. 'She's been gone a long time.'

'Not to Kait.' Branch's thoughts resembled the jumbled mess of the desk in front of him. Yet, he had a gut feeling he was right about this. He had no proof, but he had to be right. 'She's been thinking I cheated this entire time, I'm sure of it.'

'Canton never was a fan of you,' Jason added. 'And he managed to date Kait for like two years after you left.'

Branch couldn't hide his scowl. 'I know, she told me. What I can't understand is how no one knows about it. I mean, if there are incriminating pictures and lies about me being with Holly that were bad enough to hurt Kait the way they did, to make her think I would be capable of doing something like that, then how does no one else know about it? I've never heard anything about this until now, Jay. You've lived here the entire time since the accident. Have you heard this rumor?'

His friend shook his head. 'First I'm hearing of it, I swear.' He held up the hand with the coffee mug in it. 'You know I would've called you on that kind of crap if I'd known.'

Branch did know. Jason Forrester might have been known as a bit of a hellraiser in his younger days, but that label derived from getting caught with beer out at the Hansel and Gretel House, and shooting at stop signs on the backroads with pellet guns. Jason always had the utmost respect for women, and he made no bones about letting it be known he wouldn't tolerate his friends being anything but good to their girlfriends. He adored his mother, and he was loyal to his friends. If Jason had caught so much as a sniff about Branch's supposed infidelity, it would have been the first thing out of his mouth when he showed up at his front door, regardless of the time that had passed.

'So, I've been in town three weeks, you've been here eleven years, and yet no one, not one person, has ever mentioned the rumor that I was cheating with Holly on the night of the accident, which everyone knows about?' Branch wanted to see if his friend was on the same wavelength he was. 'She was in the truck with me, Jay. It's not adding up.'

'In a small town where some folks thrive on rumors and gossip,' Jason added. 'Kind of hard to believe. Unless that rumor was meant for one person and one person only.'

'Kait.' Branch had a sick feeling rising in his stomach. His friend was definitely thinking the same thing he was. 'So, Zach takes pictures of me getting Holly into my truck or something, then makes Kait believe the photos he has are proof enough that I'm up to no good. He deletes them after showing them to her, and Kait breaks things off with me the moment I show up at the hospital, believing I already knew what I'd done, and too humiliated by the entire thing to talk about it again. Until today, when Zach gave her supposed proof that I was selling the house and leaving town.'

Jason set his coffee down and raked his hands through his hair. 'It all sounds so crazy,' he muttered. 'But plausible, and that's even crazier. Who knew secrets could actually be kept in Port Landon?'

Branch clenched his jaw. 'They can't,' he stated. 'Kait said it earlier; secrets don't stay secret forever. She just didn't realize it wasn't my secrets she was referring to.'

'What are you going to do, Sterling?'

Branch let a long breath out, then headed for the door. 'The way I see it, if the secret was meant for only a few select people, then the truth can be, too. I'm not out to ruin anybody, Jay, I just want my name cleared.' He turned, his hand on the door handle. 'And I want my second chance. I want Kaitie.'

The Northland Realty office was downtown, dangerously close to the diner, so Branch made sure he avoided passing by The

Port's front windows, taking Hemlock Street instead and bypassing the Main Street stretch all together. Navigating the Escape to the side of the street, he saw that he was in luck. The sporty BMW was parked out front, along with a few other more modest sedans.

Normally he would argue that the people who worked there were just like everyone else, trying to make ends meet and get by. With regard to Zach, however, Branch was more inclined to believe there was no rest for the wicked.

Having once been a residential home, the tall building with its long windows and elegant moldings held a lot of similarities to his grandparents' house. The huge house had been renovated to become the Port Landon site of Northland Realty years ago, with its main office in North Springs, but the building looked shiny and new and modern despite its architectural history. The beauty of being in the real estate business, he assumed.

He felt uncomfortable as soon as he walked in and an electronic buzzing sound announced his arrival. Not only because of the troubling reason he was there, but because the office was all stainless steel and dark wood and crisp colors that reeked of embellishment and professionalism. Branch held neither of those things in high regard. He worked hard, at a mining site, within a team of other men and women who did the same. A stuffy real estate office wasn't in his comfort zone.

'I'm here to see Zach,' he advised the receptionist when she addressed him. 'Zach Canton.' He felt silly. How many Zachs could there be here? It was Port Landon.

'Do you have an appointment?'

He shook his head. 'He'll see me. Just tell him Branch Sterling is here.'

The way she looked at him, he wasn't sure if she was affronted by his brisk response or if she knew him. He didn't recognize her. Either way, the receptionist disappeared down a thin hallway and Branch heard murmuring. She reappeared a minute later, Zach following close behind.

'Sterling, you changed your mind, I take it?'

His smug grin made Branch want to go against everything he stood for and smack it off his face. 'Something like that.'

'Come into my office.' He motioned down the hall. 'We'll get this figured out.'

You're right, we will.

Branch followed, silent. Zach's office was more of the same: stainless steel, dark wood, and an air of professionalism. There were also enough pictures of himself on the walls and shelves to give it an air of egotism, too. When he continued to move behind his desk and sit down without making a move to close the door behind him, Branch took it upon himself to do it for him.

No one else needed to hear this.

His move caught Zach's attention, but the realtor played it cool, steepling his fingers in front of him and wearing that ridiculous grin. And that's what it was, ridiculous. Because now that Branch had come to the conclusions he had, he could see beyond the facade. The man wasn't as dignified and superior as he made himself out to be.

'So, Sterling, you're ready to take me up on my offer.'

Branch disliked the way he said it, as though it wasn't a question so much as a command. 'Actually, no. But I've already told you that twice before.'

'You don't become a successful businessman without at least some persistence.' He grinned wider.

'You don't become the one somebody loves by lying to them, either.'

Finally, Zach's smile faltered. Not completely, but the smug mask had been penetrated and Branch could see the questions in his eyes. 'Excuse me?'

'You heard me,' he insisted. 'I know you lied to Kait to make her hate me. Then, and now.'

Zach shifted in his chair, chuckling. 'You can't blame me for your shortcomings when it comes to Kait, Sterling.'

200

Branch set his jaw tightly. 'Maybe not all of them, but I can think of a few things you've had a hand in. Let's talk about the pictures on your phone, for starters.'

He wouldn't have seen it if he hadn't been watching for it, but Zach's face grew a slight shade paler. 'I have no idea what you're talking about.'

'Oh, so now Kait's lying, too?' Branch scoffed. 'I know, Zach,' he added. 'I know what you did.'

He saw the man's jaw clench as he mulled over what to do next. His lies were only strong as long as the secrecy was maintained. If Branch walked out of here and managed to get Kait to explain what she knew, the foundation on which his deception was built would crumble. It already had.

'Enlighten me.' Zach leaned back in his chair, feigning comfort. His eyes betrayed him, however.

'That night,' Branch began, 'Kait couldn't go to the party with me because she had to work. But you didn't know that.' He watched him from across the desk, his eyes never deviating. 'She didn't want me to miss out, so she told me to go anyway, knowing I had friends who'd be there. So, I went. But I was sober, Zach. Stone cold sober. But you didn't know that, either. I hadn't touched a drop of alcohol that night. Haven't touched it since, if I'm being honest.'

So many folks in town had assumed alcohol had been a factor in what happened, because of the seriousness and because of his passenger's intoxicated state. Branch couldn't even smell the pungent scent without being transported back in time.

'How noble of you,' Zach muttered, his expression twisting slowly into a scowl.

'I'd planned to tell Kait about my new job offer,' Branch continued, ignoring his jab. 'But I figured I'd do it after the party when I picked her up from the diner. So, I stayed as long as I could, celebrating with Jay and the guys, but it wasn't as much fun without her. I decided to leave. That's when I saw

Holly Raynard practically passed out on the couch near the door, with a group of jocks from the football team dripping beer on her for fun. I was disgusted, so I decided I'd take her home. That was the good deed that helped you make me look guilty, wasn't it?'

Zach, surprisingly, stayed silent. Which was fine, because Branch didn't need him to confirm or deny it. Just saying it out loud and watching his face fall with each accurate point in the story told him everything he needed to know.

He forged on, pacing in front of the realtor but watching him closely. 'On my way outside, I ran into you. I was basically holding Holly up, arms draped around her to keep her standing. You asked about Kait, and I—'

'And you went off on me like I had no right to be saying her name.' Every word dripped with disdain.

Branch winced. 'I did,' he agreed. 'I was dragging a drunk girl out of a party, saving her from whatever those jerks inside were going to do, and you showed up out of nowhere, making no move to help me with Holly. You just wanted to know where Kait was. So, you're right, I was rude about it.'

He was putting it mildly, if he remembered correctly. In no uncertain terms, Branch had told him that if he was only there to follow Kait around like a lost puppy, and if he wasn't going to be the least bit helpful, he needed to get the hell out of the way. He had felt guilty about his unwarranted outburst the entire way to his truck.

'I didn't deserve that,' Zach replied briskly. 'And you didn't deserve Kait.'

'You're right on both accounts.' He would never hear Branch argue with him on that. 'I was a jerk to you, I know that. I was already frustrated and preoccupied, and considering the circumstances, I guess your questioning set me off.'

A scoff from Zach was his only reply.

'I'm not condoning what I said. But my unjustified blow-up

202

must have set you off, too,' Branch countered, 'considering what you did next.'

Zach's eyes narrowed, silently daring him to say it out loud. But Branch didn't need to be challenged. He had come too far not to say it, and too much was on the line.

'I was distracted, pissed off at myself for chewing you out, and frustrated from trying to get Holly out of that house and into the truck. Once I got her into the seat and buckled in, I went around the back of the truck. The back, Zach. I know there was no one anywhere near that truck because I'd looked around to see if anybody was going to come and help me with Holly. No one was there.'

Branch swallowed, a bad taste in his mouth. 'I climbed in and turned the key, but Holly kept falling over to one side. Against me.' He had stopped pacing, couldn't move. Couldn't do anything but let his gaze burn into Zach's. 'Those are the pictures you took, I'm sure of it. You stood behind my truck and used your phone to take photos of Holly flopping over against me, through the rear window of the cab.' He could almost visualize what those pictures looked like, hazy and unclear thanks to the darkness of night and only the dashboard glow to illuminate their silhouettes. He cringed, thinking of what Kait must have thought when she saw them.

'I'll never forgive myself for not paying attention, Zach. For being so distracted and letting my mind get so flooded with my frustration regarding you, and about Holly, that I threw that truck in drive and slammed my foot down on the accelerator.'

Something changed in Zach's features. A sliver of surprise mixed with confusion. 'You didn't put the truck in drive.'

Solemnly, Branch shook his head. 'It was in reverse,' he explained weakly. 'And you were behind my truck, taking photos to ruin my life.' His throat was thick, dry. He let his statement hang between them, thick and suffocating.

Zach cleared his throat, visibly shaken. 'Even if it was an

accident, it happened, Sterling.' But his bravado was gone, stolen along with his certainty. Branch wondered if Zach had repeated his lies so often that he had begun to believe them himself.

'It did. Is that how you justify sitting in a hospital bed and still being so hell-bent on ruining my chances with Kait that you had to show her those pictures and spin your web of lies, all before I even managed to get to the hospital?' A crack split in the foundation of Branch's calm resolve. 'I was at the police station, Zach, just trying to find out if you were okay, trying to make them see it was an accident. And the entire time, not even being hit by a truck could stop your quest to make her see that I was no good for her. I've spent eleven years feeling so goddamn guilty for what happened to you because of my negligence, and yet it never would have happened if you hadn't been standing there, taking pictures to break Kait's heart.' He pointed a long finger at Zach. 'And *that* was no accident.'

Branch didn't need to tell Zach any more. He had witnessed the rest himself, from the moment Branch sprinted into the hospital hallway just outside Zach's room door, desperate to know if Zach was all right, to the moment Kait screamed at him, inconsolable, and yelled at him to leave and never come back.

'You used everything good in my life to ruin me. You overheard me at the party, I'm sure of it. So, my best guess is that you knew I hadn't told her about my job offer yet. You knew I adored that girl, and that I'd just gotten myself a job that was going to help me build a good life for me and her. And still, you made her think I had some kind of secret life, with a job I was going to take and a girlfriend I'd been seeing behind her back. Am I close?' Branch shook his head, sickened by the thought. It was one that had just come to him, but he believed it with every fiber of his being. 'All because you loved her,' he added. 'Yet, by ruining my chances with her, by breaking my heart, you had to break hers, too. And you still did it,' he choked out. 'You broke Kait's heart that night, Zach, not just mine.' His chest was so constricted he fought to breathe. 'And now you're doing it again, all in the name of love.'

'I do love her!' The words burst from Zach's mouth, offering up more emotion than Branch had ever seen him convey. 'I'd do anything for her, don't you see that?'

He nodded. 'Then, let her go,' Branch whispered, defeated. 'Let the idea of her go. You've got her friendship, and if that's as strong as you think it is, then it'll withstand the truth. But, Zach, if you love her half as much as you say you do, you've got to tell her the truth – the whole truth – and let her make her own decisions. About how she handles it, and about who she loves. Kait deserves that much.'

'She'll hate me.' Zach's shoulders were slumped, everything about him suddenly wilted and melancholy. Gone was the confident businessman. In that moment, only a ghost of the gangly, unrefined teenager remained.

'Kait's the most forgiving woman I've ever met,' Branch replied, his breath coming out in short bursts. 'Give her time. But, damn it, give her the truth.'

'You're not going to tell her?'

'I never want to mention the events of that night again, and as long as you're honest with her, Zach, we'll never have to. You have to be the one to tell her. It'll help your cause if it comes from you.' He refused to mention the fact that Kait probably wouldn't listen to what Branch had to say, anyway. 'It's time to let the past be just that – the past.'

It could have been seconds or minutes or hours that passed as they stared at each other, the tragedy of another lifetime both dividing them and binding them together simultaneously.

'I'll talk to her.'

Chapter 21

Kait

A month ago, the mention of Christmas had instilled a sense of childlike anticipation in Kait. As a kid, the events surrounding the holidays had never been huge and lavish in the Davenport family, usually consisting of a few gifts under a scraggly artificial tree Kait's mom had bought from a garage sale when she and Janna were still in elementary school and a precooked roasted chicken from the grocery store's deli that they heated up in the microwave and paired with instant potatoes and canned cranberry sauce. Regardless, every year without fail, they spent it together. Their mother always managed to be sober and even a little bit fun on Christmas Eve and Christmas Day, taking them to Addie's house on Christmas Eve for the festive dinner that had become a household tradition in many families within their small town, then bringing home premade cookie dough that they baked while Christmas cartoons played on the television the entire day in a cheerful loop. As they grew older, Kait looked back on those days with fondness.

The past couple years changed how Christmas was done, however. She and Janna had always taken their holiday decorating seriously, but once the twins were born, it became their mission to pull off the kind of Christmas season that the boys would hold dear when they someday looked back on it, too. Decorating began early, and their tabletop tree was lit up from the first of December through to New Year's Eve. The boys couldn't reach it, but they spent many an evening playing beneath its multi-colored glow, a sight that gave both Janna and Kait a heartwarming pause, then matching grins.

Four stockings hung from the electric fireplace's mantle, embroidered with initials of their names. She and Janna could be caught at any given moment humming or singing Christmas carols to the boys, much to their delight. They both baked – boy, did they bake! – as much as they could fit in the freezer, starting to make sporadic batches of cookies and fudge in November as they found the time to do it. There had been no Christmas Eve dinner held at Addie's place last year, for the first time in Kait's lifetime, but the year before, despite being only infants, Janna had stopped by Addie's for a few minutes, just to introduce the boys to the woman who held more Christmas spirit than all of Port Landon combined.

It was a tradition, after all, and Kait found solace in knowing Addie had gotten a chance to meet the twins.

Christmas was busier now, with two little boys scurrying around and creating havoc with wide eyes and high-pitched giggles, but all in all, it was still tame. Christmas Eve was met with two bleary-eyed sisters staying up to wrap gifts from themselves and from Santa, and Christmas morning brought toys and games for the twins that she and Janna saved for months for, drinking warm coffee and cookies from sunrise till dark.

It had always been a fun and pleasant time of year for Kait, creating memories she would hold on to until she was old and gray.

This Christmas was different, though. There had been so many ups and downs that she didn't know if she should be thankful for it or try to request a do-over from Santa Claus himself.

This Christmas had started as it normally did, with the light-hearted feelings and the antsy urge to decorate every room and surface she came near. With the sound of Christmas songs floating through her mind even when they weren't playing, and the excitement as she dreamed about the fun things she would purchase as gifts and the decadent treats she would bake. Now, the morning before the big reveal of Addie's tribute dinner Kait had so painstakingly planned with Branch, she yearned to be under the covers in her bed, warm and comfortable as she hid from the world and all the sadness that came with it. There wasn't a thing that was jolly or festive about this time of year to her, now. Maybe her Christmas spirit was broken.

Just like her heart.

She wished she hadn't been so proactive and switched her diner shifts with Eve for today and tomorrow. She wished Eve hadn't been so willing to work so she could prepare for the Christmas Eve dinner alongside Branch, a knowing smirk on her face the entire time as she nodded, scratching out Kait's name on the schedule and replacing it with her own.

She wished she could go back in time and do it all again. How far would she go? There was a certain appeal to retreating to the beginning of the month and handling everything differently. She could have pointed to the door when Branch walked into the diner that day, telling him he wasn't welcome there, that she had nothing to say to him, didn't want to see him, and would never forgive him for his lies and betrayal. A few simple, sharp-tongued words would have changed the course of events between then and now.

But perhaps the answer was to rewind the hands of time further, going back to her teenage years when she was so impressionable and willing to believe in all the things that he promised. Willing to believe in love. If Kait went that far back, she could turn away from him when she saw him in the hallways of their high school, ignore his soft-spoken voice and his alluring espresso eyes. She could have kept her distance, and managed to keep her heart safe from the likes of Branch Sterling.

Even as Kait thought about all the *what ifs* and *might-have-beens*, she knew things would never have been able to change the trajectory of their love. She would have fallen for him in any scenario she could conjure up. She would have welcomed him back into their hometown, and into her heart, regardless of his past indiscretions.

Because she loved him. No number of years could change that. And feeling something – even the pain that accompanied their brand of unconditional love – was better than feeling nothing at all.

At least, Kait had thought so. The numbness that crept in under her skin and anesthetized her wasn't exactly a welcomed feeling, either, especially considering the cheery mood she was supposed to be buoyantly displaying during the holiday season, but it was better than the bouts of excruciating sadness that overtook her, coming on with the tiniest reminder of Branch and the lies that came with him, and only abating once her tears ran dry. It was a vicious cycle, feeling nothing and then being consumed by every emotion all at once. As much as Kait wished she had her diner shifts to occupy her body, she knew that not even physical labor and overwhelming crowds would occupy her mind. She was better off at home, where she could wallow in her own sadness without having to put on a brave face and pretend she was fine.

Because she wasn't fine. She didn't know if she ever would be again. Buried amidst her heartache, she had so many questions. Not only for Branch, but for Zach. For herself.

Maybe she always had.

Because the more she thought about it, something didn't add up.

Maybe it never did.

There were so many maybes whirling around in her brain, Kait couldn't think straight. She was beginning to struggle to remember which parts of her memories were real and which parts were what she had told herself to get through it. Or which parts she took at face value when she should have delved deeper and demanded answers.

But that was the thing, wasn't it? Even back then, all those years ago, Zach had an answer for everything. No wonder he was such a successful businessman. He went after what he wanted, and he wasn't afraid to ask the tough questions or give the hard answers. Had those hard answers been the truthful ones?

Guilt swarmed her. She was doubting Zach, after everything he had been through. Everything they had been through.

Janna was, too, though, and Kait's older sister didn't fully trust anyone. She might have been on the sidelines of this situation, but Janna had watched it unfold through a spectator's eyes, not completely objective but definitely less subjective than Kait was. She had picked up on the discrepancy immediately. Why hadn't Zach mentioned his two previous meetings with Branch before slapping that contract down in front of her as proof? She had been so caught up in the *who* that the *why* hadn't managed to even make it on to her radar.

And that could have been exactly what Zach was banking on.

Goodness, she sounded like a conspiracy theorist. If only she had been rational enough to demand answers from Branch outside the diner instead of losing her cool in the heat of the moment.

Déjà vu was creeping in. Kait had already lived through a similar situation once before, and look where that had gotten her. Standing still, afraid to do anything that might move her own life forward or change things in any way, and afraid to say things in fear of rocking the boat, keeping her mouth shut and her head down, to keep herself protected from the outside world.

In retrospect, all she had done was put off the inevitable. She knew that now. Back then, she might have screamed at Branch to leave, out of sight but definitely not out of mind, but more than a decade later, all those unspoken questions still needed answering and all that love she had locked away had come pouring out at the first sight of him.

Kait needed to find out what was really going on. Her head wasn't in the sand anymore, and she wasn't hiding from the truth. She couldn't. This time, there was a time limit; Branch would leave Port Landon by the end of the month, and the answers she so desperately needed would be gone with him.

She showered quickly and dressed, tossing her wet hair up in a messy knot despite the icy chill outside. Janna would turn into Mom-zilla if she saw her head outside like that, but the furthest thing from Kait's mind right now was whether or not she might catch a cold.

Shuffling into her thick jacket, her stomach churned violently. Her gut instincts were rarely wrong, but she had a funny feeling that she had been ignoring those instincts for a long, long time. Now, she wasn't turning away from that churning sensation. It proved to her that something was wrong, and that she was right to face it.

No makeup, eyes puffy from her tears, Kait reached for her purse and shoved her feet into her shoes. She should have been over at Addie's house, working alongside Branch to prepare for all the festivities tonight would bring in that household. Instead, she was heading out into the cold to hunt down the truth, something she should have done a long time ago.

She swung the door open, prepared for the blast of frigid air to wrap itself around her, pinching at her bare cheeks and making her eyes water. What she wasn't prepared for was the man standing in the middle of the front step, hand raised to knock. She barrelled into him, gasping as her mind struggled to catch up with her physical surroundings.

'Oh!' She let out a strangled sound of surprise, her mitten-clad hands dropping her purse onto the snow-covered concrete as she tried to push herself away from his chest. 'Oh, I'm sorry—' Her brain finally registered his presence. 'Zach?'

'Hey, Kait.' He greeted her with a small smile that didn't reach his eyes. 'Let's go inside, if that's okay. I think we need to talk.'

The way he said it, the way his eyes betrayed him, she knew then that it wasn't okay. Things might never be okay again. But that was the price of the truth, and she had a sinking suspicion they were both about to pay dearly for it.

Chapter 22

Branch

Branch didn't know what he had been thinking.

As he spent the entire morning recleaning the main floor of his grandparents' home after Googling how to cook a turkey – it took just as much time for him to find the roast pan and turkey baster as it did for him to run through all the steps listed on the cooking website he found, and he still hadn't figured out exactly what the baster was for – he finally decided he had been crazy to ever think he could pull this off on his own. Trying to walk a foot in Grandma Addie's shoes was impossible, let alone attempting a full mile. He didn't know why he ever thought he could do it in the first place.

Scratch that. Branch knew exactly what he had been thinking, and he remembered why he'd been so confident he could pull it off.

Kait.

The woman had the ability to make him feel like he could do anything. Like it was possible for them to pull off the biggest, greatest, most festive dinner Christmas Eve had ever witnessed, bringing Port Landon together and reminding them of all the good Branch was capable of, not just his mistakes. She made him feel like this event mattered more than anything else in the world. Like he mattered.

And now he didn't even know if he was going to be able to make it happen.

Considering the circumstances, he didn't blame her for not showing up. She had the next three days off; she had said so numerous times over the past couple weeks, excitement gleaming from her seafoam eyes as she advised him that she didn't remember the last time she had that many days off in a row. She was home, on Christmas Eve.

And being anywhere in the vicinity of Branch had gone from the top of her list to the very bottom. Or, maybe he had been erased from the list completely.

This wasn't at all how he envisioned this day would go. What was supposed to be a fun-filled day of seeing all their plans and holiday wishes come to fruition together was now one hour that stretched into the next, alone, fumbling through the things he did know how to do and struggling to quickly learn the things he didn't.

He could only imagine what Grandma Addie would be saying to him right about now.

The day was a certifiable recipe for disaster in the making. Which seemed to be the only recipe he could successfully handle at the moment. The ingredients were all on the countertop, somewhere, for Grandma Addie's bread pudding, but Branch didn't know a thing about making good bread pudding. Kait had planned to tackle that dessert, with him as her wingman if needed.

He swallowed, reminding himself that she didn't need him anymore. For anything.

He had been a fool to rely on Zach to go to Kait and tell her the truth. What did it matter to him if she still believed Branch was a conniving liar with no conscience? The reality was that, if Zach wanted to, all he needed to do was keep his mouth shut and he would get exactly what he always wanted – Kait would continue to hate Branch more than ever, and she would continue her friendship with Zach like nothing had ever happened.

Like Branch had never been there at all.

Except, that wasn't enough for Zach. It never had been. He loved Kait, and Branch would never blame him for that. Frankly, he didn't understand how the whole world wasn't in love with her. But the man had gone about it the wrong way, trying to remove Branch from the picture by dishonorable means and hoping to make Kait love him back by … what, exactly? Process of elimination? Branch would never understand his reasoning, or the fact that he thought it might actually work.

But Branch was betting everything he had, including his own heart, on the flicker of uncertainty in Zach's eyes. He had ended up seriously injured the last time he'd tried to force fate to work in his favor, and then spent the following years without Branch around to meddle in his relationship with Kait. It still hadn't been enough. He and Kait were still friends, but friends only. Everything he had gone through during the accident and afterward, including what sounded like a one-sided romantic relationship, had been in vain in his eyes. Zach and Kait were still friends, and friends they would remain.

Then, Branch had shown back up in town like the ghost of Christmas past, only to pick up where he and Kait had left off, effortlessly. Even Branch realized that it must have been a vicious slap in Zach's face.

He got it, he really did. Branch was furious with the man for the lies he told and the underhanded things he had done, to Kait and to himself, but he understood, in a messed-up kind of way. Love made people do crazy things, rash things. As he glanced around the kitchen, unsure what to do next, he reminded himself that he and Zach were no different in that regard.

All he could do was hope that Zach followed through on his word. There was nothing more Branch could say or do, save for getting a grip on his concentration and doing what he said he would, too – host a true Addie-like Christmas Eve here, tonight.

He had a lot of work to do.

Disgruntled by the amount of food he didn't know how to make, he went about working on something he did to boost his morale a bit. He pulled the different kinds of cheeses from the fridge, found the assortment of pickle jars on the countertop, then went in search of Grandma Addie's crystal-cut platters. He found the three small ones he'd been looking for underneath the antique hutch in the dining room, and piled one on top of the other. Rising from his crouched position, eager to feel like he accomplished something, he turned with a renewed determination. Whether it was his lack of grace or the unsteadiness of the tower of glass in his hands, the top platter slid between his fingers. In painstaking slow motion, Branch watched, horrified, as the glass glinted in the incandescent light of the chandelier above the dining room table as it somersaulted in mid-air, then crashed to the floor, shards and pieces scattering wildly across the hardwood floor.

'No!'

It was too late. He stood there, eyes wide and heart pounding, as the glass glittered like icy frost in the streams of sunshine stretching across the floorboards. Gripping the remaining two platters so tightly that his knuckles turned white, Branch couldn't tell if he couldn't breathe, or if he was getting too much oxygen from the heavy panting he couldn't seem to control.

Motionless, he let a new, unabashed wave of grief consume him. It was just a platter. But as his throat grew thick with pent-up emotion, he knew it wasn't. It was Grandma Addie's platter. A piece of his history. A sliver of the memories he had left of her that was now shattered. That was now gone forever.

Like Grandma Addie and Grandpa Duke. Like Kaitie.

He blew out a long breath, hearing the quiver of it as he released it. In unbearably slow movements, he set the remaining platters on the dining room table and stepped away from the mess. The distance helped to slow the thump in his chest a bit, but it did little to fill the void the broken crystal had managed to rip open inside him.

Tears burned his eyelids as he turned away from the shattered glass that mirrored his heart so well, and Branch found himself drawn to the Christmas tree in the front window. The first thing he had done that morning when he woke up was plug it in, counting on the twinkling lights and shiny tinsel to cheer him up and keep him forging on. So far, it hadn't worked as well as he had hoped.

He approached the tree with caution, reaching out to let his fingertips touch first one sparkly ornament, then another, blinking rapidly as he attempted to keep his tears at bay. He couldn't cry over this. He refused to. If Grandma Addie were here, she would remind him that a glass plate was nothing to shed tears for.

It was more than the broken platter, though. It was the loss he felt in this big old house, the constant reminders that the two people who loved him like a son were gone and that all he had left were things—ridiculous, menial, tangible things that surrounded him and weren't ridiculous or menial at all. If they were, he wouldn't be two seconds away from crying his eyes out over a cheese platter his grandmother had last touched.

He sniffed, shaking his head to free himself of the emotional wave threatening to engulf him completely. Squeezing his eyes shut, he took a deep breath in and let it out slowly. Upon opening his eyes again, his gaze landed on the ornament pressed into his palm, a tiny glass teddy bear with a cardinal nestled in its paws.

Cardinals are supposedly messengers from heaven. They show up when you need them most.

Branch heard Kait's voice as clearly as if she were standing there with him. Fingers enclosing around it, he let his eyes close again, focusing on the warmth of the glass in his hand and the vivid image of his grandmother that was never far from the forefront of his mind.

'I can't do this without you, Grandma Addie,' he whispered painfully. 'I can't do this alone.'

It crushed him to admit it, knowing there was no way he was going to be able to pull a Christmas Eve dinner off the way his grandmother had done for so many years, so effortlessly. But he couldn't, and in that moment, he grieved his inabilities almost as much as his loss and loneliness.

He opened his eyes slowly, letting the light of day back in and the silence of the house take over once again.

It wasn't the silence or the sun's rays he noticed first, however. Facing the Christmas tree, Branch had a clear view out the window it stood in front of, a large bay window that jutted out in front of the house and showed off the entire front yard between its elongated panes.

It allowed an unobstructed view of the driveway, too, which was why he was struggling to comprehend why there were a bunch of vehicles parked behind his rental SUV and Grandpa Duke's Bronco. He recognized Jason Forrester's Dodge truck a split second later, only compounding his confusion.

He got to the door just as a loud knock reverberated through the quiet house. Even before he opened it, Branch heard the muffled sound of voices. Their words were obscured, but the hum of anticipation and excitement penetrated the steel door with ease.

'Jay?' But it wasn't just Jason. His friend was there, all right, but he was squashed between a group of older adults. It took Branch longer than it should have to recognize Jason's parents and grandmother, accompanied by another elderly woman he didn't know.

'Happy Christmas Eve, man!' his friend exclaimed, his smile glowing as brightly as the midday sun. 'We're here for the party.'

Ashamed, Branch's head hung slightly. He didn't know what to say to that. 'I … It's not supposed to be until later tonight.'

'We know.' Jason's mother, Bettina Forrester, radiated so much enthusiasm that she was shaking from it. 'So, we'd better get started.'

'When Jay told us you were holding a dinner for the town, like Addie used to, we thought you might want some help with the preparations,' his father, Roderick, explained, holding up a few canvas shopping bags. They all had similar ones clutched between their fingers, except for Bettina, who was holding a covered pan of some sort.

'You're here ... to help?' Branch stared at them, bewildered.

'Well, who in tarnation do you think helped Addie all those years?' Branch had only met Jason's grandmother, Mary-Jean, a handful of times, but he remembered her outspoken demeanor. For such a little lady, she sure was a force to be reckoned with. He remembered thinking, even when he was a teenager, that she was pretty cool for her age. 'Addie certainly wouldn't want you to be doing this alone, either.'

The old woman's statement rendered him speechless, and he managed to keep just enough of his wits about him to have the manners to step sideways and motion the group of people inside.

As they shuffled inside out of the cold, Branch stood there, hearing the agonizing words he had just spoken aloud to his grandmother float continuously through his mind.

I can't do this without you, Grandma Addie. I can't do this alone.

But his plea was quickly followed by the sentiment Jason's grandmother had just offered him, and as he played it over and over on an endless loop, Branch swore the voice who said it began to sound less and less like Mary-Jean and more and more like his own grandmother.

That was when he felt it, the warmth in his palm. Branch glanced down and opened his clenched hand. In it, a tiny glass teddy bear sat, nestling a crimson red cardinal in its paws.

His own little messenger from heaven.

Chapter 23

Kait

Kait thought she was an emotional wreck before. Heaven knew she had more than enough reasons to be one throughout the years. Even during the times where she seemed cool as a cucumber on the outside, she had a tendency toward being a chronic worrier. Looking after everything, and everyone, was her way of dealing with her worries. As long as she was the one in charge, she knew there was no one else who would care more or do more than she would to make things right. Organization was key, as well as routine. Which was why Kait had welcomed the almost mundane life she had built in Port Landon – same job, same daily schedule, same four walls she hid behind so that nothing bad would ever befall her and her family again.

And it had worked for over a decade, until Zach showed up on her doorstep and brought the something bad inside her home. She couldn't hide from emotional upheaval when she was the one to invite it inside and offer up its messenger a piping hot cup of coffee.

The moment she opened that door and saw the look in his eyes, she knew things were about to change forever. The truth was coming, bringing with it a new brand of turmoil she had never experienced before.

Still, there was a sense of relief, albeit fleeting, that accompanied the reality that things were about to change, and once they did, life was never going to be the same again. Kait had hid from that kind of change for so long, ducking her head in the sand and letting unanswered questions and intuition go by the wayside. It had been easier at the time to focus on other people, to do things and keep herself treading water instead of facing the reasons she wasn't propelling herself forward.

As Zach's words tumbled from his mouth, picked up speed, and hit her with the force of a hurricane, phrases like '*I lied to you …*' and '*I made you think …*' piercing her heart and making her chest sting violently, she realized that, as much as she wanted to, she couldn't solely blame him for what had happened.

Because Kait had lied to herself, too. She let herself believe his lies despite her gut feeling that it couldn't be true. It was her own debilitating fear of the truth that led her down this path, and she had no one – not Zach, Branch, Janna, or anyone – to blame for it but herself.

Still, to sit at her kitchen table, the cup of coffee in front of her long since cold, listening to him relay how he argued with Branch on the night of the accident, how he watched Branch struggle to get Holly to his truck in her intoxicated state, how he used Branch's good deed to glean supposed evidence that finally proved Branch wasn't good enough for her …

Whatever was left of Kait's heart was shattered completely. It was all a lie. The pictures he had taken back then, and the real estate contract he had shown her now. Branch hadn't signed anything to sell his grandparents' house. He hadn't even seen the papers.

His confusion when she had confronted him had been very, very real.

'Kait, I'm so sorry,' Zach insisted, leaning forward in an attempt to see her eyes, shielded behind the curtain of hair that had fallen over her face as she hung her head and began to cry freely. 'I am, I mean that.'

'Why?' She choked on the word, her head snapping up. 'Why confess all this now? I don't understand.' She didn't understand any of it, how he could have done it in the first place, how things had all gone so horribly wrong.

'Branch,' he replied simply.

She stared at him through puffy eyes, bewildered.

Chagrined, Zach's throat moved. 'I … I think I might have been wrong about him.' Pain marred his features, and Kait knew how much it had to hurt to admit that aloud.

He wasn't the only one sitting at that table who had been wrong about Branch Sterling.

'We've lost all this time,' she whispered, shaking her head at the unsurmountable sadness of it all.

'I know.' Zach's voice was only a ghost of the confident baritone he had so often possessed.

Kait stared at him, unable to see him clearly through her blurry eyes. Even if she could, she wasn't sure she would recognize the man sitting across from her. The man who was supposed to be her friend, who claimed to love her. Who admitted he'd been wrong about Branch. She needed to focus on that right now.

Silence ensued, and Kait let it drag out between them. She needed to give Zach every opportunity to fully understand what had been lost, what he had truly done to all three of them. Not just say it, but feel it, realize it, and be as completely horrified and devastated by it as she was.

'Go get dressed, Kait.'

Her gaze narrowed, the silence so deafening that she wasn't sure if she truly heard him say the words or imagined them. 'Excuse me?'

The corner of his mouth lifted. 'I know you, so I'll bet my

next commission that you've got a pretty holiday outfit picked out for this evening. It is Christmas Eve, after all.'

Her stomach clenched at his note of familiarity. He was correct, there was a little red cap-sleeved dress upstairs hanging on the front of her closet door, a find she had unearthed on a clearance rack months ago and stowed away in case she ever had a special occasion to wear it.

The idea of Christmas Eve with Branch had been enough for her to finally pull the tags off.

Kait had managed to stay surprisingly calm throughout Zach's entire heartbreaking confession. Anger swelled inside her, now, blazing and fueled by fury. He had a lot of audacity. 'If you think for one second that I—'

'I'm not suggesting you spend Christmas Eve with me,' he interjected, hands raised in surrender. 'I'm suggesting you go get all dolled up like you'd planned, so I can drive you to Addie's house. From what I hear, there's a dinner party going on over there, and you're invited.'

'Now you want me to spend time with Branch?' she seethed. 'After I've hurt him so much, for the second time?'

'What I want is for you to be happy.' His shoulders sagged, defeated. 'I've come to terms with the fact that it's not me who's going to be able to give you that, so I want to give you the next best thing – a chance to fix things with the man who will.'

She couldn't believe her ears. 'You want to take me to Branch.'

'I want you to be happy,' he said again. Boldly, he reached out and cupped her hand in his, squeezing encouragingly. 'It's been a long time coming. Too long. And I know I've played a huge part in that. So, let me help the only way I can.'

Every fiber of her being vibrated with the need to scream at him that she wasn't some kind of plaything to just be handed off to another person, that he had a lot of gall thinking she wasn't furious enough to want to lash out at him and make him see that his decisions had stolen a decade from her that she would never get back. But there was a voice reverberating inside her head that was louder than those caustic thoughts, and stronger than her will to despise the man in front of her who was supposed to be her friend.

Let me love you, Branch had said to her only days before. He pleaded with her, and now Zach sat here, begging her to let him help her find her happiness.

All Kait wanted to really do was confess that she knew where to find her happiness, and that she yearned to let her guard down, let herself have everything she ever wanted. It took only seconds for her to realize that meant a life with Branch.

She stood. 'Give me half an hour.'

If it was possible to have déjà vu on top of déjà vu, Kait was pretty sure that was what she was suffering from by the time Zach stopped his BMW in front of Grandma Addie's house.

The time she spent changing into her dress and fighting with hair products and makeup to make herself feel readily prepared was eerie enough; a constant battle of nerves and guilt rising up and warring inside her as she did her best to stamp it down. The nervous buzzing that hummed in her veins felt an awful lot like the fluttering anticipation she had felt years before as a teenage girl, primping her hair and reapplying lip gloss before heading out to meet up with Branch. Many times, they spent their evenings watching movies at his grandparents' house, drinking Grandma Addie's sweet tea, and listening to his grandma hum a melodic tune from the kitchen. Kait couldn't recall the titles of those movies, or what they were about, but she remembered the stolen glances, the innocent way his fingers traced along her palm; the whispers under their breath, words meant only for each other.

The idea of preparing to meet up with him now, at that same house, was dizzying.

Add in the line of cars on both sides of Crescent Street and the full driveway in front of Addie's house, and Kait was having a full-blown case of the past crashing into the present. As a child, she recalled the abundance of vehicles on this street every Christmas Eve. So many folks made it a priority to at least stop in at the big Victorian house, all decked out in twinkling lights and decorations like a real-life gingerbread house, that one of the memories that went along with the annual event was the inability to find a parking spot if you didn't arrive early enough. By the looks of it, half of Port Landon had come out for the dinner.

Even from the road, in Zach's car, Kait swore she could hear the laughter and merriment happening inside. She was convinced the house was somehow beckoning to her, with its brightly lit Christmas tree in the front window and the fireplace with its dancing flames in view just beyond it. The smell of smoke wafted into her nostrils, and the sparkle of the candle decorations that lined both sides of the driveway seemed etched into her vision long after she looked away.

She might have been inside the car, with the windows rolled up and the heat on high, sitting beside the man who had tried to ruin her chances with Branch in a misguided attempt to prove his own love, but she had never been more certain that the sight before her was exactly how she remembered it.

And it was exactly where she needed to be.

'Thank you for bringing me here.' As soon as she whispered it, she felt silly. She didn't have a clue why she was keeping her voice barely audible. Hopefully her sincerity made up for the lack of decibels.

'It was the least I could do.'

They had been through so much together. So many ups and down that she couldn't say for certain whether there were more good times than bad. Kait didn't know what to believe when it came to him anymore. Not right now, at least. And yet, as she sat in the passenger seat of his car, her heart thumping in time with her thoughts of Branch being just beyond the front door a matter of feet away, she had to resist the urge to invite him in with her.

The holiday season must have been getting to her. Not even the acute knowledge of what Zach had done was enough to rival the fact that it was the night before Christmas. No one deserved to be alone on Christmas.

'Wait here, okay?'

'I'm in the middle of the road—'

'Just wait.' Kait scrambled from the car and slammed the door, preventing any further argument.

She hadn't rehearsed what she was going to say to Branch, and even as she took careful steps up the snow-packed, candlelit driveway to the front door, she was at a loss for words. Her thick jacket might have withstood the chilly air of the evening, but the skirt of her dress did little to protect her legs. Still, she stood on the front step longer than necessary, staring at the oversized wreath hung on the door, with its dusting of snow and frosted winter berry accents.

Finally, she rang the doorbell. An uproar of voices sounded from inside, some cheering and a multitude of others calling out, 'I'll get it!' She was surprised anybody heard the bell over the cheery Christmas carols blaring over the children's shrieks and giggles mixed with a steady cacophony of voices and laughter from the folks milling about.

'Merry Christmas!' Jason Forrester opened the door, shouting out the greeting before he even looked to see who was on the other side. The crooked Santa hat on his head only added to his jubilant demeanor. 'Kait, you're finally here.' His grin grew wider. 'Let me guess, you're not here for the bread pudding.'

Her cheeks flamed as red as the holly berries adorning the wreath. 'I—'

'Better late than never, Davenport,' he chuckled. 'Come in, I'll go find him.'

He disappeared amongst the crowd of people before Kait could

226

change her mind. She was still wondering how much Branch had confided in Jason when his voice infiltrated her thoughts and made them scatter like butterflies.

'I didn't think you were going to come.'

She turned. Branch wore no Santa hat, but there was a gleam in his eyes just the same. It wasn't the jovial, fun-loving glint that had sparkled in Jason's gaze only moments ago, but a glimpse of pure, unadulterated hope.

'I didn't think I was going to, either.' There was no room for anything but honesty at this point.

The Port Landon residents, with cider in their cups and cookies pinched between their fingers, faded into the background. The chatter dulled, and the vivid colors around them dimmed, leaving Kait and Branch the only ones left in the room.

Kait, Branch, and a glimmer of hope.

She cleared her throat. 'Zach ... he told me everything.'

Words must have escaped him because he only nodded, waiting, still as stone, to find out where that left them.

'He told me he was wrong about you,' she continued in a shaky voice, afraid it might crack at any second. 'I was, too. Branch, I was so cruel to you.'

'It's okay, Kaitie.' He took a step forward, the emotion thick in his throat, giving his voice a husky quality. She held up her hands.

'But it's not!' Shaking her head, she struggled to remain composed. 'I wish I could change everything. I wish I could go back and believe you and trust you and listen to you. Branch, I'm so sorry.'

He caught her under the arms as she collapsed against him, wrapping her arms tight around his waist and holding him against her, finding solace in the warmth of his chest.

'Kaitie, will you listen to me now?' Branch cooed in her ear. The softness of his tone melted her resolve like nothing else ever could.

She pulled away just enough to peer up at him through tear-rimmed eyes. She nodded, not trusting herself to speak coherently.

'It's okay,' he repeated, pushing a stray strand of hair out of her eyes. 'You're here, and you know the truth. That's all that matters to me. I'll never hurt you. I swear to you, I won't.'

'I know.' She choked on the words.

Branch's hand stayed cupped around her cheek, holding her face up to his. His dark eyes searched hers frantically. 'Are you okay?' he whispered. 'Now that you know what really happened that night?'

'I will be,' she promised. 'But you—'

'Then, we don't need to talk about it now,' he replied. 'I don't want or need apologies, just tell me I'm not the only one still in love like a teenager here.'

Kait choked out a chuckle. 'You're definitely not the only one.'

'Then my Christmas wish has come true.' Branch leaned forward and kissed her softly. The pressure of his mouth against hers was sweet and inviting, tinged with the bygone years as well as the time they would spend making up for those years, but the simple sweetness of the gesture might as well have been an explosion the way it burst through the armor around Kait's wounded heart and made her whole again.

'Come in,' he whispered against her lips. 'Spend Christmas with me, Kaitie.'

'As long as you make my Christmas wish come true, too.'

'Anything.'

She knew he meant it, unconditionally. 'Promise me this isn't our only Christmas together, Branch.'

The upturned curl of his lips broadened. 'It's definitely not the only one.' He kissed her again. 'Let's make it the first of many. For us, and in this house.'

'You're staying.' It came out as a rush of relief, fortifying Kait. She wasn't too late.

228

'I'm staying if you are.' He pulled her against his chest again. 'You're stuck with me now.'

Thank goodness. She reveled in the warm strength of his arms.

'Come in. Let's get you some cider and a plate. You wouldn't believe the food Jay's entourage whipped up today.'

She offered him a questioning glance as he helped her out of her coat. 'Jay's entourage?'

He tossed her coat onto the already overfilled rack by the door. 'Long story. Where'd you park?'

'Oh!' Kait scrambled for the door. In the intense emotion of it all, she had forgotten about him completely. 'Zach drove me here.' Hand on the door handle, she winced at the mention of his name in Branch's presence. 'I'll let him know everything's okay in here.'

'Zach's here?' He gently removed her hand from the handle and opened the door himself.

'Branch, I—'

Astonished, she watched as Branch swung the door wide and waved a hand in Zach's direction. Except, he didn't wave him on, dismissing him. Branch waved him *in*.

'What are you doing?' Kait didn't bother to hide her surprise.

'Inviting him inside.' He waved a second time, more vehemently. This time, Zach rolled down the window and offered him a gracious nod of the head before disappearing further down the road at a slow crawl, undoubtedly in search of a parking spot. Branch closed the door with a satisfied nod of his own.

'Are you sure?'

He reached for her hands again, enveloping them tightly. 'I meant it when I said it's time to let the past stay in the past. Tonight, if we're going to talk, Kaitie, let's talk about the future. About the life we're going to build together, here in this house. Here in Port Landon.'

Her heart swelled. The sound of the word *future* on Branch's lips was intoxicating, a dream she never thought would come true. 'I'd like that.'

'Good.' He nodded toward the door where Zach was somewhere on the other side of it. 'I won't belittle what's happened between all of us, but for tonight, let's spread a little holiday cheer and focus on what's right in front of us – friends, family, and the future.' A crooked grin played on his mouth. 'It's Christmas, after all.'

Even after everything, he was willing to offer his house, his food, and his Christmas Eve crowd to the man who had been the catalyst for their sordid past. But he was right. No one person was guilty, and no one person was innocent, and it didn't matter who was what because it was the past.

And it was Christmas. She beamed up at Branch, proud of him for the gesture toward Zach. Silently, she thought that Grandma Addie would be proud of him, too.

'I'll call Janna and make sure she's bringing the twins over.'

'I'd love to meet them,' he replied. 'Oh, just one more thing.'

Her eyebrows arched, but her confused gaze was met with another sweet kiss that left her dazed and floating.

'Merry Christmas, Kaitie.'

She stared up at the man who had been the love of her life even when she didn't want him to be, then around the room at all the festive decor and glittering lights and smiling faces. She had never felt more certain of her path in life than she did in that moment. After all, it had brought her full circle, proving that her heart had been right where it was supposed to be, all along. With him.

Right here in Port Landon.

'Merry Christmas, Branch.'

Epilogue

Branch

Port Landon was nothing if not a town that thrived on traditions. And while Christmas Eve might have been Grandma Addie's claim to fame, New Year's Eve was the Port Landon Recreation Committee's time to shine.

Once spearheaded by Jason Forrester's grandmother when he and Branch were kids, Mary-Jean had since stepped down as the chairwoman, handing over the reins to someone else whom Branch had learned more than a few colorful things about.

Sonya Ritter.

Tonight, Sonya was in the limelight. While Branch and Kait had spent so many days of December organizing the finer details of their Christmas Eve dinner, Sonya spent every minute she wasn't at the Portside Coffeehouse planning the New Year's Eve dance, as she had every year for the past five years, Kait had said.

Over the Christmas holidays, Kait caught him up to speed on Sonya's recreational activities, mostly meddling and persistent matchmaking, which Branch wondered if weren't two sides of the same coin, and the older woman's exceptional party planning abilities.

'We have to go to the dance, Branch!' she had insisted. 'We just have to!'

Like there had ever been a question as to whether he would deny her something she wanted. She could have asked him for a pet zebra and he would have found a way to smuggle one into the country. If she wanted to go to a party held at the community centre, that's what they would do.

Besides, having a birthday on December thirty-first made it a little tricky to get out of celebratory antics. Especially when that birthday was the big three-oh.

Thirty years old. It seemed surreal to be such an age, considering he remembered when he once believed it to be, well, old.

He was just getting started.

Before December, he might have had himself a decent career and a place to hang his hat when he wasn't working, but he realized now, so clearly, that the life he had built for himself had been no life at all.

Life had been waiting here, in Port Landon, all along.

The unabashed gratitude and welcoming he received on Christmas Eve was proof of that. Kait was right, the only one disappointed in him for his reckless behavior as a teenager was himself. Not one person who came through the door of Grandma Addie's house, whether young, old, or in between, mentioned the accident. Not even Zach, who had merely nodded to him from across the living room, a silent but glaring understanding passing between them.

What had happened in the ten-year span between then and now was over. The truth was out, and things would never been the same, but if Branch was honest, he didn't want them to be. He only wanted civility between Zach and himself. By the looks of it, he'd got it. All Branch hoped was that Kait could heal from her friend's betrayal someday, too.

It was both strange and exhilarating to know that a month

ago he had pulled into the driveway of his grandparents' house, broken and unsure how he was going to make it through the next few weeks, unable to say for sure what he planned to do once the house was organized and cleaned. The only thing he had been confident about was his departure. He had every intention of leaving Port Landon in his rear-view mirror.

His intentions on the last day of December were so drastically different they could cause whiplash. The only thing he planned on leaving behind him was the past. As for being broken and uncertain, Branch had never felt so alive, and there was no question about his plans for the future.

His future was standing in front of him, wearing a strapless black dress with sparkles along the bottom hem. Blonde hair twisted up on top of her head and a daring red lipstick painting her lips, Branch's breath caught in his throat.

'You look gorgeous.' After all these years, she still had the ability to take his breath away.

Playfully, she sashayed this way and that, showing off the swing of the dress's skirt. 'I haven't been dressed up since Allison's wedding,' she replied. 'Thank goodness Paige has such an extensive wardrobe.'

He didn't care where the dress came from. Branch was convinced it was Kait that made the dress, not the other way around. 'You look like a princess.' The sentiment toppled from his lips without realizing he said it out loud. The sparkles on her dress only seemed to accentuate the sparkles in her eyes, and it was getting to him, big time.

She closed the gap between them, tugging on the collar of his dress shirt. Like her, he didn't own much in the way of dressy clothes. Spending more than half his time at a mining site didn't call for it, and he had refused to wear the only white dress shirt he had since it happened to be the one he purchased for both his grandparents' funerals. Tonight was a new start, a new year. Branch wanted only happy memories of this evening.

233

'You don't look too bad yourself.' She grinned. 'So, you're my prince, then.'

'I am, if you want me to be.'

'I absolutely want you to be.' Her heeled shoes gave Kait the extra height she needed to easily lean in and kiss him lightly. Chuckling, she rubbed her thumb against his bottom lip. Branch was going to have to keep in mind that her shade of lipstick was going to leave evidence of any stolen kisses throughout the night.

'Kaitie, I—'

'Come on, lovebirds! If you don't hurry, we're going to be late!' Allison's voice was loud and shrill from the bottom of the staircase. For a split second, he regretted suggesting that Kait invite her friends over to get ready together. He liked them all just fine, and he was grateful she had found such a close-knit group of folks to build friendships with, but he had to admit, it was going to take some getting used to having to share her attention with other people, especially since he'd just found her again.

'We'll be right down!' she shouted. Turning back to him, her wry grin was in place once again. 'You ready for this, Sterling?'

Humor danced in her emerald eyes, causing a wave of anticipation to flood Branch from head to toe. It wasn't the first wave he had experienced so far, and he was certain there would be many more to come by the end of the evening.

The truthful answer was no, he didn't think he was ready at all. He didn't think Kait was, either. He didn't think they had ever been, or ever would be.

But that didn't mean he didn't want this night to happen with every fiber of his being.

He nodded. 'Let's do this, Davenport.'

Branch hadn't been in Port Landon's community centre for more than a decade, and from the outside it looked exactly as he remembered it. What once was an old manufacturing warehouse during the 1950s had been transformed into a well-maintained spot where crowds gathered on most major holidays. The exterior boasted only simple white sidings and built-in window boxes on each sill, currently filled with snow and ice, but the covered front step that had been added on to it, with two thick columns and a ramp going up one edge of it for wheelchair accessibility, gave the whole building a grander look, accented with ornate corner moldings and strings of white lights twisted around each column.

The inside, however, was nothing like he remembered it to be. Sure, the music poured out onto the street each time the heavy double doors at the entrance opened, just like it always had, and the industrial linoleum under Branch's feet was the same worn, faux woodgrain pattern that had been there when he was a teen. But the party itself ...

Sonya Ritter had outdone herself.

He stood at the front entrance, folks bustling past him on both sides, waiting for Kait to hang her jacket up. He welcomed the moment to just stand there and bask in the changes time had allowed in one of Port Landon's oldest industrial buildings.

It was hard to tell the place had ever been considered plain. There was nothing plain about the ropes of glittering white mini-lights that hung from each corner of the massive room, draping across the wide expanse to meet in the middle, where a gigantic chandelier in the shape of a wagon wheel hung, with eight large globe lightbulbs hanging from it.

The entire room seemed to sparkle, with little white lights winking from the round glass centerpieces on the tables that lined each side of the room, and strings of lights twirling the length of every load-bearing metal post. The tables were situated in line with the posts, so their glow announced the spot where the sit-down area ended and the dance floor began.

There was no question about it, this was a dance party. The far wall of the room boasted huge speakers, strategically positioned to offer up the clearest beat and melody regardless of where folks were in the room.

The kitchen was the only room that was brightly lit. Harsh fluorescent light beamed across its open doorway into the main room. The overhead lights had been turned off, leaving everyone to rely solely on the glittering mini-lights and oversized chandelier. The result was dim, but the ambience it created was seductive. And perfect.

It was *all* just so perfect. Branch couldn't contain his elation.

'Ready to party like it's your birthday?' A punch landed on Branch's arm. 'Oh wait, it is your birthday!'

It looked like he wasn't the only one to rummage through the back of his closet for something that would be deemed dressy enough for a special occasion.

'That, it is,' he replied. 'Man, this place looks great. It's nothing like I remember it.'

Jason shrugged. 'Sonya goes nuts over this event every year. She's a party planner extraordinaire, that one. Besides, I think by now you should've learned that not much is like you thought it would be.'

Touché. 'Everything's so different, yet—'

'Exactly the same,' Jason finished for him. 'Yeah, you'll get used to that, too. Especially since you're staying, huh?'

Branch's smirk matched the one his friend wore. 'Yeah, turns out the home I was looking for was the place I'd been trying to avoid all along,' he admitted. 'I hate that I've got to leave Kait for the next two weeks, but I'm coming back. We'll get through it.'

'You two have been through fire, man. Two weeks is child's play for you guys.'

'Here's hoping it's as easy as you think it is.'

'It is,' Jason replied, holding his gaze. 'And if it's not, you can come and work for me.'

He hadn't seen that coming. 'You're serious?'

236

His friend slapped a hand down on his shoulder. 'I'm running with a skeleton crew, and you're the most reliable man I know. If you need a job to test out that mechanical aptitude of yours, you know where to find me.'

Dumbfounded, Branch could only nod. 'Thank you, Jay.'

'If you take me up on the offer, that's all the thanks I'll need.' Jason offered him another solid slap on the back. 'Happy birthday, Sterling.'

Branch's childhood friend disappeared into the crowds just as Kait's singsong voice sounded from behind him.

'Only two more hours until the clock strikes midnight,' she announced. 'What ever shall we do?'

Scanning the crowd, his eyebrows shot up. 'If Allison is any indication, it looks like you're going to dance until they turn the music off.'

They had been there only a handful of minutes, yet somehow Allison had already managed to convince Paige into the middle of the dance floor, breaking out dance moves he was pretty sure were just as old as the building they were in. To his relief, a quick glance to his right revealed Allison's husband, Christopher, whom he vaguely remembered growing up with despite their difference in age, and Paige's fiancé, Cohen, whom Branch had been formally introduced to a couple of hours ago. The men had taken up refuge at one of the tables that lined the edge of the dance floor.

Branch pointed toward the men at the table. 'Go join your friends,' he said. 'I'll be over there, with the rest of the guys who can't dance.'

'Are you okay?' She looked up at him, her gaze narrowed. In the dim light, the smoky makeup on her eyelids only increased the gemstone-like brightness of her irises.

The woman could see through him like a newly polished windowpane.

'I've got the most beautiful woman in the room holding my

hand, Kaitie. I'm more than okay.' Nudging her playfully, he pushed her toward the middle of the floor. 'Go dance, will you?'

Kait's laughter rang out above the music, but she relented, kicking her fancy shoes off and handing them to him before she scurried across the floor into the waiting arms of Allison and Paige.

He had never been much of a dancer, but even as Branch took his time getting a cup of homemade punch from his grandmother's punch bowl – Sonya had practically begged him to loan it to her for this event after she oohed and ahhed over it on Christmas Eve – taking slow, measured steps as he took in the sights around him and let the nostalgia sweep over him like a warm blanket, he couldn't deny he was having a good time. Seeing Kait so carefree and buoyant, seeing friends from his past and new friends alike …

He was making the right decision. He *had* made the right decision. He'd never been more certain of anything in his entire life except for one thing.

His love for Kait Davenport.

'You make her happy, you know.'

The words blasted through his thoughts like a needle pressing against the delicate surface of a balloon. Branch turned, unable to mask his shock at seeing Janna standing there. Her dress wasn't as formal as her sister's choice, but she resembled Kait in so many ways it was hard not to think of her as a taller version of her younger sibling. Her eyes, however, possessed a harsher, poignant glare. Despite everything Kait had been through in her young age, he had never seen that kind of irrevocable regret and sadness in her eyes. 'Janna,' he said cautiously. 'I didn't know you were coming out tonight.'

'For an hour or so, that's it. Mom is with the boys. They're already asleep, and I haven't made it to midnight in years, but I figured I'd make an appearance.'

Another shock followed when Branch thought he saw the

flicker of a smile tug at her lips. 'Well, I'm glad you could come for a bit,' he replied, staring into his cup. What did you say to someone you knew hated your guts the way she did? 'Look, Janna, I—'

She held up a hand. 'Don't.' Her gaze narrowed, and he braced himself for the onslaught of angry words. Instead, when Janna spoke, she sounded just as surprised as he felt. 'I was wrong,' she said. 'Took me a long time to realize it, but I was wrong about you. Kait told me … what happened, I mean. I just wanted to say I'm sorry, Branch. For what you and Kait have been through, and for thinking the worst of you.'

Never in a million years would he have expected a formal apology from Kait's older sister. Words failed him. It took a few attempts to get sound to emit from his throat. 'I'm sorry, too.' And he was. For what happened between him and Kait, but also for the raw hand Janna had been dealt. 'I've made mistakes, but I'm hopeful things are going to start to work out now.' He held her gaze. 'For everyone.'

No sound came from her mouth, but Janna's eyes evoked an understanding that resonated deep within him. 'If there's one thing Kait's taught me, it's not to believe in mistakes.' There was that hint of a smile again. 'And if you ask me, it looks like your mistakes got you here,' she said, gesturing toward the dance floor where Kait laughed and swayed to the music with her friends, 'Which is right where you belong.'

This time, Branch's shock went beyond mere surprise and straight into a state of speechlessness. He didn't hear it straight from her lips, but he felt what she said in a manner that was clearer than any sentence could have been – she was laying down her weapons. A truce. A ceasefire.

'Thank you,' was all he could choke out beyond the lump that had formed at the base of his throat.

His stunned silence was enough to pull a real, honest laugh from Janna's mouth. She reached out a hand and patted his arm.

'Don't thank me. Just do right by her; that's all I ask.' She gave his arm a gentle squeeze, then released him. 'Happy birthday, Branch.'

She left him standing there, mouth partway open and thoughts reeling from what might have been the most heartfelt words he had ever heard come from Janna Davenport's mouth.

Kait's shoes still dangling from his fingers, Branch made his way to the table with Christopher and Cohen. Surprisingly, conversation came easily between them. He never would have expected he had much in common with a graphic designer and a veterinarian, but then again, he knew now that for the past eleven years, he hadn't expected much. Just like he hadn't expected the outcome of his return to Port Landon, and yet, here he was, dressed to the nines, with Janna's apology still ringing in his ears and Kait's shoes tucked under his chair and—

'Oompf!' And Kait sitting on his knee, evidently. Allison and Paige followed suit, Paige taking up the chair beside Cohen, and Allison falling into Christopher's lap dramatically.

'I should have taken these treacherous heels off before breaking out my signature moves on the dance floor,' she shouted above the incessant thump of the bass. Paige just quirked an eyebrow in Kait's direction.

Branch got the feeling Allison's love of dancing wasn't discussed, just enjoyed and appreciated.

'I need a refill on my drink,' Cohen announced, tipping his cup to peer inside. 'Anybody else?'

'I'll go with you,' Christopher said. 'Even if I have to carry my lovely wife with me to do it.'

'Oh, how romantic!' Allison swooned.

Paige rolled her eyes, but her amusement was evident. Allison's theatrics were a common theme in their outings, Branch figured. From the little Kait had told him and the bit he'd witnessed, he thought the woman was kind of fun.

'You want anything, Kait?' Paige pointed a thumb over her shoulder toward the refreshment table.

'I'm good, but thanks.' She turned her head just enough to allow her whisper to be heard by Branch alone. 'I've got everything I want right here.'

He couldn't hide the goofy grin her comment evoked. He was so engrossed in watching her watching him that he didn't even see the other couples leave the table.

'You sure about that?'

Her gaze danced with so many emotions, but hesitation wasn't one of them. 'I mean every word of it.'

'I know exactly how you feel, then.' Confessing it only solidified it for Branch. He didn't think it was humanly possible to love someone as irrevocably as he did Kait. Then again, he had been wrong to think he could never love her more than he did when they were eighteen. At thirty, his adoration had only intensified, proving that time wasn't some cruel entity that forced love to fade, but instead let it smolder away until it was a blaze that could never burn out.

'It's crazy, isn't it?' she whispered. 'You and me. Now.'

'It is,' he agreed. 'But I wouldn't change this for the world. None of it. I might not have believed it before, but I'm a firm believer now – everything happens for a reason. You just happen to be my reason,' he said. 'For everything.' He never thought he would say it, but maybe Janna was right. He needed to have a firmer belief in fate than he did in mistakes.

'I know exactly how you feel, then,' she mimicked. 'You're my everything, Branch.'

'I want to give you something, Kaitie.' It sounded more rushed than he meant it to, but if he didn't say it now, he would lose his nerve. It might not be the right moment, but there was never going to be a moment that was as perfect as Kait deserved.

He shifted in his chair, his arm snaked around her waist to hold her in place as he dug his wallet from the back pocket of his dress pants.

'You want to give me money?' Kait joked, unable to look away.

241

Her voice sounded jovial, but her eyes were sharp and curious.

Her choice of words struck Branch funny. 'You know, in a way, yes, I guess I do,' he laughed. He fumbled with his wallet, unable to get his hands to work properly. 'More than a decade ago, I spent every last penny I had on something for you. Life might have gotten in the way for a while, preventing me from giving it to you, but it's been pressed inside one of the pockets of my wallet all this time, just waiting to be handed over to its rightful owner.'

He found what he was looking for, managing to hide it in his clenched hand before opening the wallet pocket wide to show her the round indent worn into the leather. Kait's eyes resembled that circular impression.

He opened his hand, revealing the simple gold band with the miniscule diamond. Scratched and dulled by time, it looked even worse for wear than Branch remembered, but he continued. 'At the time, it was all I had to offer you. It might not look like much, but this promise ring stands for so much, probably even more now than it did back then.' His throat grew thick, and he paused to clear it, overcome by the parallel between the battered ring and their scarred hearts. 'It's been through a lot, but so have we.'

Through the pounding of his pulse in his ears, Branch could hear hoots and hollers as the folks around them began to count down from ten.

'Someday, when you're ready, I will get you a nicer ring, Kaitie. A bigger one, a fancier one like you deserve.' He held the ring out. 'But this ring means something a little different. It's withstood the same things we have, and it'll still be here ten years from now, twenty years, sixty years. Just like we will be. You don't have to wear it, but it's yours. It's always been yours. And I want you to have it so that when you are ready, you can slip that promise ring on your finger and know that we might be battered and bruised, but we're still us. There's nothing stronger than my love for you.'

Kait, through happy tears, took the ring gingerly from his

fingers. She stared at it, wiping away the waterfall of tears she couldn't seem to control. 'There's nothing I want more,' she choked out, 'than you, and *this* ring.'

'Is that a fact?' Branch cracked a joke, anything to keep his own tears from breaking free.

An eruption of applause and cheering surrounded them, and the huge netting of balloons hidden by the light strings on the ceiling was let loose, colorful pops of color bouncing and floating everywhere. The clock struck midnight as Kait slipped the ring on her finger.

'No, Branch,' she cried, cupping his face in her hands and kissing him as though they were the only two people in the world. 'That's a promise.'

Swept away by Branch and Kait's whirlwind romance? Don't miss *The Forget-Me-Not Bakery*, another unputdownable Port Landon novel from Caroline Flynn. Available now!

Acknowledgements

First, thank you to Erica Christensen. You know exactly why this book is dedicated to you. Thank you to Belinda Toor—your guidance and patience does not go unnoticed. To the Metamorphosis Literary Agency, HQ Digital, and HarperCollins teams, thank you for all your hard work on my stories' behalf. I said it before but I'll say it again—working with you all is a dream come true. To Dennis, thank you for your unwavering love and support. To Mom and Dad, there are no words to show my gratitude for all you've done and continue to do for me. And to Jazz, you're the best writing partner I could ever hope for.

Thank you to the readers, the bloggers, and the unabashed bookworms I've come to know on this incredible journey. You're phenomenal, every one of you.

Keep reading for an excerpt from
The Forget-Me-Not Bakery …

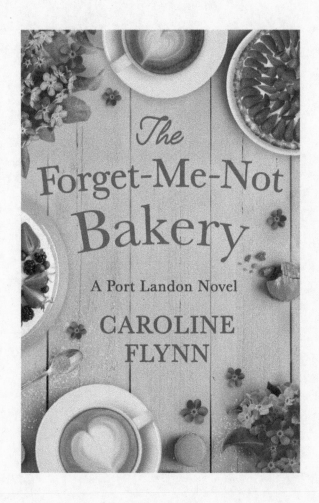

Keep reading for an excerpt from
The King I shall not Betray...

Prologue

Cohen

Eight Years Ago ...

There are days that change everything. Change our lives. Change us.

Cohen Beckett didn't understand the razor-sharp truth of that statement. Until now. Now that he stood at the edge of the room, surrounded by all the people he knew and just as many that he didn't, aching with the painful loneliness of a man stranded on foreign ground without a soul in sight. Now that he was left behind, to carry on living a life he didn't know how to live alone. Now that his family of three, content and constant and perfect, was only a family of two.

Cohen didn't remember who he was before Stacey. Try as he might, he couldn't summon up recollections of his time before he'd met her by chance at university, all wide-eyed and beautiful and ready to take on the world. It seemed like a lifetime ago, yet those days, in the beginning, as he careened over the edge and fell madly in love with her, were etched in his brain with a sharp vividness that made them seem like only yesterday. He prayed that haunting vividness would never dull.

Before that, though? Nothing. The realization left him cold, and scared of what it truly meant. The thought niggled at him that he hadn't yet begun to live, to do and be anything worth remembering, until he'd met the woman he would call his wife. And if that was the case, he wasn't just scared. He was petrified. Because he would never be that man again, the one he saw reflecting back at him in Stacey's pretty emerald eyes.

Stomach in knots, shoulders tight with the facade of strength he fought to wear nobly, Cohen ached for another glimpse of his beloved wife's stare in his direction. The smile on her face that forced her long-lashed eyelids to squint with the sheer authenticity of it in the gold-rimmed picture frame beside her matching casket, the smile that seemed to follow him from across the room no matter where he stood, was a poor substitute for the beauty now housed in that closed box. No picture could do Stacey Beckett's smile justice. No memory, regardless of its clarity, would ever do *her* justice.

He'd found his one. The one who was his best friend and his lover and his rock. It pained him to think about whether he'd managed to be those things for her, adequately and fully. His chest constricted as he hoped with every fiber of his being that he had been. It hurt even more to realize that his love for her hadn't been enough to save her, hadn't been enough to protect her in the first place. The rational part of Cohen's brain understood that he could never have prevented the fluke accident that stole Stacey from him and their young son, but there were moments during the darkness of the seven nights that had followed her death when his rational mind didn't stand a chance against the grieving, guilt-stricken part that took over and threatened to drown him in his own numb disbelief.

'Dr Cohen?'

In the distance, as though through a thick veil of cotton but more accurately of dazed distraction, a voice filtered through to him. Cohen turned, and Sonya Ritter stood near him, her back turned to protect him from any oncoming folks intent on bestowing their condolences. Judging by the added lines that marred her forehead and the slight narrowed angle of her eyelids, she had said his name a few times without gleaning a response. Sonya knew nothing of impatience with him, though. As Port Landon's designated mother hen and knower of all that went on within the town's limits, the short elderly woman had taken her role more seriously when the tragedy of Stacey's passing befell their little town and rocked their community to the core. The woman was a fixture in their tiny town, and a friend to all despite her overzealous nature and overbearing personality. But she'd been a godsend to Cohen in the past week. He didn't know how he would have gotten through any of this without her. Didn't know how Bryce would have gotten through it.

Bryce. His son. The last remaining thread to Stacey that he could touch and hold. Only two years old and left without the beautiful mother he adored. Cohen didn't know how to quantify the torturous pain he was battling, but he was sure it was multiplied a thousand times over with the added weight of the grief he harbored on his young son's behalf.

'Sorry, Sonya. What were you saying?' He shook his head, desperate to hold himself together. Not for Sonya; she could handle whatever emotional turmoil Cohen – or anyone else, for that matter – tossed at her. The woman was strong and sturdy as an oak tree despite her age. It wasn't her he worried about.

The toddler in her arms was another story. The little boy he now lived solely for. Not because anything or anyone had ever come before him in his father's eyes, but because he was all he had left.

Sonya looked uncertain of Cohen's current emotional stability. She wasn't the only one. But she thankfully kept her sentiments to herself. Cohen didn't know if he could stand to hear *Are you okay?* or *How are you holding up?* one more time. People meant well, but it didn't make having to form an answer any easier.

251

'The director says he's about ready to start the service,' she informed him. 'I figured you would want Bryce with you?'

Bless the woman's heart. She was giving him an out, phrasing it as a question and allowing him the chance to admit he couldn't handle sitting in the front row of his wife's funeral, with his son in his arms asking why Mommy's picture was on display but she was nowhere to be found. It was going to be hard. Damn hard. There would be tears eventually, though the icy numbness that spread through him like a biting frost hadn't allowed those tears to fall yet, and there would be moments when Cohen wouldn't know how he was going to get through them.

Today was one of those days. One of those moments. That changed everything. Changed him.

But he couldn't allow this to swallow him up. He couldn't let it, as easy as it would be. Bryce needed him now. More than ever. And Cohen needed Bryce just as urgently. He held his hands out, his fingers twitching with the instinctive urgency to feel the solid form of his son against him.

'I wouldn't want him anywhere else.' He hugged the boy tight to his chest as Sonya gave Cohen's jacket lapel a gentle pull to straighten it, then she pressed her lips together and headed back toward the rows of chairs, leaving him with only his thoughts and his son to keep him steady. He had more faith in his two-year-old than his own frazzled mind to level him out.

'You all right, buddy?' Cohen pressed his thumb into Bryce's palm, squeezing his fingers gently. The boy's eyelashes fluttered before his eyes fixed firmly on his father.

Stacey's eyes.

'I want Mommy.' Bryce played with the edge of Cohen's pocket, flipping the fabric up and down, his gaze flitting from it to Cohen's face then back again. Waiting for an answer. Waiting for his daddy to fix this.

Cohen felt desolate, helpless. But, despite his throat constricting, thick with all the things he couldn't find the strength to say and all the things he couldn't change, Cohen leaned forward and kissed Bryce's forehead, his soft skin warm against his lips.

'I know, my boy. Me too.' He shifted his son in his arms, needing him to focus his waning attention on him, needing him to understand the sincerity of the words he fought to say out loud. 'But we're going to be okay, me and you.' He pressed his forehead to his son's, swallowing hard past the lump in his throat, desperate for his son to believe him more than he believed himself. 'We'll get through this,' he choked out. 'Together.'

Cohen just wished he knew how.

Chapter 1

Paige

Present Day ...

Paige Henley had heard a lot of things about Port Landon. Mostly from her cousin, Allison, a long-time resident, and mostly that the tiny town was largely made up of people with big hearts and even bigger mouths. It ran on gossip and small-town gumption, and not always necessarily in that order. Of course, that was just gossip, too, when she really thought about it.

But she knew one thing for sure. When the folks of Port Landon talked about The Cakery's grand opening later on that evening, huddled back into their cozy homes with their own personal choice of sugar fix, their recollection of just how well the new bakery's grand opening had gone would be anything but exaggerated hearsay. It would be the truth.

'I can't believe this is really happening,' Paige exclaimed, bending down to pull two chocolate cupcakes with mint frosting from the glass display case. Rising to her full height, she closed the takeout box and met Allison's gaze. "I guess what I really mean is I still can't believe you talked me into this."

255

Allison expertly rang the sale through the cash register and bid the customer – Mrs O'Connor from Huntington Street was how she'd introduced her to Paige – a good day before turning to her cousin, eyes gleaming so bright they sparkled. 'Oh, please. You can pretend you're still unsure about this whole venture, but you're not fooling me. Either you've laced the baked goods with some damn good stuff that's making people *think* it tastes good, or maybe, just maybe, the people of Port Landon have spoken, Paige … and The Cakery is officially a hit!'

Paige couldn't hide her smile. Leave it to Allison to decide that the only two plausible options were either real, honest-to-goodness success or the clandestine addition of hallucinogenic drugs.

She might not have had a clue what she was doing as a first-time business owner, but, by God, she was learning on the fly. And she was doing something right. It felt like the entire population of Port Landon had left their homes and jobs on this cheery sunny day to get a chance at the free coffee and sweet treats being handed out in celebration of Paige's first official day up and running on the bustling downtown street.

Or, if Paige was honest, to catch a glimpse of the newest addition to the small portside town they all called home – *her*. Most customers weren't even trying to hide that they were just as interested in the New Yorker who had snatched up old Wilhelmina Morrison's bakery within days of it hitting the real estate market as they were the baked goods that were strategically displayed about the room. It was like they'd never seen a girl from New York before. Like she was something akin to a Yeti from the Himalayan Mountains, something they'd heard of but never truly witnessed.

Well, they were witnessing her now, a real live city-girl-turned-small-town-entrepreneur, living in what she hoped would remain her natural habitat, her very own dream come true.

And that's what this grand opening day was turning out to be – a dream come true. With Allison graciously allowing her own business, the coffeehouse too-conveniently located beside the bakery, to be solely run by her two employees so she could volunteer to help Paige 'control the impending chaos' – Allison's words, not hers – the doors had been unlocked for the very first time at nine o'clock sharp. The coffee Allison had donated for the event had been brewed and piping hot, ready to be sipped by the patrons who attended. Paige had expected there to be a handful of people who would come out, mostly for the free food that had been mentioned in the *Port Landon Ledger* advertisements, but she never would have expected the line-up of people that waited patiently outside for the heavy glass door to be unlocked, or the way the cupcakes, mini cheesecakes, and scones that had been on display had sold out in a matter of hours, leaving Paige with no choice but to begin cutting the large cakes into individual pieces and sell them by the slice so that everyone would have a chance to try the different frostings and cake flavors she'd boasted about in the ads.

If this day was any indication, The Cakery was going to need to be better stocked on a daily basis than she ever dreamed. The thought had Paige bursting with pride. Every sliver of fear she'd had about leaving her marketing career back in New York, every not-so-subtle hint from Allison that she should take a chance and follow her dreams of owning her own bakery, every doubt she'd harbored since giving her notice and selling her closet-sized condo in the heart of the city …

It was worth it. Crazy and reckless, but absolutely worth it. And it made Paige feel more alive than she had in years. Maybe ever. Even if she had to spend her evenings whipping up buttercream frosting just to keep up, she would do it, because this was her dream, and it was coming to fruition in front of her sapphire eyes.

Yeah, it was definitely worth it.

'Paige, this is Sonya.' Allison's voice cut through Paige's thoughts. She turned to see a slender woman with short, gray hair cut smartly into a bob hairstyle. She wore a black T-shirt identical to Allison's, with the round Portside Coffeehouse logo on the front. The woman looked to be at least sixty-five, which Paige hadn't expected by the way Allison talked about her.

'Oh, Allison's told me so much about you,' Paige gushed, dusting her hands on her block-patterned apron. 'You help her to run the coffeehouse, right?'

'I do what I can,' Sonya replied, nodding as she shook her hand with a surprisingly firm grasp. She leaned forward, a faint grin on her lips as she added in a whisper, 'Which is pretty much everything.'

'Easy, now. I can hear you plotting your stealthy takeover from here.' A wider grin crossed Allison's face as she placed her hands on her hips. This was obviously a running joke between the two of them. 'Taking a break, are you?'

Sonya pointed toward the brick wall to the right that divided the bakery from the coffeehouse. 'I've got Adrian running the place for ten minutes while I grab myself a treat. Got anything with peanut butter in it?'

Paige jumped into action immediately, gesturing toward the other side of the room where a long table with trays of colorful cupcakes and squares were on display. They'd been picked over a bit, but a good selection still remained. 'I put chocolate fudge cupcakes with peanut butter icing on the treat trays this morning! Help yourself to those. They're free for the taking.'

Sonya glanced back at the setup, but she quickly turned back to the front counter where Allison and Paige stood, pulling a crumpled ten-dollar bill from her pocket. 'Anything with peanut butter in it that I can *buy*?' She waved the bill in her hand.

Paige tilted her head, curious. 'Of course, but you don't have to—'

'Look, sweetheart …' The older woman leaned in as though about to reveal a deep, dark secret. 'Around here, we shop local. We help each other out as best we can. It's what we do, in case

Allison, here, hasn't told you. So ...' She slid the bill across the counter, her deep brown eyes never wavering. 'Sell me ten dollars' worth of sugary goodness, and let me be on my way, will you?'

Paige's cheeks burned hotly at having been put in her place by the older woman, but at the same time, her heart swelled with adoration and respect for Sonya ... and for the town. 'A handful of peanut buttery decadence coming up,' she announced, pulling a takeout box from the shelf behind her and beginning to place an array of sweet treats into it. She was just about to disappear into the back of the shop where the kitchen was hidden by a wall when another voice broke into the conversation.

'Sonya, are you giving this poor lady a hard time?'

The voice brought Paige back around to see who it was. It was unfamiliar and deep, the voice of a man.

Sonya had turned around at the front counter, and judging by both her and Allison's easy smiles, they recognized the owner of that voice.

He was tall, standing over by the table of treat trays, pouring himself a cup of coffee from the large coffeepot Allison had brought over from her shop that morning. The steam billowed up from the paper cup in his hands, and his hazel eyes shone with amusement.

'You got one thing right, Dr Cohen. The lady's definitely going to be poor if she doesn't start letting us folks pay for the stuff in her shop.' Anyone else might have sounded crass, but Sonya's tone was anything but. She was blunt and to the point, but there was heart behind her words, not malice. 'Speaking of that, you'd better come up here and see what you can find to buy that sweet boy of yours, yeah?'

'Don't you worry, I've been given my orders,' he assured her, placing a plastic top on the cup before making his way to the front counter. 'I don't believe we've met, yet. I'm Cohen.'

A glass display case stood between them and he jutted his hand out over it. His smile was the first thing Paige noticed about him, genuine. His eyes gleamed with just as much sincerity, and a gentle kindness seemed to emanate off him in waves. He wore dark stonewash jeans and comfortable looking loafers, but the ensemble was paired with a solid green scrub top that made the flecks of gold in his eyes shine all the more brightly.

'Hi,' Paige greeted him, shifting the box into one hand to shake his with the other. 'I'm Paige.' She could hear a sudden shyness tainting her own voice. 'Paige Henley.' She couldn't bring herself to tear her eyes away.

Cohen gave her hand a gentle squeeze, his gaze meeting hers and holding it for what could have been a minute but was probably only seconds. 'This town's been talking nonstop about you and your bakery, Paige. It's good to finally put a face and a name to all the chatter.'

'The novelty will wear off, I'm sure.' She had been living in Port Landon for the past three months, but for the first time, Paige idly wondered just what exactly the gossip was that Cohen had heard.

'As quickly as the sugar fix?' Cohen arched an eyebrow, a crooked grin dancing on his face.

'Well, hopefully not quite that fast.' She laughed.

The sound of a throat being cleared made both Paige and Cohen turn at the same time. Allison and Sonya stood there, their lips pursed, unable to hide their mischievous intrigue. It was too alight in their eyes to go unnoticed.

'Find something you like?' Allison asked, crossing her arms.

Paige didn't know if she was addressing Cohen or herself, but she quickly realized it didn't matter. What did matter was that she and Cohen were still standing there, her small hand enveloped in his.

She pulled her hand from his as easily as she could. 'Right.' She glanced down as she smoothed her apron out, giving herself a moment to compose herself and stamp down her embarrassment. 'Anything I can get you, Cohen?'

'That's *Dr* Cohen,' Sonya interjected, still rooted in place, watching their exchange with distinct interest.

Paige shot her a pleading glance, silently begging the woman to stop making this worse, but quickly tried to cover it up. 'Sorry, Dr Co—'

Cohen chuckled, shaking his head. 'No, just Cohen is fine,' he insisted. He glanced over at Sonya. 'I see what you're doing Sonya, and you can put the brakes on anytime.'

'I could.' She shrugged, waving a dismissive hand. 'But you know I won't, sweetheart.'

Paige wasn't sure whose expression was more amused, the older woman's or Cohen's, but whatever passed between them was a silent, mutual understanding. They had history, those two. Cohen turned back to Paige, unfazed. 'As I was saying,' he began again. 'I got a specific request from my son this morning for something that's double fudge, and I promised I would come and see if I could make good on that request before he got home from school. Unfortunately, I got behind in my appointments and it took longer to get here than planned. Am I too late?'

'I've got just the thing, *Just* Cohen.' She flashed him an excited smile, relieved that she did, in fact, have something that would fit the bill. She ducked down, intent on seeking out the cake she had in mind. Paige didn't even realize she was still holding the box – Sonya's box – in her hand until she was about to set it down and retrieve another one for Cohen.

Immediately, Paige stood up, her eyes wide as she came face to face with the older woman. 'I'm sorry, Sonya. I didn't finish getting everything for you! I'll be right back.' She whirled around, sending an apologetic glance at Cohen for making him wait as well, then scurried into the kitchen to add a slice of the chocolate peanut butter pie she'd made to have as her own dessert tonight, mortified at forgetting what she'd been doing the moment Cohen had entered the shop.

What in the world had come over her?

261

She knew all too well that Allison wasn't going to let her live that one down. And if her first impression of Sonya was anything to go by, she wouldn't, either.

Paige put on a brave face after slipping the piece of pie into the box and made her way back out to the counter. 'An assortment of cupcakes and a slice of gourmet chocolate peanut butter pie,' she announced, sliding the box across to Sonya. 'You'll have to let me know what you think.'

Sonya didn't bother to open the box and inspect the choices Paige had chosen. Pushing the ten-dollar bill closer to her, Sonya tucked the box under her arm. 'Trust me, Paige, I always let people know what I think.' She cast a fleeting glance from Cohen to Paige and back again, then winked. 'It was good to meet you, sweetheart.' She turned to leave, but not before adding, 'Have a good day, Dr Cohen,' as she closed the door behind her.

The void of Sonya's absence was felt the moment she left, but her words hung in the air like a thick veil. Allison had advised Paige on more than one occasion that the woman was a force to be reckoned with, but her spitfire personality was even more fiery than she'd expected.

'Now, about that order for double fudge anything ...' Paige turned back to Cohen, unable to look Allison in the eye just yet, and went about cutting an enormous slice of chocolate Oreo cake with chocolate fudge icing and double chocolate fudge drizzle on top, carefully boxing it up. She added in a pair of mocha chocolate cupcakes for good measure. 'If that doesn't fit the bill for your son, I don't know what will.'

'It looks like he's going to be swinging from the rafters till midnight once the sugar in that hits his bloodstream.'

He was smiling, but Paige immediately wondered if he thought it was too much. 'I guess the doctor in you would be worried about the effects of all the refined sugar.'

'Nah, it's the dad in me that's worried about that,' he chuckled. 'Besides, I'm not that kind of doctor. I'm a veterinarian. Believe

262

me, I understand the need for a good sugar fix every now and then. What do I owe you, Paige?'

Allison stepped back, gesturing for her to take her place at the cash register. Paige punched a few buttons, ignoring the smug grin on her cousin's face. When the amount came up on the screen, Cohen arched a brow. 'That can't be enough.'

'It's just for the cake,' she advised happily. 'The cupcakes are on the house.'

He pulled his wallet out and held out a twenty-dollar bill. 'Thanks, Paige. Looks like I owe you one.'

Paige counted out his change and handed it to him. 'You owe me nothing. I'm just glad I could fulfill the request of a boy with dreams of chocolate fudge.'

'One forkful of that chocolatey masterpiece and I'll bet you'll be seeing my son and me in here a lot more.'

'I'm looking forward to it, Cohen.'

He shoved his wallet back into his jeans pocket, his eyes gleaming when they met hers once more. 'Me too,' he assured her. 'But I'd better get back to Jazz. She's probably scaling the walls looking for me. It was nice to meet you, Paige. Have a good day, you two.' He offered a slight nod toward Allison, and then they both watched as he made his way out of the shop, the bell above the door tolling lightly to announce his exit.

With the shop empty for the first time since the doors opened that morning, Paige turned to her cousin, who was still grinning. 'What?' Paige asked, rolling her eyes. She knew exactly what her cousin was thinking. They had been best friends too long not to know. 'You're looking at me like something big just happened.'

'Something big did just happen,' Allison exclaimed. 'You, Paige Henley, just met Port Landon's most eligible bachelor.'

Dear Reader,

We hope you enjoyed reading this book. If you did, we'd be so appreciative if you left a review. It really helps us and the author to bring more books like this to you.

Here at HQ Digital we are dedicated to publishing fiction that will keep you turning the pages into the early hours. Don't want to miss a thing? To find out more about our books, promotions, discover exclusive content and enter competitions you can keep in touch in the following ways:

JOIN OUR COMMUNITY:
Sign up to our new email newsletter: hyperurl.co/hqnewsletter
Read our new blog www.hqstories.co.uk
🐦 : https://twitter.com/HQStories
📘 : www.facebook.com/HQStories

BUDDING WRITER?
We're also looking for authors to join the HQ Digital family!
Find out more here:
https://www.hqstories.co.uk/want-to-write-for-us/
Thanks for reading, from the HQ Digital team

ONE PLACE. MANY STORIES

**If you enjoyed *The Winter Berry House*,
then why not try another delightfully uplifting
romance from HQ Digital?**